"Rosche's latest novel offers a compelli[...] after losing her memory, feels like a stra[...]. The unraveling of her past takes the reader on a journey that will have them flipping pages long into the night. *With Every Memory* is a moving tale of hope and healing."

**Denise Hunter**, bestselling author of the Riverbend Romance series

"*With Every Memory* is a memorable story of damaged, imperfect people trying to rise above the rubble of tremendous tragedy. Raw and gritty, this is my favorite type of novel. It is highly affecting, and I nearly read through it in one sitting. I'm still sitting here thinking about it."

**T. I. Lowe**, bestselling author of *Under the Magnolias*

"Heartrending and redemptive, *With Every Memory* is a poignant story that follows the aftermath of loss in a hurting family and the guiding hope that leads them home again."

**Nicole Deese**, award-winning author of *All That Really Matters*

"At times messy, emotional, and altogether tender, *With Every Memory* is a story that will feel familiar to readers, a story that feels entirely true. It's also a story of forgiveness, resilience, and overcoming. This is a novel you don't want to miss."

**Susie Finkbeiner**, author of *The All-American*

"Memories are a slippery thing, especially when you have a traumatic brain injury. Even knowing her memory gap has swallowed years of her life, Lori Mendenhall isn't prepared for how lackluster her life is compared to the vibrant one she remembers. In a powerful family story about awakening and holding on to who we love, Rosche tackles the question, How would you live your life differently if you could start over?"

**Janyre Tromp**, author of *Shadows in the Mind's Eye*

# with every memory

*a novel*

## JANINE ROSCHE

**Revell**

a division of Baker Publishing Group
Grand Rapids, Michigan

Published by Revell
a division of Baker Publishing Group
Grand Rapids, Michigan
www.revellbooks.com

Printed in the United States of America

Library of Congress Cataloging-in-Publication Data
Names: Rosche, Janine, author.
Title: With every memory : a novel / Janine Rosche.
Description: Grand Rapids, Michigan : Revell, a division of Baker Publishing
    Group, [2023]
Identifiers: LCCN 2022041152 | ISBN 9780800742959 (paperback) | ISBN
    9780800744663 (casebound) | ISBN 9781493441419 (ebook)
Subjects: LCGFT: Domestic fiction. | Novels.
Classification: LCC PS3618.O78237 W58 2023 | DDC 813/.6—dc23/eng/20220909
LC record available at https://lccn.loc.gov/2022041152

The quote on page 128 is from Djurdjak Bartlett, *FashionEast: The Spectre that Haunted Socialism* (Cambridge: MIT Press, 2010), 141.

The lyrics on pages 259–60 are reprinted with permission from P. W. Gopal's song "Awaken" (from the album *Still Voices*, © 2004 P. W. Gopal).

23   24   25   26   27   28   29       7   6   5   4   3   2   1

For those who have fought the good fight—
for your recovery and healing, for your dreams,
for your identity, for your children, for the memory
of those who have passed on, or for your marriage—
whether you were able to find restoration or not,
this book is for you.

# author's note

This novel contains difficult and potentially triggering topics, such as death of a child, sexual assault, adultery, and divorce. I have tried to handle each of these issues with sensitivity while also showing the reality of trauma in the family system. If · you have experienced loss, adultery, or divorce, I recommend seeking professional help through the American Association of Marriage and Family Therapy: www.aamft.org.

If you or someone you know has experienced rape or sexual assault, please contact the National Sexual Assault Hotline at (800)-656-HOPE (4673) where you can access a range of free services, including:

- confidential support from a trained staff member
- support finding a local health facility that is trained to care for survivors of sexual assault and offers services like sexual assault forensic exams
- someone to help you talk through what happened
- local resources that can assist with your next steps toward healing and recovery
- referrals for long-term support in your area
- information about the laws in your community
- basic information about medical concerns

*one*

## LORI

Even the best makeup couldn't hide the fact that I'd been raised from death to life. A sound—half chuckle and half sigh—skimmed my lips as I placed my Givenchy powder and brush in my travel case. If Deirdre, my favorite nurse, heard my thoughts, she'd tell me to display my scars proudly, as I was "a walking testimony of the good Lord's mercy and grace." A walking testimony. She'd never caught the slip, and I'd never called attention to it.

I placed the travel case in the basket on the front of my walker and then began my trek to my chair. I'd no sooner caught my breath than a knock sounded at the door. "Come in."

"Good glory, Ms. Lori!" Deirdre sauntered through the doorway like she was wearing a gold-breasted choir robe instead of the same green scrubs all the nurses at the rehab center wore. She spread her arms wide and let the door swing behind her. "Are you excited? It isn't every day you get a second chance at life."

"I am excited. To sleep in my own bed, cook my own food, read with my childr—" I swallowed hard as reality struck. "My daughter."

"That sounds wonderful."

I checked my watch. Nearly nine. "I should make sure I have everything." I readied myself to stand, prompting Deirdre to quickstep to my side and offer her arm as a support. With a flick of my hand, I waved her off. "I must get used to doing all this on my own. May as well start now."

Using the armrests as support, I leaned forward and pushed with my legs. Fire ripped through my quadriceps—a feeling I'd learned to appreciate. Months ago, I'd felt nothing in those muscles at all. After I straightened, I waited for vertigo to come. It didn't, thank heavens. Perhaps it had slept in. Meanwhile I'd been awake since four.

"Don't push yourself too hard now or you're likely to end up right back here." Deirdre watched my slow progress. "Your baby girl may think she's grown, but she still needs her momma."

My lips were too taut for my smile to feel genuine.

Deirdre looked over the tray holding my hardly touched breakfast. "Now, now, Ms. Lori. Your hubby might be a feast for the eyes, but you've still got to eat real food."

"I tried. My nerves had other ideas. I'd rather not start my 'second chance' by getting sick all over myself or Michael." With the help of my walker, I shuffled my cashmere-slippered feet over to the large window of my suite—the best money can buy, Michael had called it once. How long ago was that? Was it even Michael who'd said it? I brushed the voile curtain back to see the sunlight sparkling on Denver's South Platte River, yet an even better image caught my attention. In the parking lot below, Michael shut the door to his Lexus. After all his visits to the rehabilitation center, I still expected to see the beat-up Honda since my brain only occasionally acknowledged the eight years prior to our accident.

I closed my eyes and went through my mental checklist: the month and year, the current president, my age, the names of the living members of my family, and the facts of my situation. Each answer tugged harder on my heartstrings, but I wouldn't give in to tears. This was a big day, so I shoved away the consuming sadness and focused on that tall, dark, and handsome man casually walking toward the clinic's entrance.

"Why are you anxious?" Deirdre asked.

My stomach twisted. "Because I know it won't be how it was."

"What if it's better?"

She tried to pat my shoulder, but I shirked away from her touch. "Better? After all I lost, how could it possibly be better?"

"I'm only thinking the Lord's not through with the Mendenhalls yet. With the way you helped us redecorate these rooms to look less like a morgue and more like one of those flippity-flop home shows, I bet you could make quite a name for yourself as an interior designer."

"I don't know. I'm not sure I can handle any more of his plans."

"After all you've accomplished here? 'Course you can. When the hospital transferred you in January, you couldn't walk, talk, or remember your name. Look at you now."

I cast a glance at my reflection in the window's glass. Like I did dozens of times a day, I fussed with the hair near my scar, brushing it forward. Did I have time to grab a scarf from the wardrobe? I had to try. The leg of my walker caught on the chair when I went to turn. It took several jarring shimmies to get it facing the other way.

While Deirdre prattled on about the importance of slow, deliberate movements, I shuffled to the wardrobe as quickly as possible and pulled the door open. Empty.

"Where—"

"We packed most of your stuff yesterday." Deirdre knew better than to add the "remember?" part because, clearly, I didn't. "I'll pack up your toiletries so you two don't linger here one minute longer than you have to. Mr. Handsome is bound to be in a hurry to get you home." She winked at me as she headed to the bathroom.

Warmth flooded my cheeks. My eyes caught something on the top shelf of the wardrobe. I slid the paper toward me and picked it up, finding one of the family photos they'd used for my memory work. My favorite memory. The moment I'd recovered it in therapy had been almost as happy as the day it had occurred. It was Easter Sunday, and the church had set up a backdrop for pictures. Austin and Avery were three. He wore light blue-and-white seersucker overalls with a hand-embroidered turtle on the front pocket. Avery wore a blue dress with pink tights, black Mary Janes, and a sparkly red bow—always the fashionista. They sat together on a bench, holding hands. Austin had insisted on it. And Michael? He was the most dashing man who'd ever dashed. He'd opted for his favorite pose with me. He'd stood behind me, slid his hands over mine, then wrapped me in an embrace.

"Hey."

The voice jolted me, and the photo slipped from my fingers as I looked up. Fifteen years after that photo was taken, Michael stood on the threshold, not an ounce less handsome but much farther away. His gaze wasn't on me but the stack of Michael Kors suitcases he'd had delivered last week. "Are you ready?"

"Yes, I believe so. Deirdre is getting the last of my things from the bathroom."

Finally, his focus found my face, and his eyes widened. He closed the distance between us in only two strides. His fingertips gentled my neck, turning my chin slightly. "When did you get this bruise? What happened?"

"On Sunday," I said, "after visiting hours ended. It was nothing. I thought I could get to the bathroom without my walker, but I fell and bumped my chin on the floor." No need to tell him about the cut on the inside of my bottom lip or the massive headache the fall summoned.

"Why didn't someone tell me?" His glare demanded an answer. "This place is supposed to be the best in Colorado—"

"Michael." I used my softest voice, hoping to recapture his focus. It didn't work the way it used to. Then again, I was no longer the beauty queen he'd fallen for. "I asked them not to call you. It was my fault."

He looked at me from beneath his pinched brow. His hands dropped from my neck and secured my waist in his strong grasp. There was no way I could fall now. "Should you be standing? I can get a wheelchair."

"I'm fine." I wrapped my hands around his upper arms, noticing how much more muscular he was now than in our early years of marriage. When had fitness become so important to him? Since the accident? Or during the part of our life I couldn't remember?

"Don't push yourself too hard, Lori." His eyes, walnut-hued and rimmed by dark lashes, did more than ask me to be careful. They implored me to. The concern radiated through me, stunting my ability to speak.

Instead, I offered a slight nod. Not sure how much more careful I could be than living in a rehabilitation center all this time, never once leaving to go shopping or to get coffee. Maybe the command was meant for when I returned home. Or when I got in the car. With a lifetime of memories swirling about my brain like specks of dust in a tornado, I wasn't sure of anything anymore, except that no place was completely safe. Not even my husband's embrace.

After I assured him I was good to stand on my own, he kneeled and picked up the photograph I'd dropped.

"I nearly forgot that picture when I packed my things," I told him, leaving out how I had no memory of packing at all.

"Hmm," Michael said after a quick examination. "When was this, again?"

"Michael," I said, "I'm the one with a traumatic brain injury."

"You know me and these things. The kids were, what, five here?"

"They were three."

He stared at the picture the way he might analyze stock dividends.

Grief, my therapist had said, is rarely handled in the same manner by everyone, and we must be careful not to judge. That didn't make my heart ache any less.

Deirdre walked into the living area. "Well, Mr. Mendenhall, your queen is ready to leave one castle for the next." She extended the handle on the largest suitcase. "We sure are going to miss her around here."

"Not as much as she'll miss you, I'm sure." Michael's million-dollar smile—another change that had developed in the span of time I couldn't recall—had its effect on Deirdre. She started fanning herself exaggeratedly. When he glanced back at me, though, the smile fell. "I'll go get a wheelchair."

"I told you he'd be in a hurry to get you home," Deirdre said with a chuckle.

"Yes, I'm sure that's it." I fidgeted with my hair again.

After one last check passed from Michael to the clinic's administrator, the fanfare began. Patients and staff who had become my friends lined the third-floor hallway, waving their goodbyes. The ones who could stand offered hugs. Suddenly, I was thankful for the wheelchair. These people had comforted me at my lowest moments, like the day I was informed my son—my precious Austin—hadn't survived the crash that I'd just barely come through. And these people cheered for me every time I relearned something the doctors had said I'd never again do. Saying goodbye was hard.

Still, it wouldn't be as hard as the missing hello back at home.

In the car, Michael was quiet.

"I thought Avery might come with you." I ran my hand over the smooth leather upholstery. This car looked more like a New York City limousine than a family vehicle. Hadn't he and Avery been doing family things while I'd been at the clinic recovering?

Other than visiting me every other weekend, I mean. Avery, it seemed, never enjoyed the visits. It was out of her comfort zone, I told myself each time, which was okay. I was sure the place would have grown on her if I had to stay much longer. Avery wasn't nearly as happy-go-lucky as Austin, but once they had settled into a place or activity, Austin had always helped Avery come around. And when that girl smiled, the sun may as well take a rest. Unfortunately, that was a light I hadn't seen in a long time.

"This is the last day of summer," Michael said. "I thought I'd let her sleep in one more time before the school year starts."

I closed my eyes and willed my brain to work. The current year minus the twins' birth year. That made Avery—

"It's her senior year," Michael whispered as if saying it at a normal volume would embarrass me for not recalling my only surviving child's age.

"Thank you." I unlocked my cell phone and scrolled through the most recent photos that Michael had uploaded of Avery. "I hate that I can't remember."

"That's all right. I'm here to help you, babe." He reached over and patted my knee twice, then settled his hand on my thigh long enough for its heat to burn through my lounge pants. There had been a time when he'd thought I was pretty. Back in my Miss Colorado Teen days. Back when my hair had been the color of the Great Sand Dunes and there wasn't a four-inch-long *C* scar above my ear.

His hand tensed and his knuckles arched. Then he pulled his arm away entirely. Could I blame him? I looked nothing like the young twentysomething in that Easter Sunday photo.

Michael cleared his throat. "And I've hired the finest home health-care professionals to come over while I'm at work to get you settled in."

"You're going back to work? How soon?"

He kept his eyes on the road. "I have a meeting this afternoon across town. I can cancel it if I need to."

I swallowed my disappointment like it was a chocolate-covered toad. "No, I'll be fine. It's been a tiring morning, so I imagine I'll rest. Maybe read a book." I laughed coarsely. "Do I still like to read?"

"I hope so. I uploaded the latest book from that author you love onto a new e-reader. You know, the one who writes those love stories set in the 1920s. Do you, uh, remember what an e-reader is?"

"Only because one of the nurses had one."

"You loved yours, but it was in your purse when we . . . Anyway, this one has far better features. Top of the line. It's plugged into the charger on your bedside table."

"Michael, thank you."

He stiffly nodded as we headed north on Highway 93 toward Boulder. Funny how I couldn't remember our address, but I knew every hill and curve of this road. Perhaps funny wasn't the best word. I gazed out the windshield at the mountains rising unapologetically from the plains, capturing the focus of anyone looking west and beckoning them toward their cragged beauty. Thank the Lord I could still recall my childhood climbing boulders and befriending foxes outside our cabin, all while promising Mom I wouldn't skin my knees ahead of pageant day.

We passed the neighborhood where our three-bedroom ranch stood. According to Michael, we moved out of our "starter" house four years ago. Was it too much to hope we'd found a quaint home nestled into a secluded mountainside?

My heart leaped when the Lexus turned west onto a road I didn't recognize. Soon, absurdly large homes came into view. The kind in the home decor magazines I used to fawn over after researching the week's best deals on diapers.

Michael steered the car between sprawling estates, many

of which had horses in adjoining pastures. "Does any of this look familiar?"

My chest tightened, forcing my no out on a breath.

We pulled onto a driveway that led to a sleek home, mountain-style but modern, with sharp eaves, large windows, and textures of lumber and stone. Beautiful and entirely unrecognizable. My eyes stung, and I turned away from Michael.

"Lori, it's okay." His typically deep voice rose in pitch and softened. "Take it one day—"

The car stopped abruptly, and my body pitched forward until the seat belt lashed my chest and neck. I threw my hands up to shield myself from the steel and glass I expected to strike my face. Piercing noise assailed my eardrums as my vision went blindingly white then black.

# *two*

"You've gotta be kidding me." Michael cursed.

I opened my eyes to daylight and lowered my hands slowly. A woman with pretty, yet quite unnatural-looking red hair stood in front of the car's nose and waved at me.

"Are you all right?" He curled his hand around the back of my neck, his warmth providing instant calm to my muscles.

"Yes," I said. I'm okay. I'm safe. It was . . . a memory, I think.

"Wait here." Michael jammed the shifter into Park and jumped out of the car, letting the door's slam add an exclamation to the unflattering word he called the woman. The woman rounded the bumper, heading toward me. I leaned away from the window.

Michael stepped between the stranger and my door. "I told you to come by next week. This is already a lot for her to take in. She doesn't need to worry about entertaining neighbors."

"I'm her best friend, Michael, and I've missed her."

"You can see her next week." Slightly muffled, Michael lowered his voice. "She may not even remember you."

"All the more reason to let me talk to her. For goodness' sake, at least let me hug her." She reached for the door handle, but Michael blocked her way. "What? Are you afraid of what I might tell her?"

I strained to hear Michael's response. There was only silence though. After a long pause, the woman responded. "Fine. I'll wait another unnecessary week to see her. Tell her that I'll drop off a cooler on the front stoop tomorrow night with salad and

18

gazpacho in it. She should know that someone actually cares about her."

After the woman had crossed the neighboring lawn and disappeared inside a Spanish-style, stucco home, Michael reclaimed the driver's seat. "Sorry about that. Let's get you inside." He drove the car into the opened garage, ensuring the door was shut before he cut the engine.

"She doesn't seem to like you much," I said, unbuckling my seat belt and turning toward him. "Who is she?"

"Enid Lowry. Her husband is a professor at the university. Margot, her daughter, was in band with Austin. You and Enid were close the last few years."

The tears I'd held back all morning grew angry and hot as they raged down my cheeks. I closed my fists and dug my knuckles into my thighs. "I can't remember my best friend. I can't remember my home. I can't remember losing my son."

As my body shook with sobs, Michael left the car, left me. How was I expected to do this? I shouldn't have been discharged from the clinic. I'd told Dr. Klein I wasn't ready for this, but he'd insisted I was. What did he know anyway?

My door opened. Michael leaned inside and stroked my face. "It'll be okay. I promise you, it will." If I searched hard enough, I could still see that fresh-faced boy who'd said those exact words to me years ago when I was a frightened, pregnant beauty queen in a borrowed veil. He slid one arm beneath my legs and one behind my back, scooping me up like I was a child. I curled into him. This Michael I remembered. This Michael was the man I loved.

After carrying me to the entry door, he fumbled with the doorknob, using the hand of the arm under my knees. He pushed the door open wide, revealing a brightly lit mudroom. "It's like the old days—me carrying you over the threshold."

"I remember." And I did. I held his gaze as long as possible. He carried me through the mudroom and into a generously spaced kitchen with hickory floors, open shelving, and copper accents. Beyond that, a cozy family room brought the out-doors in with large windows and an unobstructed view of the mountains. Michael situated me on a suede couch the color of a caramel macchiato. Everything was so lovely I was afraid to touch it. This place even smelled expensive, like bergamot and rum, although I didn't see a single candle.

Warbled rock music—"Free Fallin'," maybe—blared from the upstairs. Not all things had changed. With the help of the familiar chorus, I relaxed, allowing the pleasantly worn couch cushions to cradle me in comfort. Due to Avery's loud music, I didn't hear the slow and rhythmic clacking sound until it was nearly upon me. Before my brain could process the sound, a white-blond dog lumbered over.

"Wynton?" Whenever I had imagined coming home, I had expected the Labrador to greet me with puppy kisses and an-noying tail thumps. Instead, the old boy took his time coming my way. Though it seemed to have lost its power, his tail still wagged happily. I welcomed him with a hug and dug my fingers in the dog's soft fur. Austin's dog. He'd begged us for one for his tenth birthday. That was only seven years before the accident. Seven. Progress. I kissed Wynton's forehead, leaving a mauve lip print between his eyes.

*Bang, bang, bang.*

I jerked my head up to see Michael pounding on the wall of the staircase.

"Avery, Mom's home!" Michael turned back to me, a sheep-ish expression rippling his brows. "Sorry. She can't ever hear me over her music." He crossed the room and kneeled before me to remove my shoes one at a time. After that, he retrieved a blanket from a cabinet. He unfolded it and placed it over my legs with care and strange precision, tucking it around my feet and knees. He must've caught on that I never seemed to be warm enough these days. The title lyric to Salt-N-Pepa's

"Whatta Man" randomly popped into my head, then saddened me. After all, I could remember a song from high school better than my supposed best friend. When Michael had finished caring for me, he straightened, pinning his hands to his hips and peering up the stairs.

There was a time when my homecoming would have been greeted by tiny feet pitter-pattering as the twins jockeyed for the first hug. These footsteps were slow. Hesitant, even. Avery descended the steps and came around the couch, finally pausing in front of me. My little fashionista now wore plain black shorts and a cropped T-shirt that read "Colorado Bandmasters All-State Band." Like when she'd visited the clinic, her hair hung limp against her pale skin and indifference seemed to mar her once-smiley face.

"Hi, Mom."

I extended my arms to her. "I've missed you, sweetie."

Her chin puckered, and her bottom lip pushed forward. She flung herself down, practically onto my lap. "You too," she whispered, softening against me. She buried her nose in my blouse and the steam of her breath warmed my skin through the fabric. I heard her sniffle.

The longer she held me, or perhaps the longer I held her, the more my eyes blurred with tears. How many times in the hospital and rehab center had I longed for these mommy hugs from Austin and Avery?

She pulled away and returned to standing before I had time to fully soak in the embrace. Avery swiped at her cheeks. "Can I go back to my room now?"

"Avery." Michael's warning tone earned him a knowing glance from the girl.

"I'm glad you're home, Mom." Hurriedly, she retraced her path back to the stairs and out of sight.

All kinds of questions caught on the tip of my tongue. What had my girl been going through since the accident? What had it been like for her to lose her mother temporarily and her twin brother . . . for life? And when had our bond become so strained?

"Don't worry about her," Michael said. "It's all that teen angst. She'll come around."

"I hope so." I scratched Wynton behind his ear while Michael stood across the room, unmoving, for a good thirty seconds until an Aerosmith song began blaring.

"I'll tell her to turn it down," Michael said.

"Don't bother. I don't mind. So, she still has a thing for the '80s?" My heart squeezed remembering the night I drove Avery out to the Red Rocks Amphitheater when she was in third grade. We couldn't afford concert tickets so we parked on the shoulder of a private road, sat on the roof of our car, and listened to Tom Petty and the Heartbreakers off in the distance.

"She inherited that from you. Awful stuff, but it's better than what's popular now. I think it's how she feels closest to you." His hand raked through his thick hair once, twice. Strong as he was, he seemed unable to bear the weight of his shoulders, and they hunched forward as he paced the room. Finally, he sank onto the couch cushion by my side, caressing my blanketed knee with his thumb. "I didn't want to worry you with this while you were at the clinic, but Avery's going through a rebellious stage. She doesn't listen to me. Doesn't hang out with any friends. Doesn't want to go to school."

"Is it angst or grief?" I asked, careful to keep my voice from carrying.

"Honestly, I don't know."

"Don't you two talk? You've been alone here for ten months."

"If I let her, she'd never leave her room."

"Maybe things will get better now that I'm home. I have faith."

"That's good. Your faith has gotten us through hard times before." Michael forced a smile but just a quick one. He dropped his hand from my knee. When had he grown so weary? Was it after the accident? Before?

22

"Besides," I added, "if her room is as amazing as the rest of this house, I can't say I blame her for never wanting to leave it."

"It is amazing. You designed it, after all. You designed this entire house. Every light fixture, every faucet. You worked closely with our builder to make it your dream home. It kept you busy for nearly three years."

"Oh." The home was beautiful. But it was also . . . excessive. Like there had been an emptiness I'd been trying to fill with swanky finishings and magazine-worthy couture. An emptiness that seemed to hover just below the faith I carried, waiting for the ice to crack and for me to fall into its abyss. I squeezed my eyes tight and recalled snippets of a conversation we'd had during my stay at the clinic. "How can we afford this again?"

"The switch to wealth management has been bountiful. I manage the portfolios of some high rollers all along the Front Range. With big risk came big rewards."

"I see. You must have worked very hard for this."

"Absolutely." He didn't smile or show any sense of pride in his accomplishments. Instead, there was a lingering sadness in his expression.

"Don't you miss teaching at the high school? You used to love it."

"I don't miss worrying about how I'd provide for you and the kids." He expelled a breath.

A phone buzzed. Michael retrieved his from his pocket and stared at the screen. "I have to take this. Excuse me." He'd barely gotten his words out before he left through the front door.

Upstairs, Aerosmith yielded to U2's "With or Without You." Oh, my sweet, hurting girl.

Despite the August sunlight outside, this house felt cold. Where was the texture? The welcoming paint colors? Houseplants? Family photos? Hotel rooms felt more personal than this space. And the kitchen looked brand-new. Hadn't anyone cooked a meal in it? He'd said I designed every detail. My head spun. Who on earth was I in those lost years?

Michael returned only to jog up the steps. Bono went silent, and Avery's groan sounded in his place.

Michael's voice came next. "I need you to watch your mom while I go to a meeting. This isn't a question. You're doing it or you're grounded."

Her coarse laugh sent a barb straight into my chest.

"How about this, then? You're doing it or I'm making you go out."

I didn't hear her response.

Wynton padded to the bottom of the steps and looked up. As heavy footsteps descended, his tail wagged. Michael passed right by him. "One of my clients is in the hospital," he told me. "His family is after his money, so I need to see what's going on with his account. Avery will be down soon." He went to the kitchen table and gathered items into a laptop bag.

A minute later, Avery reappeared in the room. She flopped down into the easy chair, then fumbled with the television remote and started scrolling through an assortment of movies until she landed on *Girls Just Want to Have Fun*. "This used to be one of your favorites. A long time ago."

I nodded. "Why do you say it like that?"

Avery shrugged while giving me a sidelong glance. "People change."

Michael returned to kiss the top of my head, nearly touching my scar. Instinctually, I ducked to the side a bit. It wouldn't do to gross him out on my first day home. Michael, however, didn't notice. After a quick check of his watch, he rubbed his hands together. "Is there anything I can get you? Water, coffee, uh, toast? I think there's some pad thai in the fridge."

"Nothing right now. Thank you."

"You sure?" he asked.

"I'm home now. I'll be fine."

# three

## AVERY

"I can't believe you're making me do this."

Also trapped in the principal's office, Mom looked frail as Dad helped her into a chair. When he sat down between us, his arm touched mine, and I pinned myself as close to the wall as I could, crossing my arms over my stomach so tight my breakfast threatened to redecorate the principal's desk.

"Can't Mom just homeschool me?" I asked.

"Your mother needs to focus on her recovery."

"Okay, so hire me a governess like in *The Sound of Music*. She can teach me trigonometry, singing, and the birds and the bees all at once."

"Nah, I don't think lederhosen will go with your fashion sense," Dad said.

"Oh, ha ha. You're so funny." I leaned forward to catch Mom's eye. "Mom, tell Dad to take us home. Please?"

Mom merely looked to Dad for guidance. It served me right for expecting her to stand up to Dad as she'd finally learned to do before the accident.

"You need to be in school," Dad interjected. "I've let you stay home too long. You have to play catch-up." With each syllable of the last sentence, his right hand karate-chopped the flattened palm of his left hand, like it made the facts clearer.

I wasn't dumb. I knew I needed to get my high school diploma somehow. But if Dad thought I would happily prance into a school where I no longer had any friends, he was crazy.

The office door swung open. In his department store suit and loafers without socks, Principal Wright strutted in like he was Ryan Seacrest. He stopped behind his desk, placed his hands on his hips, and smiled. Just smiled. Was he expecting us to clap?

Beside me, Dad stiffened. I don't blame him. I hate the no-sock trend too.

"Avery, I'm happy to see you've come back. Hello, Michael. Lori," he said, looking at each of us. When he didn't get a bubbly greeting back, he took a seat and jiggled his mouse to wake up his computer. "While I'm pulling up Avery's records, may I ask how you're all doing?"

I waited for Dad's overconfident response. I'd heard him say the same things on the phone starting about two weeks after Austin died—even when Mom was still in the ICU. Things like, "We're doing great" and "The stocks are trading high, aren't they?"

Now, he said nothing. I couldn't know why. He and the principal worked together before Dad went all Leonardo DiCaprio in that Wall Street movie.

Mom didn't answer either. She was too busy fidgeting with the scarf covering her hair. I figured anything I said would dig me deeper into the pit I was already in.

I guess Principal Wright decided to surge ahead, despite our silence. He turned to Mom. "Lori, I know the PTO is hoping you'll return as president this year. Enid Lowry stepped in to cover your responsibilities, but the parents and the faculty have all felt the loss."

Mom's cheeks pinked, making her deer-in-headlights look even sweeter.

Dad cleared his throat and placed his hand on her knee. Gross. "As you've probably heard from every gossip hound in town, my wife has retrograde amnesia. She doesn't remember anything or anyone from the past seven or eight years. She must focus on her recovery this year. Enid will have to keep covering for her for the foreseeable future."

Principal Wright grinned before looking back at his computer. He swiveled his screen to show us my academic records. Straight As until last fall. "Avery, you're a capable student. If anyone can work hard enough to graduate on time, it's you. All you need is some additional resources. We'd like to provide them for you."

Yippee. I searched outside the window for anything to take me away from this place. The mountainous skyline, the beautiful mural on the side of the gym memorializing victims of gun violence, and the community garden complete with a fluttering butterfly? Nope. My focus found a wasp climbing up the window screen, doing what it needed to do to survive when all anyone wanted it to do was go away.

"What additional resources do you have in mind?" Dad asked. "We're willing to do whatever it takes."

Still facing the window, I rolled my eyes as Principal Wright answered. "I've spoken with some of the teachers, and they believe having an honors student—one who excelled in the courses Avery missed last year—tutor her regularly would be the best option. I have someone in mind who knows your family well."

I jerked my head back to the principal. "Who is it?"

"Alexander Dixon."

"No way," I spit out.

"Mr. Dixon is in the running to be valedictorian, so he's qualified. Plus, your parents seem to approve."

"My father is too obsessed with his work to know any students here. The only reason he knows Xander is because the pest infested our home every day for a decade. And my mother can't even remember what year it is."

27

"Avery!" Dad scolded.

Pain shot through the tip of my thumb, and I realized I had been biting my nails. I pressed my hands into my lap, as the pain led to a dull throbbing where I'd already nibbled to the nail bed. I couldn't let this happen. It would be better to drop out.

The principal rose from his chair and went to the door, opening it wide. "Ms. Crandall, can you call Alexander Dixon down to my office, please?"

I tugged on Dad's sleeve. "I'll work with a tutor. I promise I will. Just not him. He isn't nice to me."

Dad looked annoyed. "How was he not nice to you? Because he used to tease you? Pull harmless pranks on you?"

My eyes burned. Don't cry. Don't you dare cry. "His pranks weren't harmless," I spoke through gritted teeth.

"He was Austin's best friend, and Austin had great insight into a person's character. Besides, have you ever heard the phrase 'beggars can't be choosers'?"

I angled my body until my face was practically kissing the back corner of the office. Lederhosen weren't sounding so bad anymore. While the principal explained how the catch-up work would coincide with my senior year courses, I imagined myself sneaking off to the Alps and meeting some gorgeous Swede. Scratch that. Who needed a man? I'd join the convent where Maria got her start. Climb every mountain, indeed. And I'd never, ever look back.

What felt like an eternity later, footsteps preceded the shutting of the door. I didn't turn.

"Xander," Principal Wright said, "I believe you know the Mendenhalls."

"Uh, yeah." That voice grated against my skull. Not only was it ridiculously deep for someone who barely met the height requirement for roller coasters, but most of the time, it was also full of sarcasm and insults, all aimed at me.

Except once. That one time I was more alone than I'd ever been, he'd shown up. And here he was again, showing up.

That couldn't make up for wrecking my reputation.

"Oh my. Xander, you're so grown." Mom's voice held a kind of sad joy I didn't know was possible. "Can I give you a hug?"

"Sure," Xander said. I risked a peek and found him leaning down for Mom's seated embrace. Her features seemed to melt in the warmth of someone familiar. "Mrs. M, how are you doing?"

"I'm doing well," she said with a small sniffle. I took the box of tissues off the desk, set it on Dad's lap, and resumed my position.

"Awesome. My mom will be glad to hear that. And your hair looks great. Like the chick in that *Rosemary's Baby* movie."

"Mia Farrow," Principal Wright clarified. "She absolutely does."

Out of the corner of my eye, I saw Dad replace the tissue box, knocking over the bobble-headed replica of the principal, bad hair and all. "Thanks for coming, Xander. Avery's in quite a difficult spot. She needs to catch up on her schoolwork this year or she won't be able to graduate in May. We called this meeting to develop a strategy. I know you're a strong student, and having been Austin's best friend, we hoped you'd consider tutoring her."

The bell rang. First period was over. Maybe I could stretch this meeting out to last all day. Even this was better than being surrounded by other classmates.

"I know you're very busy," Dad continued, "and this would be quite a time commitment, but we wanted to ask before we move on to more, shall we say, unfortunate options." He talked as though striking a business deal. "We would pay you. Very well, in fact. Consider it a part-time job."

Please say no.

"Only if Avery——" My name caught on his tongue. He cleared his throat. "Only if Avery wants me to help her."

How chivalrous. Feeling four sets of eyes on me, I slowly

turned my head. Thankfully, I'd fought off tears so far. I could hold my head high and show Xander, the principal, and my parents that I wasn't as broken as they thought. But nothing could've prepared me for what I saw.

Xander was much taller than the last time I'd seen him. My gaze had to travel upward to meet his eyes. Remarkably, they weren't hidden by that mop of hair. It seemed he'd discovered hair gel, so his dark waves swooped up and over. And that was the slightest change about him. Broad shoulders, arm muscles, clear skin, and a pronounced jawline. Total glow-up. Why, why, why did he have to get all attractive and stuff? It would only inflate his ego even more.

Yet, when we held eye contact, I only saw compassion. That made literally no sense. Unless it was compassion by way of pity.

"It doesn't matter if she wants help or not. She's getting it," Dad said.

"Whatever." I was resigned to my fate. I had survived that *Fast and Furious* marathon with Jake sophomore year. I could make it through this.

Still locked in my gaze, Xander lifted a corner of his mouth in a bit of a smile. Did he find some sick pleasure in lauding his academic supremacy over me?

I pursed my lips and narrowed my eyes. He must've gotten the message because his smile grew into a smirk. That was the Xander I remembered.

"I'll do it."

◆

Stupid, dumb, idiotic waste of time. After that nightmare of a meeting, I waited with Mom out in front of the school until Dad pulled the car up. I folded Mom's walker and stuck it in the trunk while Dad helped her into the car. Seeing her exhaustion only made the situation worse. I moved to her door. "Thanks for coming, Mom." I even managed a smile.

"I'm glad I was able to be here. I'm proud of you, sweet girl," she said.

Not as proud as she would've been of Austin. I decided to let that one slide. She wasn't the villain here. Dad, on the other hand . . .

I waited until Dad shut the passenger-side door before I spoke. "I'm eighteen. In the state of Colorado, I can legally quit school. I don't need to go back in there."

He checked his phone for notifications. "Yes, you do. You aren't just going to sit around your room making those fashion videos." Dad took his focus off work long enough to discover my video channel?

"Wow, Dad, you knew about that? It's like you're actually part of my life."

He tucked his phone into his pocket. "You're going back to school. And you'll accept Xander's help." He held me gently by my shoulders. "Look, honey. This has been a horrendous year, but we can't give up. You're a Mendenhall. You have too much intelligence and talent to keep hiding away from the world."

I dragged out a sigh until my lungs begged for a new breath.

"Avery, you and I have always been the strong ones. I need you to remember that."

"What am I supposed to do? Act like you and pretend nothing happened?"

He dropped his hands. "That's not fair, and you know it."

"Sorry, Dad." Lie. I wasn't sorry for telling it like it was.

I backed away, then leaned against the brick wall, beneath the words "Front Range High School," and watched my parents leave the lot. On my left, one of the front doors opened. I didn't need to look to know it was Xander. He had, like, no boundaries or self-awareness. A quick glance showed him mimicking my exact pose a few yards away.

The least he could do was say something. I'd never known

him to bite his tongue, but the silence dragged, making things super awkward.

"You got taller," I stated, still staring straight ahead.

"Uh, yeah. My mom said I had a real growth spurt. Thanks for noticing."

This was getting way too friendly. "You're still ugly though."

Xander snickered. He'd always been smug and overconfident, even when he was short and had big ears, bad hair, and braces—the awkward-stage trifecta. I couldn't tell if the braces were still there, but it didn't matter. Xander Dixon was hot.

"And you're still mean," he said. "It's nice to know that hasn't changed."

Now it was my turn to laugh. "I'm the mean one?"

"Let me guess. You're still mad I told everyone you scored the role of Quasimodo in the live-action version of *The Hunchback of Notre Dame?*"

"If only that was it."

Xander rolled to face me and picked at the brick quietly, long enough for me to feel like I'd swallowed that wasp and it was now swirling inside my belly. "I stopped by your house a bunch of times," he said. "Why wouldn't you see me?"

The answer to that would take the rest of the school day.

"I didn't even know if you were home," he continued when I stayed silent. "No one did. I tried my best to squash the rumors about where you'd gone. Cross-country move, rehab, suicide attempt, psychiatric ward. . . . My favorite was that you'd joined a family of gorillas in the Congo. That sounds pretty fun, actually."

"Why are you telling me this?"

"So you know you were missed."

"Austin was missed. Not me." The simple mention of his name was enough for grief to swarm over me and for pain to etch into my skin. I pushed off the wall and strolled to the student parking lot.

"Where are you going?" Xander asked, following a few feet behind me.

"None of your business."

"Shouldn't we talk about tutoring?"

"I don't need your help."

"But you won't graduate. What will you do without a high school diploma? How will you get a job?"

"I'll go back to social media influencing."

"How do you know brands are still interested? You've been offline a long time."

Shows how much he knows. "I guess I'll wait tables or something."

"With your chipper personality?"

I paused, debating on whether to challenge him. Deciding not to, I stepped quickly between two cars, making him fall behind. When I reached my Wrangler, I opened the driver's door and tossed my bag onto the passenger seat.

Xander finally caught up to me. "Avery, are you okay?"

This couldn't go on. I looked him dead in the eye. "Don't do that."

"Don't do what?"

"Pretend you care."

He stepped forward, close enough to touch me. Close enough for me to smell the woodsy cologne that had replaced his cheap body spray. The whole situation had a dizzying effect on me, and I didn't like it. "What if I'm not pretending?"

"Then you're the one who needs help." I climbed into my Jeep.

True to form, he threw his hand out and stopped me from shutting the door. I flattened my palm against his chest to push him back, but he grasped on to me so I couldn't pull away. His heart hammered the heel of my hand.

"Leave me alone, Xander. Or I'll make you pay."

He released me, but instead of moping about like a person with actual feelings, he smiled like an idiot. "Promise?"

Ugh. Unfortunately, he moved just far enough away that I couldn't run over his foot when I backed out. This day kept getting worse. He stood there watching me drive away with that satisfied look on his not-ugly face, acting like he had some kind of right to my feelings, my thoughts, even my time.

And not that it mattered, but yes, he had gotten his braces off.

*four*

## LORI

In the past seventy-two hours, I had gotten lost in my own home many times. And that was only on the first floor. What on earth had made Michael and I think we needed all this? Maybe I would have felt different if it felt like home, but it didn't. In a notebook, I'd already drawn pages and pages of ideas that could change that. I could add style and warmth with a small budget. It was a gift of mine. One that I hadn't lost on the train tracks last fall.

With the help of my physical therapist, I'd climbed the stairs this afternoon and taken a much-needed nap. Feeling refreshed, I was ready to explore again. As far as I could tell, there was only one room I'd yet to see, although I'd rested my hand on the handle several times. Once again, I was staring at the door marked with the green-and-white "Austin Avenue" street sign. I traced the letters.

*"Please, Mom? It would look cool on my door, don't ya think?"*

*"Austin, you already used your souvenir money on that shell. You don't have enough, baby."*

A boardwalk shop. Ocean City. Summer of 2014. Nine years ago. No more recent than other memories, but this one was sharp, not fuzzy. Austin had been so disappointed. My son didn't know that I'd had to scrounge up pennies to get Michael to agree to that vacation. I'd promised him we'd keep within our budget. Avery had been standing behind Austin, and while I took Austin out of the shop, she'd stayed a couple more minutes. When she emerged, she held the street sign out to Austin after choosing to use her own souvenir money on it.

By my side, Wynton whined, pulling me out of the memory.

"Should we check it out, boy?"

Wynton's tail wagged furiously.

"Okay. Just for a minute." Feeling strong from the recovered memory, I moved my walker out of the way and opened the door. As I cautiously stepped inside, Wynton ran past me and jumped onto the full bed. A figure popped up from the covers. I reached for something to grab, but I fell too fast, slamming my tailbone against the floor. Pain reverberated up my spine.

"Mom!" Avery scrambled off the bed and came to my aid. "I didn't mean to scare you. I'm so sorry."

"It's all right, sweetie. I'm simply unsteady on my feet." I fought off the pain-bred tears surging behind my eyes. "What—What are you doing home? Shouldn't you be at school?"

Avery glanced away. "Can I get you ice or a heating pad or something?"

"Really, I'm fine." I rubbed my lower back. Deirdre and Michael wouldn't like me moving about so much without my walker, but they weren't here, and they didn't need to know about this spill. "Please don't tell your father about this."

She plopped down beside me. "As long as you don't tell him I skipped school."

I pinned her with my best parenting look, but I was rusty. Besides, Avery's red-rimmed eyes called for compassion, not discipline. "Were you sleeping in here? Do you do that a lot?"

She shrugged and brushed her fingers down Wynton's neck.

As the pain lessened, I breathed in a familiar scent I couldn't place, but it swirled around me. A faint hint of cologne, maybe—the grassy kind you might find at a clothing shop at the Colorado Mills Mall—mixed with a synthetic smell that took me back to an elementary school band concert. Austin, but not the one I could feel hugging my waist on Mother's Day or holding my hand at the pool. I scanned the room. Only one picture looked familiar. Austin and Avery posed in front of the school bus on their first day of kindergarten. Avery had cried when she was placed in a different class than Austin—scared to be without him for even a few hours. My gaze found hers. "Avery, do you want to talk about the accident? Or about Austin?"

"Why? It's not like it would do any good."

"You don't know that. You miss him. I do too. I think it would be nice to talk through our feelings."

"Maybe for you. I'd rather not hear about how hard it was to lose your favorite kid."

The lashing gutted me. "How can you— I love you both."

"Of course you do. You're a mom. But Austin was your favorite. He was everyone's favorite. Even mine. I get it."

I started to protest, but Avery cut me off. "You don't remember how it was before the accident, Mom."

I took a deep breath. "Tell me. I want to know."

"You want me to tell you how I'd sneak out to meet up with my boyfriend? How about the time I was texting while driving and hit a mailbox? Or all the times I'd mouth off and you'd tell me I was just like Dad?"

It couldn't be true. Using my disappointments with Michael as a way to insult my little girl?

"We didn't get along, Mom. It was Austin's job to mediate."

"How could that be? You and I were close. I took you to that Tom Petty concert. I taught you to sew."

"I know. I made a skirt that was so short Dad never let me wear it out of the house." Avery picked a few pieces of dog hair off my pants. "When I started high school . . . I don't know. I don't blame you for not liking me as much. I didn't make it easy for you."

"Even if that were true—which it is not—I never could've had a favorite child. I'm sorry I made you feel that way."

"It's okay. You and Dad were dealing with a lot of junk." Avery stood and held out both hands. "Let me help you up."

Junk? Between Michael and I? Since I was in no position to deny the offer, I accepted her help and together we worked our way back to standing. While I rested against the doorframe, Avery carried in my walker so I wouldn't repeat the fall.

I thanked her, then started getting to know who my boy became in the years I forgot. This one room more than made up for the lack of sentimentalism in the rest of the house. Though organized and tidy, the room was filled with knickknacks. The shell from Ocean City. Trophies from band competitions. I picked up a snow globe with a basket of puppies inside. Avery's present to Austin for Christmas the year before we adopted Wynton.

I moved to put it back in its place. No dust circle.

"I like to come in here when I want to feel close to him." Avery's voice was so soft. It could hardly be heard above Wynton's jingling collar as he scratched his ear with his back leg.

"Are you the one that keeps it clean?"

Avery scoffed. "For sure, no. Dad hired a maid."

A framed picture sat on the dresser. The little boy from my mind had grown quite a few years. His blond hair had darkened slightly, but his eyes and smile were the same. In a typical school dance pose, his arms circled the waist of a brown-haired girl I recognized. "Sarah?"

"Yeah. They started going out in sixth grade. He loved her." Avery's words wavered but didn't break. "This picture was from sophomore homecoming."

"How is she doing now?"

She shrugged. "Don't know. I haven't talked to her."

"Why not? It seems like she might be someone who could understand what you're going through. I remember her being a charming little girl."

"She's still sweet. She and Austin were perfect together. I couldn't talk to her because . . . because . . ."

A chime rang out through the house, leading Wynton to bark and jog out of the room. I must have looked confused because Avery explained that it was the doorbell.

"Oh," I said. "It will take me a few minutes to get back downstairs. Will you answer it?"

She groaned. "I don't wanna. It's probably Mrs. Lowry with more gestapo soup."

I chuckled. "Gazpacho."

"Whatever."

The chime sounded again, followed by a knock. "Avery, please?"

She threw her hands up. "Fine."

I followed her out of Austin's room, slowly pushing my walker to the top of the stairs. Down below, the door opened.

"Avery Wheeler Mendenhall, why aren't you in school? I saw your car in the drive and thought, 'Great, another Mendenhall female is throwing her life away.'" My mother's voice could polish coal off a diamond. The nurses at rehab had nicknamed her Baby Jane after Bette Davis's iconic character in *Whatever Happened to Baby Jane?* She had the personality to match.

"It's nice to see you too, Grandma," Avery deadpanned.

"Have you given any more thought to letting me cut you some bangs? Your forehead is too big not to have any."

"Mom, Grandma Anita's here!"

"All right. I'm coming down." I pushed my walker aside and gripped the banister with both hands, sidestepping to the stair below.

"Wait. I'll help you," Avery rushed up to me, although I'm sure that had more to do with leaving my mother's firing range than having genuine concern I might fall. She held my waist as I prudently descended the staircase.

My mother watched the entire thing from the bottom of the stairs. "I knew you'd be trying to do too much. You really should be in a wheelchair."

"I'm fine. Winded, is all." With Avery's help, I made it to the couch.

"I brought enchiladas. You have to put it in at 350 for twenty-five minutes."

"You didn't have to do that."

"Oh really?" She arched her brows. "Would Michael have fixed you dinner? I seriously doubt it." My mother set the glass dish on the countertop.

"I'm gonna go listen to some music." Avery scurried upstairs before anyone could force her to stay.

Mom hardly noticed. She simply headed to the windows and opened one. "You need fresh air. It's a beautiful day outside."

"Is it? I haven't been out."

"That's what I figured. He's got you back in your granite and suede prison cell."

"Mom, I don't understand."

"Of course you don't, sweetie." With a shake of her head, my mother came to my side and took my hand, stroking it gently. No wonder she was worried. My nails were clean but short and natural, with only my wedding ring as decoration. Not pageant-ready at all. "Listen. I want you and Avery to live with me."

I sucked in a sharp breath. The outdoor air, although not exactly cold, still prompted a rash of gooseflesh up my arms. "I've already told you—"

"At least until your memory returns fully. That way, you can make an informed decision about your marriage."

"My marriage?" I shook my head. "Mom, I love Michael. We've been apart so long. Why would I leave?"

"Because he's not who you think he is, and frankly, you deserve better."

I took my hand back and rubbed my arms. The chill remained. First Avery's "junk" comment. Now this? "No. Michael is a good husband and a great father. Our family is finally together. Broken maybe, and missing Austin, but the three of us need this time to heal."

"You won't heal here. He'll break your heart again." My mother lifted her chin. "I refuse to watch it happen. It will take my last breath, I'm sure of it."

I did my best to keep my breath steady. To be sure, my mother had never liked Michael, even in the early days. In her eyes, he'd gotten in the way of her dreams for me. She couldn't care less about the dreams I had for myself.

Yet there was more fire to her hatred than I remembered from before. She didn't know Michael's true nature. How he'd stepped up during the most challenging time of my life. Despite what my mother said, or what that Enid woman insinuated, Michael would never break my heart.

"I should get going. I'm playing cards with some friends tonight." My mother went over the cooking instructions for the enchiladas again, enunciating each step like I had a hearing problem in addition to a memory problem. She gathered me in her arms for a tight, no-nonsense hug. "Think about it," she whispered in my ear. "You're always welcome."

I watched as she let herself out the way she came. The moment the front door shut, Avery ran down the steps, twisted the lock, and peeked through the sidelight. After the sound of her car faded into the distance, Avery turned around, a scowl bending her pretty face.

◆

**Michael**
Hey babe, I thought I'd be able to leave the office at six tonight, but one of my clients may be

facing a lawsuit. I need to pull some of his money
from the market. It will be closer to seven.

I hate to do this, but I need one more hour. I'll
be home soon.

Sorry, babe. This is a huge mess. Don't bother
waiting up.

After Michael's third text came in at nine thirty, I turned off
the sappy movie I'd been watching and made my slow climb
up to my bedroom with only Wynton's encouragement. I pretended that his wagging tail against the wall was the slow clap
from a movie about an underdog. The trophy was won, the
lesson learned, the crush kissed.

I knocked on Avery's door loudly since Van Halen was inside
shouting, "You Really Got Me."

"Yeah?" she called over the noise. "It's unlocked."

I opened the door and peeked in. Avery's room, where she'd
spent the entire evening except the few minutes it took her
to grab her dinner plate, was a teenage girl's dream. A low-
profile platform bed was draped in layers of white and gold
fabric. A clean contrast to the accent wall wallpapered with
vintage posters of 1980s bands. A window seat overlooked the
backyard. In the corner of the room, lighting equipment and a
tripod-like gadget leaned against the sewing table where Avery
sat, facing away from me. A satiny fabric flowed down her lap
to her feet.

"I'm going to bed. I wanted to say good night."

Avery cast a glance over her shoulder before resuming her
work. "Night."

I so badly wanted to kiss the top of her head, but with my
walker downstairs, even an extra ten feet was a stretch. "I love
you."

"You too." She kicked up the stitch speed on the machine.
And so it was.

My bedtime routine was simple: wash face, apply lotion, brush teeth, floss, apply ChapStick, and smooth cream over the grotesque four-inch scar that snaked down my scalp. I slipped out of my clothes, then tossed them in the hamper. It took three attempts to find my pajama drawer. Once I did, I found every possible type of nightwear, all neatly folded: cotton gowns, flannel tops with matching bottoms, tank tops and shorts. Only one option could genuinely be called sexy. A silky piece the color of champagne with lace embellishments, spaghetti straps, and a not-so-modest thigh slit—classier lingerie than I used to wear. Blushing, I reminisced over Michael's smile when I'd donned those old, cheap threads. Surely this could take his mind off work.

Ever since the accident, our marriage had the spice of Fred and Ethel Mertz's relationship. In rehab, when I'd regained all my motor functions and gotten strong enough physically, Deirdre and the other nurses had said they'd happily look the other way if Michael and I wanted to, let's say, reconnect. While I was more than willing to act on my ever-strengthening desires, Michael was not. Apparently, a physical rehab center wasn't the best location to get him in the mood. I'd had high hopes for the first two nights I'd been home. But again, I was game. Michael wasn't. Why?

There was once a time when we'd have taken every opportunity to enjoy each other, even when we were newlyweds with a double dose of pregnancy belly between us.

Just for kicks, I slipped the gown over my head and studied my reflection in the mirror. Although I'd need to put on a few more pounds to fill it out correctly, I looked good. This was real silk, and it felt fabulous, except for one spot. I reached between my arm and my ribs until my fingers took hold of a price tag. I found a pair of cuticle scissors in my vanity and clipped the string. I'm not sure what surprised me more: the sky-high price I paid or the fact that I'd never worn this.

I slid between the cool sheets on our bed and relaxed in the sleekness.

Sometime later, I awoke to shuffling noises. Light shone in my eyes, emanating from the slim crack outlining the bathroom door. A quick check of my phone showed 11:43 p.m. Not exactly bank hours.

I adjusted the duvet and sheet covering me. Then I brushed hair over my scar while scraping my bottom lip through my teeth to give them a bit of color and an inviting plump.

Inside the bathroom, the water turned off—my cue to close my eyes, soften my facial features, and slightly part my lips.

Barely audible, the door opened. Behind closed lids, I could see the spread of light shining on the bed. On me. I heard nothing. I felt nothing except my eager anticipation warming me from the inside out. After thirty seconds or so, the mattress rocked, dipping just enough for my right shoulder to roll forward a bit. He hadn't turned off the bathroom light yet. Was he looking at me how I'd so longed for him to see me? As a woman. Not a crash victim or a burden.

He expelled a long breath. His hand rested lightly on my hip. Kiss me, I tried to speak into his mind. Instead, I writhed slightly in reaction to his touch, inviting him to awaken me in whatever way might please him.

Again, the mattress shifted beneath me. A shadow fell over my eyelids, and breath not my own warmed my expectant lips. He lingered there for several torturous moments.

And suddenly, as if time had reversed, the warm breath withdrew, as did the hand on my hip. I opened my eyes to see him leave the bed and turn off the bathroom light. When he returned, climbing under the covers and adjusting his body for sleep, I reached for him, only to find his extra pillow creating a wall between us.

# *five*

## AVERY

Thank the Lord for school libraries. Like, seriously. If it weren't for Ms. Clemmons's willingness to keep the library unlocked during her lunch hour, I would have to face the cafeteria. As if the first five periods hadn't been torture enough. I lost count of how many shrugs, one-word answers, and dead-eyed stares I gave in response to questions from students and teachers. The librarian was the only one who hadn't prodded me for details. Maybe she could tell I was at my breaking point when I asked if I could hide out in the stacks.

The silence and a lunch packed by Mom were all that mattered in the world right now. Not gonna lie: peanut butter and jelly sandwiches tasted way better when cut into four triangles and paired with apple slices. All that was missing was a bag of Cheetos and I'd be right back in second grade. Plus, the sticky note Mom had packed inside telling me she loved me would make a great bookmark for me and Austin's journal.

Okay, it was less a journal and more a spiral-bound, wide-rule notebook with two cartoon aliens on the cover. When Austin first attended band camp, he wrote me letters in this notebook, but he didn't have stamps or envelopes, so they remained inside. He placed it on my bed for me to read through when he got home. The next month at cheer camp, I did the same. Thus, we began writing letters to each other when spoken words would be too loud or too painful.

Since he'd been gone, of course, there'd been dozens of Dear Austin letters added, but no Dear Avery letters. Such is life. Or death. I opened to the first blank page and let the blue ink in my pen spill my thoughts about the day.

*August 26*

*Dear Austin,*

*I'll never forgive Dad for making me come to school today. Because I'm clever, I've managed to keep clear of classes for three days now. So this morning Dad took my keys, drove me to school, and walked me to the door so I couldn't escape.*

*Of course, my locker has to be in the center of the main hallway. Remember the bathroom that overflowed toilet water into the hallway freshman year? I'm right next to that. You should have heard everyone whispering. They were like, "I can't believe she's back," and "I thought she killed herself." Oh yeah. They also laughed about the way I looked.*

*My golden mane and meticulously made-up face are long gone. What's the point? My roots are long and dishwater blond and I haven't worn makeup in forever. You used to say I didn't need it anyway. Still, it was hard walking in there without you. Remember when I made you hold my hand in kindergarten?*

*Anyway, when I got to my locker, guess who came up behind me.*

*Sarah. Your Sarah.*

*In case you're wondering, she hasn't changed much. Her hair is still cut to her shoulders, but now she has bangs. Can you see her from where you are? If not, just know she's still super pretty. And sweet, of course. Before I knew it, I was locked in a hug.*

*She smelled like a spring meadow, cotton candy, and the color pink all rolled into one.*

46

*Unfortunately, Xander was there too. He keeps staring at me. I know what you're thinking, and no, it's not like that. Mom and Dad are making him tutor me so I can get caught up with my classes. I'm not happy about it. He's not a good person. Do you know how I know? Because after I walked toward my first-period class, I looked back and saw him hugging your girlfriend. And you thought he was such a faithful friend.*

*I'm sorry to be the one to tell you. I promise it isn't payback for that mess about Jake after the football game. About that, I shouldn't have gotten so mad. You were only trying to protect me. I should've let you, just like that first day of kindergarten. I'll forever regret my last words to you. I promise I didn't mean them. Please forgive me.*

*Love you always,*
*Avery*

I bookmarked the page and slid the journal into my bag. Knowing I had another twenty-five minutes of lunch left, I pulled out my already-twice-read copy of *Emma*.

Three triangles through my sandwich, one of the library doors opened. I glanced up, leaving the village of Highbury to see the one person I despised more than Xander.

When Jake Powers stepped inside, his focus dead set on me, my appetite plummeted lower than the neckline of a Regency-era gown. I closed my book, then tossed the remainder of my food back into the lunch bag.

I was too late. When I stood, I practically collided with Jake. The fumes of his cologne were noxious, and my stomach roiled. I had not bought him that. Must have been a gift from Courtney.

"Hey."

After all that time, after all he'd done to me, I got a hey.

I pushed past him, intentionally shouldering his arm. Wishful thinking I could cause him any pain since he was too big of a lug to hurt. All it did was give him the chance to grab my elbow and keep me within reach.

"Come on, now. I haven't seen you in forever. How have you been?"

I shot a look at the hand grasping my arm. "I've been studying assault."

A shy look overtook his usual cocky expression, and he let go. "Sorry. I just want to talk to you."

"About?"

"Things, I guess. How's your mom?"

"Fine."

"I heard she doesn't remember who she is or something."

"You need to find a better source for your gossip. She's still working on retrieving memories from before the accident, but she knows her identity."

"That's good, I guess." Jake lifted onto his toes, then settled back on his heels. "And your dad?"

"Fine. We're all just swell."

"Avery, I'm sorry"—he blew out a breath and looked me in the eyes—"for everything."

The sting I'd worked so hard to numb fired back quickly and angrily, centering deep in my chest. "Whatever. I'm over it. Considering all I lost last fall, you were the easiest to forget. As Jane Austen would say, you are not really necessary to my happiness."

Why he looked like I hurt his feelings, I'd never understand. He was the one who threw me away. "Okay, then . . . I'm glad you're doing okay."

"I am."

We stared at each other.

Again, the library door swung wide. It took several seconds to realize the girl with bleached blond hair, fake lashes, and hideous fashion sense was my former best friend.

"Avery. Hi." Courtney looked more terrified than when Xander dressed like the Slender Man and ran through our sleepover. So I was scarier than a mythical internet villain? That made perfect sense. I wasn't the one who stole my friend's boyfriend at the worst time of her life for no understandable reason. Courtney and I had been inseparable for the first half of high school. I'd trusted her with my secrets, and I'd thought she trusted me with hers.

I rolled my eyes and tucked my hair behind my ears. Emma never had to deal with this junk.

"Jake?"

Shocking that she didn't trust him. "You better go," I said. "Your girlfriend's waiting."

He nodded. "Thanks for talking to me. I'll see you around school." As he walked to the doors, Courtney shot him a death glare.

Fortunately, I held my laughter in until the door shut. Once I started, I couldn't stop. My shoulders shook, my breath escaped with each wheezing hoot, and a tear slid down my cheek.

Are you paying attention, God? I prayed. I'd hate for you to miss even one minute of this pathetic life you gave me. Can't wait to see what you do next.

My phone vibrated. I retrieved it from the side pocket of my book bag and checked my notifications—a text from Slender Man himself.

Hey. It's Xander. When do you want to start our tutoring?

Yep. Can't wait for what's next.

*six*

## LORI

Peonies. Salvia. Monardella. Poppies. Perovskia. Columbine. How was it that I could name every flower in our pristine garden but not remember planting them? Fortunately, Michael had hired a gardener this spring and summer. He said he couldn't bear to see it all go to the weeds after all my hard work.

So that morning, when the gardener had pulled into the drive, I'd told her we didn't need her services anymore.

Somehow, I felt alive, kneeling on the grass with my hands in the dirt. Perhaps it was the fresh breeze traversing the mountains. Perhaps it was the morning sun bathing my arms and face with warmth. Perhaps it was the slight burn in my muscles as they instinctually cared for these plants.

The delicate, herbal scent of the lavender to my left wafted past as I pinched off the spent salvia blooms. I hummed a melody, then realized I had no clue what the song was or where I'd heard it.

"Hi there!" Rounding the patio, Enid neared with a large basket on the crook of her arm. "Is Kaiser Michael here to kick me out?"

I offered a courtesy laugh, although I wasn't sure if that was the correct response to her question. "Michael's at work. I was hoping time in the garden might jog some memories for me."

Enid stood above me, blocking the sun. "You remember me, right?"

I worried my lip, trying to come up with a kinder response than no. "Um, well, not exactly. I'm so sorry."

She waved off the apology. "Don't you dare apologize, honey. I put together this little gift to remind you. I would've come by earlier, but Michael forbade me."

"Why would he do that?"

"I stopped trying to understand that man years ago." Enid set the basket on the patio table and then helped me rise from the grass. What Enid lacked in height, she made up for in strength, as evidenced by her outfit—spandex shorts, a halter top, and a six-pack of abs.

The basket overflowed with goodies someone else might get excited by. Not me.

"Okay, we've got not one but two bottles of wine. Rosé all day, baby."

"That's nice," I fibbed. Wine had never been something I enjoyed. I didn't think so, at least.

She withdrew a book with small tags sticking out of the pages. "The latest Sanna Bristow novel. I went ahead and marked the best scenes. You may have forgotten me, but I know you remember the hot plumber from *Taking the Plunge*. He's back."

Oh my. I moved to the closest chair, then sank into it. Wynton wandered over and stretched his body beneath me before sighing heavily.

Enid prattled on, "Your favorite nail polish. Cashews. The last four issues of *Tarry & Dwell* in case you get the itch to redecorate. Finally, a plane ticket to head to California with Laney, Ruth, and me in October."

"I can't—"

"Of course, that's what you say now. But after you've been home awhile, you may remember why you love getting away."

"You and I took vacations together?"

"At least twice a year. We've been to San Diego, New Orleans, the Bahamas, New York." Enid's sparkle-tipped nail circled the shirtless model on the book's cover, and she gazed dreamily at him like the act could conjure the model to life. "Oh, and Key West, although even I don't remember that one, thanks to that margarita stand." She winked at me.

"And we spent a lot of time together at home too?"

"Oh yeah. Book club, hot yoga, PTO. And I never would've made it through all those band competitions without you."

"That's right. Your daughter was in the band with Austin?"

"Yes, Margot. I always wanted her to date Austin, but Sarah got to him first."

"Are Margot and Avery friends?"

Enid laughed. "No. Avery's not in the same group as Margot. Avery's more popular, or at least she used to be."

My spine stiffened. I leaned on Michael's explanation from the day I returned home. "Avery's having a hard time."

"Of course she is. She lost everyone close to her on the day of the accident, or soon after. Austin, you, Jake."

"Jake?"

"Yeah, Jake Powers. Her boyfriend. Margot said they'd dated for a year or two. A week or so after the funeral, Avery returned to school and discovered Jake had hooked up with her best friend. It caused this whole scene. Avery locked herself in the teachers' restroom. People thought she was going to, you know, harm herself."

My heart absorbed this information the way flesh welcomes shards of glass.

"It probably didn't help with you in a coma at the time. Poor girl's whole world fell apart." Enid clucked her tongue.

Her boyfriend and her best friend? No wonder she'd stopped going to school. How humiliating. "At least she still had Michael."

When Enid snorted a laugh, Wynton startled, bumping his

head on my chair. I reached down and rubbed his forehead with one hand and scratched his neck with the other.

"Michael was a stranger in your house before the accident. I can't imagine he was any more present afterward."

"A stranger?" I shook my head. "No. Michael was always home for dinner, always helping the kids do their homework."

Enid put her hands up and pursed her lips. "All I know is what you told me. When he switched jobs and the money started rolling in, he changed."

I peered down at my hands and futilely picked at the dirt caked beneath my nails. Distant stares, long work hours, and distracted conversation. I'd seen enough since I'd been home to think Enid may not be completely wrong. "That's when you and I became friends?"

Enid nodded. "I'd seen you around the school before that, but we never spoke. When you moved in, we got to know each other. You were always sad, like you were still waiting for your old husband to come home. You did everything for your kids, but I think it took a toll on you, especially—"

"Mother!" Enid's mini-me stomped across our lawn. "Have you seen my Spanish textbook?"

"Why are you asking me? I took Spanish twenty-five years ago. It isn't my textbook."

"Can you help me look for it?"

"Margot, you're being rude to Lori."

"Sorry, Mrs. Mendenhall," Margot said before turning back to her mom. "Please? I need to do my homework before practice."

I leaned back in my chair, wishing I could escape this conversation. "I should head inside. Avery will be home soon."

◆

I made pesto with basil from the garden. I mixed that into pasta and served it with grilled chicken for dinner. I even poured myself a glass of Enid's rosé, but after one sip, my taste buds protested. A glass of skim milk was in order. It also helped settle my nerves.

I tried engaging Avery in conversation, not that I was expecting her to pour her heart out about what happened last fall with that Jake boy. Even a simple "How was your day, dear?" "It was great, Mom" would be better than the current level of communication.

Avery had always been more closed off than Austin. How often would he speak for the two of them? Whether it was about wanting a pet or needing ketchup for tater tots, all Avery had to do was give him a whisper or a particular look, and Austin would step up. Had anyone stepped up for her that day she locked herself in the faculty bathroom?

Poor, brokenhearted girl. It was the only personality trait Avery and I had in common. In all other ways, she took after Michael.

The door to the garage shut, and I stood.

Michael appeared and sniffed the air. "It smells good in here."

"Thanks. I've set the table for us. Avery wanted to eat in her room." I held on to my chair for balance. I'd managed the past few days without my walker, but I still wasn't confident, especially when my mind wasn't focused on my steps.

Michael set his bag on the floor. He gave Wynton a pat hello. When he kissed my cheek, I knew Enid had been wrong. He held my chair steady as I lowered my body into it. Yes, Michael was caring—a good husband. He settled across the table from me and immediately grabbed the fork to dig in.

"Can we pray?" I asked. Michael peered at me from beneath a quizzical brow. "For the food?"

"Sure."

We hadn't prayed before a meal since I returned home. I got the feeling it hadn't been our custom for a long time.

Michael bent his head but said nothing. I grasped his hand—awkwardly since it still held the fork—and closed my eyes. After a few more painful seconds of silence, I spoke. "Lord, we thank you for this food and our family, both here and in heaven. Amen."

Halfway through our quiet meal, I wiped my lips with a napkin. "How was work?"

"Good." Michael bobbed his chin. "I picked up a new client. He's a lawyer in Littleton. I'm hoping I can impress him so he'll steer his partners my way."

"How many clients do you have?"

"Not enough." His lips curved a bit as he glanced my way, a sliver of the flirt I once knew emerging.

"You've explained this to me before but I'm still not sure I understand. What exactly does a wealth management company do?"

Michael sat back in his chair. "Big picture, it's simple. I help my clients build, preserve, and transfer their financial assets. My services are more nuanced for each client."

"What do you like about it?"

"I like getting to know the people I help. They let me peer into their finances—their past mistakes, their hopes. It means a lot that they trust me with that information. And then I get to help them meet their goals."

"You make money seem almost romantic."

"I wouldn't go that far." He quirked a brow and chuckled. "Another reason I like my job is I'm finally able to provide for you and the kids."

"You've always provided for us, even when you didn't have to."

He stabbed a bite of chicken with his fork and drummed it against the rim of the plate. "As a high school economics teacher, I couldn't provide the life you deserved. Now I can."

"So, money is romantic after all," I quipped.

"I guess so." He looked at me from beneath his dark lashes, his stare weighted with something that sent a flash of heat through me. Then, like a switch had flipped, he turned his attention back to that bite of chicken. "How was your day? Did I see your garden shoes out?" he asked before continuing his dinner.

"Yes. I picked basil for the pesto."

"It's good. Thanks for making it."

"Enid came over too."

His chewing stilled for a moment. He resumed, then forced a swallow. "What did she have to say?"

"Michael, what was our marriage like during the years I can't remember?"

Confusion flickered in his eyes. "Good." It sounded more like a question than an answer.

"Just good?" I asked. "It used to be amazing. Or is my memory playing tricks on me?"

With a set of his jaw, he pushed his plate forward and rested his elbows on the table. "Lori, our marriage is and always has been strong. Whatever Enid claims to know about us is likely a product of jealousy."

"And my mom? Is she jealous too? Because she doesn't seem to like you either."

"Anita has never liked me. You know that." He folded his hands and pressed his knuckles to his mouth as his eyes darkened. After a few uncomfortable moments, he rose from his chair and kneeled before me, taking my hand in his. "I know times are strange. Our marriage hasn't been perfect. I haven't been perfect. But I'm asking you to trust me so we can get through this together. Do you think you can do that?"

Those brown eyes held such earnestness, yet all I could wonder was if I even had a choice in the matter.

# *seven*

## AVERY

I turned my Jeep into my neighborhood, letting it coast while I fed Wynton another french fry. I relaxed back in my seat and enjoyed the sun on my face and the wind in my hair. Why couldn't life feel like this all the time? People would be a lot happier.

At the sight of Xander's Bronco in the driveway and him leaning against the side of it, that moment of joy disappeared quicker than a fry in front of Wynton. Tuesday had come way too fast. I hadn't had enough time to plan a way out of this. Too bad he'd already seen me. I opened the garage and pulled the Jeep inside. After cutting the engine, I unbuckled Wynton's safety harness and lifted the big boy to the ground. Sure, he could probably make the jump, but I couldn't bear it if he got hurt. The moment his paws touched the pavement, Wynton took off, barreling toward Xander.

"Hey, buddy!" Xander kneeled and patted Wynton's back as the dog pranced and danced in front of him, something I hadn't seen since Austin was alive. "I've missed you, boy!"

"What are you doing here?" Maybe feigning ignorance would work.

Xander looked up at me. "I'm here for our first tutoring session."

"You know I don't need your help, right?"

"You don't need it? Or you don't want it?"

"Both. Come on, Wynton. Inside."

The dog looked at me and whined before sitting to Xander's left.

"I said inside," I commanded.

Still nothing. Xander took a step forward and patted his thigh. Wynton popped back up and trailed him into the garage.

Awesome. Add Wynton to the list of people against me. "Fine. You can come in, but you aren't tutoring me." I grabbed the shopping bag out of the Jeep and walked into the house. I didn't bother to acknowledge Mom, who was chopping vegetables in the kitchen.

Of course, Xander did. "Hi, Mrs. M. I came over to work with Avery."

"I remembered." She smiled at him. "I'm so glad you're here, honey. Are you hungry? I thought you might be, so I made you your favorite—grilled cheese, no crusts."

"Aw, you didn't have to do that."

"I wanted to." Mom handed Xander a plate holding a sandwich and sliced carrots.

"Okay, but in the future, you can leave the crusts on. I try to act more mature now."

"Do you still like your Nesquik to have an extra spoonful of powder in it?"

Xander laughed. "Yeah, but don't tell anyone."

I sat on the couch with my canvas shopping bag and perused my haul from the thrift store while Mom chatted easily with Xander. I told myself the tightening in my stomach was simply a craving for the grilled cheese that Xander was scarfing down. If I hadn't already eaten a drive-thru cheeseburger, I would've accepted when Mom called with the offer to make one for me. But, no, this was more than just craving a sandwich.

Somehow, Xander knew exactly what to say to get my mom to smile, to laugh, and to joke. I couldn't do that. Neither could

Dad. Was I jealous of him? The boy who chugged a half glass of chocolate milk and then wiped his sleeve across his mouth? Or was I jealous of Mom?

It felt like a lifetime since Xander Dixon and I were able to talk like that. Back when I believed he climbed into the sky and hung the moon and stars, all because I was scared of the dark. He looked different now—better looking and more mature than before. Yet he still resembled the boy I first developed a crush on in kindergarten—and the boy who had broken my heart over the past three years with every tease, scoff, and snide remark. It was hard to reconcile—despising someone while being drawn to them, even after he started a hurtful rumor about me. He made me feel like I wasn't good enough, smart enough, or nice enough to be in his presence.

Until that night in the hospital. And every visit he'd paid to the house in the months following, asking to see me. He'd been the only one to check on me. And now he sat on the opposite end of the couch, eating his sandwich with one hand and stroking Wynton's head with the other.

"I've missed Wynton," he said. "How's he doing?"

I waited for Mom to answer but she'd left the room. "Better than the rest of us, I think."

"Is there anything I can do?"

"It is so like you to think that you can help. Your cologne might as well be called Arrogance."

For a brief second, his face registered hurt. I opened my mouth to apologize, but that smirk flooded his smug face. "You noticed my cologne?"

When he didn't get a response from me, he placed his plate on the coffee table and dug into his book bag. "I didn't see you at school, so I went ahead and picked up the work last year's teachers need you to complete." One after another, he withdrew binders labeled with classes from my junior year schedule: Biology, Spanish 3, Trigonometry, Psychology,

American History, and English. "They said you should still have all the textbooks, either at home or online. Where should we start?"

I studied him. "How much is my dad paying you to do this?"

"It isn't about the money."

I ignored his attempt at deflection. "I hope it's a lot. At least one of us should benefit from this torture."

"I won't see it. We arranged for it to go into a college fund." Xander averted his eyes. Back when we were friends, he was embarrassed by his family's situation. His father was a struggling musician and burned through his mother's salary as a restaurant manager. I imagined his home situation was only slightly better now after his mom's remarriage. "But I'm not doing this for the money."

"Then what?"

"Nothing." In his irises, medium gray, turquoise, and coastal blue swirled in a mélange better suited to a silk brocade. It would be impossible to find a matching thread. Seriously, could this guy get any more complicated?

"Tell me or I won't let you in the house next time."

Xander scowled. "Spoiled girl."

"Stubborn boy."

Before I could think of a better insult, he turned and bounded up the stairs. Wynton went too, acting like a puppy. I leaped to my feet and followed Xander, acting like a crush-struck sixth grader again.

The door to Austin's room was open and the light spilled into the hallway.

"You have no right to be in here! Get out now." My words were breathy and broken. I yanked the collar of my shirt away from my throat, hoping to stop whatever was choking me.

He didn't listen. Instead, he remained in front of the closet, sifting through my brother's clothes. After a pause, he yanked something off its hanger and tossed it to me.

I caught the garment against my chest and neck.

"That's why I'm doing it." He stepped away from the closet and leaned back against the wall.

I unwadded the article of clothing. Hunter green enhanced nylon formed the MA-1 bomber jacket. On the left breast, Austin's trumpet pin. On the right, his name. I traced the hand-embroidered *A*.

"He didn't want a flashy letterman jacket, so you made this for him. Why?"

Because he was an amazing musician. I was proud of him and wanted him to show off his talent around school. I kept it humble—one solid color, a darker hue than the school's Kelly Green, and left off the big block letter *F*. Austin said it was the best Christmas present he'd ever received.

"Because you could," Xander said when I didn't respond. "For as long as we've known each other, you've wanted to be a famous fashion designer, styling clothes for celebrities and musicians. I mean, in fourth grade, you sent hand-drawn patterns of clothes to the White House and offered to sew outfits for Sasha and Malia to wear."

I buried my face in the jacket. Not to take in Austin's scent as much as to hide my embarrassment. I never did hear back from the Obamas. When I looked back up, Xander was sitting on the bed. He'd pressed his palms together, steepling his fingers like he was ready to start praying or something. Good luck. He'd find out quick that God was silent regarding the Mendenhall family.

"That dream will be much harder if you don't graduate high school. You asked what's in it for me? I've already seen one life lost because of that accident. I don't want to see it ruin another one."

I threw the jacket back at him. "When did you start caring about my quality of life? You did enough to ruin it and my reputation before the accident."

"Is this still about the gum in your hair? I've felt bad about that since it happened, and I've apologized for it."

"It's not about the stupid gum!"

He had the nerve to look confused. "Then what?"

"Forget it." I stepped forward, ripped the jacket out of his arms, and turned my back to him. Fuming, I returned the jacket to its hanger in the closet, then slid each apparel item along the rod until they were equidistant from each other.

"Let me help you." He stood behind me now, not close enough for me to land an elbow to his ribs but close enough for his cologne to weaken my defenses. "At least let me come over for two hours on Tuesdays and Thursdays. You don't have to acknowledge me if you don't want to. We'll do our own thing. If you change your mind and want help with schoolwork, I'll be here."

---

Two days later, I lowered the sewing machine's presser foot onto the shiny gold fabric and prepared to stitch. But first, I brought my lips close to the microphone beside me. "When sewing the points of darts, especially on thin fabric like this lamé, you don't want to finish with a reverse stitch or you'll get a bump and ruin the silhouette. Instead, shorten your sewing machine's stitch length."

The needle rose and fell in a smooth rhythm as I slowly fed the material beneath it, following my own instructions. "And now, I'm going to do a symmetrical dart beneath the other arm opening." I scooted my chair back and collided with something.

That something was Xander, and he was now bent over and groaning.

"What are you doing here?"

He didn't answer. With the way he was coughing, talking was probably out of the question. He simply showed me his watch.

How was it already 6:30? Panicked, I pressed the stop button on my tablet to pause the recording, then yanked the ring light's electrical cord from the outlet. "Why were you standing right behind me?"

Gingerly, he straightened up. "I knocked. You didn't answer." He scanned my filming setup. "You're making videos again?"

I jumped up, and he flinched. "Sweet Swayze, I'm not going to hurt you. At least, not again." As quickly as I could, I gathered the tripod, lighting stands, and microphone and shoved them in my closet.

Xander lifted the edge of the fabric I'd been sewing. "What are you working on?"

"None of your business," I said, popping his hand and making him let go.

"Sorry. It was just cool to see you so passionate about something." Xander grasped the straps of his book bag and tapped his foot at a rapid pace. "I thought you'd stopped making those ModernCher videos."

"What, do you miss trolling me and making ugly comments on them?"

"Oh, come on. I was always joking."

"You asked me if I got style inspiration from Pennywise the clown."

He tried to bite away his grin.

"And you wonder why I no longer want to give style advice on the internet."

"If you aren't advising your lemmings to spend their allowance on two-hundred-dollar skirts, what are you doing now?"

"Like I'd tell you." I nudged him out of the way, then climbed onto my bed.

"Come on. I'm curious why a person with eighteen thousand followers would stop posting videos."

"Just a guess. Maybe her twin brother was killed in a collision between a car and a train. Maybe her mom spent months in the ICU and woke up not remembering her. Maybe her dad disappeared into his job, leaving her all alone." Ugh. Word vomit. I opened the music app on my phone and hit Play on my favorite playlist, losing myself in the opening chords of Peter Gabriel's "In Your Eyes."

Xander stood awkwardly in the center of my room, like he just realized he was in a girl's bedroom. The guy looked like a vegetarian tiger at a monkey meat buffet. Funny. He'd never been shy about going in my room before, like when we were eight and he stole my teddy bear and held it for ransom. "Did you, uh, ever see that movie where the guy held the radio over his head and played this song?" he asked.

"*Say Anything*? I watched it once."

"I don't get why girls think that's so romantic. Maybe if he played an instrument or sang it, but just playing a song? That's lame."

"Did you ever consider that not everyone is an all-American marching band drummer?" I regretted the words the moment they dove off my lips. I soo did not mean to flatter him right then.

The song ended and Paula Abdul's "Opposites Attract" began before Xander moved from his spot. He still didn't sit down anywhere—just made a slow lap around the perimeter of my room.

"Where should I sit?"

"Wherever. You can sit on that end of the bed."

"The floor's fine."

I smiled. Should I tell him he can't get pregnant by sitting on a girl's bed?

As per our agreement, we each did our own thing. I flipped through a vintage *Seventeen* magazine—August 1984. Xander seemed to be watching something on his laptop. At least until I stole a peek over an Esprit ad and made eye contact with him. Awk-ward.

Almost an hour later, Xander stood and stretched. "Okay, I must ask. What did you do to Austin's Macy's Thanksgiving Day parade shirt from freshman year?"

The shirt was situated on the dress form near my sewing desk. I'd been too busy hiding the video-making equipment to remember that was in plain sight. I shrugged. "I've started altering his shirts to fit me and my style."

Although the shirt once had a boxy shape, it now had a narrower, more defined waistline, a shorter hem, and an irregular neckline. It would look amazing under a jean jacket and flipped-up collar.

"Let me know when you wear it. We can be twins." Xander's face reddened. "Not that I'd ever try to take Austin's place or anything. I meant we could have matching shirts, is all. I'm sorry."

"Xander, it's okay. That's not the most offensive thing you've ever said. What did you used to call me? Butterface? As in, 'she's cute but her face . . .'?"

"You know I never meant that. I like your face." He smirked. "It's way better than your personality."

## *eight*

**LORI**

"Thank you for joining us, Michael. I always love to see my patients surrounded by the support of loved ones in their recovery." Dr. Leo Klein opted for a handshake with Michael over the hug he'd given me. He and I had grown close during my stint in rehab. I might even call us friends except he'd merely been doing his job.

I took a seat on the worn leather couch I'd come to love, then patted the spot next to me—an invitation for Michael to drop his tension at the door and relax. He accepted but remained rigid in his stature. Shoulders back, chin high, with a canyon of space between the back of the couch and his shirt, faintly dotted with perspiration.

"You've been back home for a month," Dr. Klein said to me. "How are things going?"

"Good. I don't need my walker anymore, as you can see. My headaches have lessened in number and intensity. I think it helps being home." I rested my hand on Michael's knee. "Michael has been great. He's been giving me a lot of alone time to reminisce."

"Alone time?"

Waiting for Michael to jump in, I bit my tongue. He didn't. "Michael has a demanding job." Guilt twisted my stomach. "When he's home, though, he's very caring."

Dr. Klein steadied his focus on Michael. Could he hear the concern in my voice? Michael spoiled me. A new silk robe, a personal shopper, a housekeeper. He'd even arranged for a masseuse to come every Friday morning. Who wouldn't love that?

Me, I guess. I'd trade a professional massage for five minutes of uninterrupted time with my husband in a heartbeat.

Dr. Klein turned back to me. "Good. Let's talk about your recovery. What is your latest memory pre-injury?"

"I remember taking the kids to the pumpkin patch. Austin rolled his ankle in the field, and we had to take him to Urgent Care. That was six years before the accident. That's my first full memory. I've had glimpses of others, but I can't place them."

"That's perfectly fine. Recovery isn't linear. Your brain prioritizes your oldest, most significant memories. Austin's injury at the pumpkin patch has more meaning than, say, what the kids dressed like for trick or treat. Did you bring your journal?" Dr. Klein asked.

I pulled the small spiral notebook out of my purse and set it on my lap.

"Did you find that useful for recording snippets of memories?"

"A little. I'd get a feeling that something important happened once, but the details live just out of reach."

"Are you able to talk to Michael about it? To try to flesh it out?"

I stole a glance at Michael, but he stared straight ahead. "Uh, not really. He's busy. And I'm not sure what I could even say to start that conversation."

"You could always start by saying, 'Michael, I've retrieved a memory, and I would like two minutes of your time to help me decode the meaning of it.' Surely, he could find two minutes during his busy day, right?" Considering the edge in his voice and the way Dr. Klein lasered Michael with his eyes, it was less a question and more a command. After all, this wasn't

Michael's first visit to the clinic. Each time he'd greeted me with a kiss and intently listened to the progress I'd made, but as Deirdre once said, he always had a constipated look on his face. In fact, Dr. Klein had been the first one to help me process the difference between the marriage I remembered and the marriage I had.

I nibbled my nail. While Michael hadn't fought me about attending this appointment, he certainly hadn't been excited about it. If Dr. Klein pushed him too hard, he may hire someone else to accompany me.

Michael swallowed, his Adam's apple struggling with effort. Then he turned his gaze on me. Backlit by the window, I couldn't read his eyes at all. So when he took my non-nibbled hand in his and gently stroked my wrist, my heart pirouetted. He directed his answer at me. "I want you to bring those memories to me, even if they are incomplete. Do you have one in there?"

What choice did I have? I opened the notebook and skipped a few pages until I found one I felt comfortable sharing. "Escargot. I saw a plate with escargot on it and there's a lot of light around me."

"And how did that memory make you feel?" Dr. Klein asked.

"Happy, which doesn't make sense because snails aren't exactly my favorite snack."

"Michael, can you provide any clarity?"

"About four years ago," Michael began, "I had a conference in San Francisco and Lori came along."

Dr. Klein pointed his pen at me. "Don't tell me. Tell her."

He nodded, then faced me. "The last night, we went out to a nice dinner with a client of mine. Escargot was served as an appetizer, and you started feeling ill at the sight of them. But then Herschel Irving and his wife joined us."

My jaw dropped.

"Who is Herschel Irving?" Dr. Klein asked.

"My favorite interior designer," I said.

"You two got to talking," Michael continued, "and he told you that if you ever wanted to come back to the field, you should give him a call."

"Stop it!" I begged myself to remember more of that dinner than just those snails. "Did I?"

"Eat the snails?" Michael grinned.

"No," I said, squeezing his hand. "Did I ever call him?"

"I don't think so. The twins were in the throes of middle school. You were always taking them to band practice, dance, cheerleading, church, et cetera. Plus, my business was demanding a lot from me. It wasn't good timing, I guess."

All I could do was blink in response. My chance for an actual career, come and gone.

"Lori," Dr. Klein said, "you look resigned. What are you thinking?"

"That it sounds typical of me. My family is my world."

"Do you feel sad at all?"

What a loaded question. "I feel like I've always supported Michael's dreams. It would be nice to have dreams of my own one day."

"I agree," Dr. Klein said. "This is a big improvement. Even if only a sliver, that recollection was from four years ago. Fantastic. Your brain's neuroplasticity is allowing new connections to form, making way for memory retrieval. What's another thought you've had?"

I chewed my lip.

"Don't be embarrassed. These are all pieces of a puzzle."

"You told me that our sense of smell is tied to our memory, right? There's a smell I've imagined more than once. I have no idea what it could be linked to."

"What smell?"

"Wood. Freshly cut wood."

"Hmm. Could be a home improvement store or the building of your house. What do you think, Michael?"

He snapped to attention like he'd mentally checked out already. "I don't . . . know. Probably the house."

Annoyance flashed over Dr. Klein's features before he focused on me. "Are there any emotions you feel when you go back to that smell, Lori?"

A small chuckle pushed past my lips. "Adventure and a little fear. Like when you're riding on a motorcycle with the wind in your hair."

Beside me, Michael shifted in his seat. Was he thinking of our first date too? What a ride that had been. Two college kids with nothing but blue skies ahead of them. How could the smell of wood shavings fit into that?

"I think this time at home has been good for you." The doctor twisted his pen. "We need to keep looking for items that could jog your memory. Family photo albums or a journal?"

"Our pictures are all digital, but I could get them printed into a book," Michael explained. "Lori never kept a journal."

Dr. Klein jotted down a note on his tablet. "What about social media? That could be an excellent way to jog your memory, Lori."

I waved off the suggestion. "I'm not a fan of social media. I've told you all before. I don't have Facebook, Instagram, Momentso, or any other. Neither of us do. Right, Michael?"

It took a pat on his knee to shake Michael from his daze. "Right," he said. "Right."

---

"I guess I'll choose Peach Chiffon." I handed the ring of polish samples back to the nail technician, then leaned over the armrest and whispered to Avery. "How much does this cost, again?"

Avery didn't bother to open her eyes as she relaxed into her chair. She looked more serene than I'd seen her in the month since I came home. "Mom, you don't have to worry about it.

Dad wants us to spend his money so he doesn't have to give us his time. You know how bad he is at that."

"It feels frivolous. I can soak my feet in the tub and paint my own nails."

"That's not the point. Besides, you used to come here all the time. Sometimes with me. Sometimes with Mrs. Lowry—you know, Enid. I have a feeling the wine you two drank during your visit cost more than the actual mani-pedi."

"I can't imagine that. I don't understand how I could've become that different in only a few years."

Avery rolled her head my way and opened her eyes. "I do. When Dad switched jobs, everything changed. It wasn't all bad though."

"How so?"

She shrugged. "You guys stopped arguing."

"We never argued before."

"Not how other parents argued. Not like Xander's parents before their divorce. But you guys were really stressed about money."

"I do remember that," I said.

Raising two kids on the outskirts of Denver on a single teaching salary had been tough, especially as the kids got involved in activities, but we made it work with coupon-clipping and modest living. I'd been happy, and I thought Michael had been happy too. The nail tech resumed her seat in front of my feet and began applying the polish.

Avery tucked her hair behind her ears. "There was one night when I wanted to go to the summer carnival, but you said we couldn't afford to go. I pitched a total fit, so Austin used his chore money for us. When we came home, it was pretty clear you'd been crying. And Dad wouldn't come out of his office. He didn't go back to teaching that fall. After that, Dad wasn't around much. You got sadder."

"That must have been hard on you," I said, hoping Avery

would be as comfortable discussing her emotions as she was discussing mine.

"I had Austin." Avery buttoned her lips. She closed her eyes and rested her head back against the chair.

"I know how much I miss him. I can't imagine how hard this is for you, honey."

"Lori? It's been so long." A raven-haired beauty slowed as she neared my chair. Her slight curves were clothed in business casual attire, a big departure from the athleisure the rest of the spa clients wore. "Michael said you probably won't remember me." She held out her hand.

I accepted it. Never in my life had I met a woman with this firm of a handshake.

"Who are you?" Avery asked, reading my thoughts.

The woman pulled her hand back slowly, gripping the strap of her purse with the other. Her smile wavered a touch. "Jade Jessup. I work for your father. You must be Avery. I've seen photos. Your dad thinks the world of you."

Avery snickered. "Hmm. And I thought you and my dad were close."

Close? To me, the word felt like taking a nail file to my heart, but Jade seemed none the wiser. "I'm happy to see you both up and about." She turned to me. "I bet you're glad to be home."

"I am."

"I keep offering to take on some of Michael's accounts so he can get home at a reasonable time." She shook her head, and her long glossy hair made her look like a model on a shampoo commercial. "But you know Michael."

Did I? She spoke my husband's name with such familiarity. *Michael said you probably won't remember me. Michael and I are going out for Italian. Michael likes his eggs scrambled in the mornings.*

"Thank you, Jade," I forced out.

"Ms. Jessup? I'm ready for you over here," another nail tech said.

Jade nodded. "Well, I should go. If you need anything, please have Michael let me know."

I watched her cross the room, not slow and staggered like my present self. Not fluid and elegant like my old self. Jade walked with the strength and determination of a powerful business-woman who knows what she wants and isn't afraid to take it. From the corner of my eye, I saw Avery staring at me. Embarrassed by the pity dipping the corners of her mouth, I smiled. "That was nice of her."

"Yep. It sure was, Mom."

*nine*

**AVERY**

*September 29*

Dear Austin,

For English, I had to choose one of Shakespeare's works and overanalyze it to death. I chose "The Phoenix and the Turtle" for a couple reasons. First, everybody and their cousin was doing Romeo and Juliet, Hamlet, or Macbeth. This one is lesser known. And second, it's super short. I pulled out the dead brother card, so Mrs. Herman let me use it.

Turns out it isn't about a turtle in Arizona. Okay, I'm kidding about the Arizona part. But if I knew old Willy Shakespeare was talking about turtledoves, I would've skipped the assignment entirely. The whole thing is about a funeral for two birds, a phoenix and a dove, attended by a bunch of other birds. It didn't make an ice cream lick of sense, so I plugged it into my search engine. Some people believe the phoenix and dove were madly in love, but others believe they were close like friends or siblings. The phoenix represents perfection. Probably loved by everyone, good at everything, and basically, the best there was. Totally you. The dove represents devoted love. I know I didn't always show it, and I certainly didn't speak it, but I had your back no matter what. No matter what.

*So between them love did shine.*
*That the turtle saw his right*
*Flaming in the phoenix' sight:*
*Either was the other's mine.*

The phoenix, perched on an Arabian tree, burns as the sun sets the tree aflame. The dove chooses to die with him.

*Phoenix and the turtle fled*
*In a mutual flame from hence.*

Austin, I don't understand why God let me live. I should've died instead of you, but if your time was up, mine should've been too. After all, we started life together—why not end it together?

Faith always came easy for you. Maybe you know why I was forced to remain here without you, my brother, my best friend. My only comfort is that the phoenix didn't remain in the fire. It rose from the ashes. But what became of the dove? My guess is it got trapped in the fire, forever singing its mournful song.

Love,
Avery

P.S. In case you're wondering, no, I did not ask Xander for help with this assignment. He's currently trying to get Wynton to balance a Cheez-It on his nose. I'd hate to interrupt his important work. Maybe I won't complete this assignment after all.

◆

"Peter Wright called." Mom's words stretched across the restaurant table. I'm not sure who she was speaking to, but if it was Dad, she might have to bounce her message off a satellite because he seemed a thousand miles away.

Dad downed half his soda in a few gulps. I half expected him to let out a huge burp like in *Elf*, but no such luck. While I sank lower in my chair, Dad set down his glass, and his gaze took a journey around the busy Italian restaurant before making its way to Mom. "What did he have to say?"

"Avery hasn't turned in any assignments yet."

Whoops.

Dad placed his elbows on the table, clasped his hands together, and rested his chin on his knuckles, waiting for an explanation. My guess was that producing videos on thrifting and upcycling clothes was not going to pass the test for acceptable excuses, even if I was averaging seven to ten thousand views each.

"What exactly is happening during these tutoring sessions, then?" Dad arched a suspicious brow.

"Don't worry, Dad. I'm handling it." Lie number one. "I'll be turning in a Spanish project next week." Lie number two. "I should be caught up in no time." And lie number—

"It isn't that Xander isn't trying," Mom butted in. "Avery's just—"

"Being Avery," Dad finished for her.

I threw my half-eaten garlic knot on the table, and it rolled onto the floor. "This whole thing is dumb. I don't want to go to that school. I don't like anyone there."

"What about Sarah?" Mom asked. "She was always so sweet."

"Sarah is sweet, but her friends were Austin's friends. This may shock you, but I'm not the most likable person."

Dad picked up the tossed knot and placed it on the edge of the table to be cleared away. "So be more likable."

"Thanks, Dad. So helpful. I'm not like you. I can't turn it on and off when I leave the house."

Never one to turn away from my challenges, he pinned me with a glare. "What do you mean by that?"

"What's our server's name?" I let that question rest a moment. "It's Derek, remember?" I cleared my throat to prepare for my best Michael Mendenhall impression. "It's nice to meet you, Derek. We've heard your place has the best chicken parm on the Front Range. What's your take?"

"Honestly, Avery. There's nothing wrong with being friendly with people. And I don't even sound like that. If you're going to mock me, the least you could do is get my voice right." He sighed. "I only want what's best for you."

"Then let me get my GED."

"So you can continue to hide away behind locked doors? You need to be around people. Your gift, although you may not see it, is inspiring people."

"Austin was the inspiring one."

"Okay," he said. "Then let's call you the influential one."

Derek approached the table to take our order. Mom ordered a salad. Dad ordered the chicken parmesan, of course. I asked Derek whether the beef came from responsibly and sustainably raised cattle. As he stumbled through an answer, I pondered Dad's words. He was right about one thing. If it were up to me, I'd never leave my room again. Even tonight, he'd forced me to choose between the high school football game or this dinner. Sulking on my window seat and listening to power ballads wasn't an option.

"Does that answer your question?" Derek asked.

"Yeah, it does. I'll have the cheese ravioli."

After Derek left the table, Dad reached into the bread basket and took one of those brown rolls with random oats on top. Better him than me. He cleared his throat loudly. "Lori, did Peter say anything else?"

"Not about Avery." Mom smiled slyly. "He encouraged me to come back to the PTO. That was it."

"Of course he'd suggest that. Is that something you want to do?"

"Why do you ask it like that?"

"Lori, you have a generous heart. You'd offer your shirt,

shoes, and jeans to anyone who asked. In the past, people have taken advantage of that, the Parent-Teacher Organization included."

"You don't think I should?"

Dad bit into his roll and chewed slowly, probably regretting his choice. Then he spoke, but not about the gross bread. "I want you to do whatever you think is best for you."

While Dad started telling stories about his job, I dazed out for a while, playing a game on my phone where you pop colored bubbles. Not to brag, but I'm on level 362—a total beast. Finally, Derek delivered our meals to the table. Several bites in, Dad spoke again. "There's a conference in Dallas coming up in a couple weeks. One of the main speakers had to back out because his wife went into preterm labor."

"Oh no." Mom had told Austin and I about her time on bed rest toward the end of pregnancy and about all the prayers she'd said for us.

"Mom and baby are fine, but he doesn't want to leave them yet. He asked me to fill in for him and I said yes."

"What are the dates?"

"October 12th through the 15th."

Mom rested her fork on her plate and stared at him. "October 15th. The anniversary of the accident."

"I thought about that. You and Avery can come with me. That way we'll be together."

"What would we do with Wynton?" I asked, my shrill voice hurting my own ears.

"Board him. Or have Anita watch him."

"Over my dead body." I scowled. "Grandma is literally the worst. Plus, she still thinks his name is Winston after all these years. No way. I won't leave him on that day."

"That's ridiculous," Dad said. "Wynton's a dog. Calendars and anniversaries mean nothing to him."

"But they mean something to me."

"And to me," Mom said, lifting her chin and eyeing me with so much girl power I thought she might start singing a Spice Girls song.

"Fine. If Avery wants to stay home, we'll make it a trip for just you and me. How does that sound?"

Awesome, Dad. Great plan. Way to help me be social.

"I won't leave Avery alone that day. You shouldn't either, Michael." That's my Momma Spice.

"Lori, we can't stop living our lives. Austin wouldn't have wanted that."

Maybe Dad meant well, but I couldn't take one more second of him talking down to Mom. He'd done that for years, ever since he started his dumb business. And Mom had been a sweet waif of a woman until even she'd had enough. In the months leading up to that awful moment on the railroad tracks, Mom had finally become what I wanted to be one day, strong and independent. There was still a glimmer of that woman in her.

"Dad, did you know Mrs. Lowry practically begged Mom to go to California with her and Mom's other friends, but she said no?"

Dad glowered at me. Was he mad I brought up the fact that Mom had a life outside of our house once? "That's completely different. Those women aren't good for her."

A groan emerged from the pit of my stomach. "Don't you think she should be the one to decide that? You know what? Mom should go with them."

"No," he said, locking horns with me, "she shouldn't."

The noise of Mom pounding her hand on the table jerked our attention to her. "Please don't talk about me like a child. I have a traumatic brain injury, but I can still think for myself." Atta girl, Mom. "Avery, I don't want you to be alone."

The image of Mom moving hauntedly through the house searching for lost memories of Austin on the anniversary of his death sent chills up my spine. I'd end up spending the entire time pretending I was fine, she was fine, everything was fine. The only thing worse than being alone on October 15th was being with others on October 15th. I needed Mom to go on that trip.

"I'm not a child either, Mom. And not gonna lie, I'll probably spend that entire weekend in my room listening to music with Wynton. But you can go and spend time with women who, for better or worse, were a big part of your life before the accident. They might help you remember something Dad and I can't."

"That's not a good idea," Dad said. "But Avery brings up a good point. October 15th is just another day you can't remember. Making it a big deal here, in Dallas, or in California will only add to the pain we're already carrying."

Just another day you can't remember. My jaw nearly fell into my marinara.

Mom pushed her salad around with her fork, but I could see a plume of red mottling her upper chest and strangling her neck.

"I'm sorry. That wasn't fair," Dad said, about point two seconds before I would have picked up his chicken parm and thrown it across the room.

Dad downed the rest of his soda, leaving the ice to clank back to the bottom of the glass. He wouldn't, couldn't be as cold as that ice, could he?

He looked at Mom. "I can't miss this speaking opportunity, Lori. I'm sorry. I just can't. Besides, we'll all be better off when October 15th becomes just another day."

# *ten*

I double-checked my book bag. No lunch. Mom, already a stress ball over her trip tomorrow, must have forgotten to make it. No matter how busy she'd gotten and no matter what she'd been going through, she'd never once forgotten Austin's lunch. The realization pinched my heart a little bit. Maybe I just failed to grab it off the counter. I had been running late this morning. I even skipped breakfast.

Forget growling. My stomach straight-up roared. All I had to do to tame it was walk into the cafeteria. It would be way easier to cut out early and grab some fast food, but I told myself I'd make it through the entire day. I stared hard at the doors as the voices of the entire senior class rumbled through them.

The last time I'd walked in there, the last remaining thread of my life had been severed. Having already cried enough for a lifetime in the two weeks after the funeral, I had decided to return to school. It had been lonely without my brother, and for some reason, none of my friends were responding to my texts. Not even Courtney. Some best friend she was. Jake had been weird too. "Death freaks me out," he'd said. Like all the rest of us were perfectly comfortable with it? As my hero, Cher from *Clueless*, would say, "I don't think so."

I'd even worn my favorite Cher-inspired outfit for my return: a yellow plaid skirt and top. No knee-high socks though. That was way too '90s for me. I'd taken a deep breath and stepped into the cafeteria. My gaze went straight to my lunch table where friends from the cheer squad mingled with the cutest guys from various sports and clubs. They were chatting away, many of them laughing. I was confused. How could they be laughing? Sure, none of them were close friends with Austin, but didn't they know the pain I'd been going through? How could they all be acting like nothing had happened? I stood there for what felt like forever. Not a single person from that group noticed me.

My heart lifted when I spotted Jake standing with his back to me. I moved forward. What was he doing? Then I saw a hand slide over his shoulder.

"Avery." Xander blocked my way. It was the first time I'd seen him since the funeral. A heavy frown tugged at the corners of his lips. "Don't go over there."

I pushed past him in time to see Jake turn and look my way. Courtney peeked her head around his body. When she and I locked eyes, she clasped her hands around Jake's waist. I froze. Not her. Not him. I waited for the others to come forward, to come to my defense. No one did. Instead, they all stared at me. Even Jake.

My stomach roiled. I backed away from the spotlight, running to find the closest restroom. Luckily, the faculty one had a lock so I could get sick with dignity. After the nausea used and abused me the same way my closest friends had, I leaned against the wall. I pulled my knees into my chest and the tears returned. Outside the door, I heard Xander's voice, then a woman's, both asking me to unlock the door. But I hadn't. Not for hours. Not until the firefighters removed the hinges. Through all of it, I hadn't heard a word from my boyfriend or my best friend.

"Hey."

I spun toward the mousy voice in the hallway. Courtney, in a cornflower-blue plaid dress, inched closer to me.

"How are you?" she asked tentatively.

If only I were in the mood for surface-level conversation. That wasn't possible with her, especially not so close to October 15th. "Not great."

"Oh." Courtney twisted the fingers of her left hand. "Are you going to start eating in the cafeteria?"

I glanced at the door. "I forgot to grab— Courtney, why'd you do it? You were my closest friend. We did everything together."

Her expression hardened. "I don't think we should go into that."

I shook my head. "It's been a year. When should we go into it?" My brows pinched together so hard they brought on an immediate headache.

She tried to slip past me, but I grabbed her hand. I'd always been the stronger one. I could keep her here if I wanted to. Fortunately, she stopped in her tracks, and I dropped my handhold. This wasn't going to be one of those reunions.

"Why'd you do it?" I repeated.

"You really want to know?" Her voice pitched higher. "I was sick of you. We all were. I mean, we all felt bad about what happened to your brother and mom and stuff. But those two weeks you weren't here? It was better. For once, the world didn't revolve around you."

All I could do was grit my teeth and blink. While I was mourning, my friends were . . . celebrating?

"You were the pretty one, the smart one, the cheer captain, the homecoming princess." She cursed loud enough for me to worry the rest of the students might find their way out here. That faculty restroom probably required a key now, so hiding wasn't an option. "Did you ever think about what it was like for me? No, of course you didn't. Because you were too focused on yourself to ever truly care about me or any of your other friends. Even at Austin's funeral, you cried like a total baby so all the attention would be on you, not him."

"I wasn't—" My words came out as croaks. "I didn't—"

"Stop pretending you don't know what you're doing. Everything you do is to make people jealous of you or feel pity for you. Remember that anonymous post that said you were easier than riding a bike with training wheels? I bet you made that yourself. Then you cried about how all the boys suddenly wanted to date you for only one thing."

At the far end of the hallway, the library door opened. Xander appeared on the other side. He raised a hand to wave. I wiped hot tears off my neck as my self-pity turned to anger. That anonymous post wasn't anonymous to me. And I certainly wasn't the one who wrote it.

"If it makes you feel better, people don't think you're easy anymore. They don't think about you at all." Courtney stepped closer. "But I know what you really are—a tease. You strung Jake along for almost two years, and the fact is, he got tired of waiting for you. So he called me. He didn't need you anymore after that. None of us do."

With Xander approaching and each word from Courtney lashing my skin wide open, I decided promises to myself were overrated and left before the noon bell rang.

◆

It was close to 8:30 that night when Xander shut his copy of *Animal Farm* and set it on the floor. He said something I couldn't hear, so I removed one of my earbuds.

He spoke again. "I'm worried about you."

I'd gotten used to having him around. During every tutoring session I would let him in and lead him to my bedroom where he'd ask the usual question, "Do you want to do any schoolwork?" I'd shake my head and resume doing whatever it was I felt like doing. Right now, that was bingeing the latest season of *Outer Banks* on my tablet. Then, after two hours, he'd pack up his stuff and leave.

"It's not your job to worry about me," I said. That should be my parents' job, but in the two weeks since that Italian dinner more tension had built up in my home than on a teenage soap opera. Dad was already gone, and Mom had an early flight tomorrow morning.

"You've gotta stop leaving school early every day."

I was afraid this lecture was coming after today's incident in the hallway. Telling him why I left school would only validate Courtney's harsh words. She was wrong about me. Delusional, actually. One hundred percent.

Having listened to his concern, I put my earbud back in and repositioned myself to lay on my stomach with my heels kicked up in the air. At the foot of the bed, Xander stood perfectly still, not leaving although it was now 8:31.

I was watching him in my periphery when he lunged forward and took my tablet from me. He held it close to his chest and took a step back.

He seriously underestimated my stubbornness. I found my phone beside me, unlocked it, opened my streaming app, and picked up the show right where I left off. Xander placed my tablet on my sewing desk. I pretended not to notice him coming to the side of my bed, but when he dove to grab my phone, I was ready. I tucked it beneath my chest and curled my body protectively around it.

"Avery, stop being a brat." He took hold of my shoulder and tried to roll me over.

I straightened my body and heel-kicked him. Without any leverage, the kick was embarrassingly weak, so I did it repeatedly just to be annoying. Bad move.

He dropped all of his body weight on my back, crushing me. "Stop messing around. You need to take this seriously." His words, whispered against my cheek, weren't spoken angrily. They were pleas. "If you won't do it for yourself, do it for Austin."

My blood heated to boiling in record time. I bucked my body and rocked it side to side. "Get off me, Xander Dixon."

Shockingly, he obeyed.

"You are the most infuriating person I've ever met," he said. "Austin was right. You won't be satisfied until you've run your life into the ground."

He may as well have slapped me across the face. "Austin wouldn't have said that. He thought the world of me."

"You're so self-absorbed," he muttered.

I sprang off my bed and, straightening to my full five feet and five inches, stood nose to nose, or rather, nose to throat with him. "Say it louder."

He took my challenge. "You are self-absorbed, conceited, immature, reckless, and spoiled. Everything in life has been handed to you, and you're throwing it away."

My hands balled into such tight fists my wrists ached with the tension. First Courtney, now Xander. Me, me, me. That's all they thought I cared about. "Maybe I have been given everything. But I've also had it all torn from my hands. You can't even imagine what that's like."

"I lost him too!" Xander flinched at his own yell. He backed away from me and swiped his hand across his eyes. His chest heaved in time with my breaths. "For a long time, he was the only brother I had. I knew him well enough to know that no one could break his heart like you could. And I hope, no, I pray Austin can't see you now, because if he could, you'd be breaking his heart all over again with how you're acting."

My face was probably cherry red, and my nostrils were likely flaring, but I couldn't care less. He had no right to stand in my house, my room, and speak to me like that. He knew nothing. Nothing except how to hurt me. "I hate you."

The same last words I'd screamed at Austin in the car, the ones that shocked my Dad so much he missed the flashing lights signaling an oncoming train. Now they scattered the pieces of my already-broken heart into every dark, hidden place inside me. And just like Austin's had, Xander's eyes filled with pain. I winced and looked away, preferring the darkness outside the window to the light that illuminated everything wrong with me.

"Avery." The sound of my name flowed out of him like a sewing needle, piercing my heart with every syllable "Why are you meanest to the people who care about you most?"

"Leave me alone." The cliché command was all I could muster. And somehow it was the one command I didn't want him to obey in this moment.

He was quiet for several seconds. Finally, he gathered his belongings and left me, just like I'd demanded.

# *eleven*

## LORI

I never should've left the house this morning. That fact smacked me square in the face about thirty thousand feet above Nevada, when, next to me, Ruth's ability to turn anything into a sex joke became my traveling companion. I wouldn't call myself a prude, but I preferred to keep references to anatomical parts locked behind bedroom doors.

Enid had known I was nervous about this girls' weekend since I still did not have any memory of her, Ruth, or Laney, so she created a photo book for me to peruse on the plane. Enid's captions were sweet—"Hiking in Yosemite," "Laney's Fortieth Birthday Party at Texas de Brazil," "The PTO's Miracle Mania Fundraiser"—but Ruth's commentary on the exact same events was scandalous. It didn't help that she had one of those voices that didn't have a volume down button.

I missed Michael. I missed Avery. Shoot, I even missed Mom. At least her difficult personality was familiar to me.

Upon arriving in Napa, the girls wanted to walk the trail through a vineyard. I declined since walking up my stairs at home still left me winded. I suspected they'd leave me behind. Instead, the three of them exchanged looks.

"Let me work some magic," Laney said. She sashayed over to the concierge at least twenty years her senior and leaned flirtatiously over his desk. She returned a few minutes later with a set of keys to one of the property's golf carts.

Soon we were cruising between rows and rows of vines from which Ruth had no problem foraging.

"I can't get over it," she said through a mouthful of Petite Sirah grapes. "You're so different, Lori. Way quieter. Subdued, almost."

"She'd be the one driving, for sure," Enid added.

"And cutting through the rows to make it more exciting." Laney snaked the golf cart to the right, the left, and then the right again. By the time she'd straightened out, all the blood had drained from my knuckles where I gripped the roof of the cart, not sure whether I could let go yet.

"I don't believe it," I said.

"It's true. Remember that time we were snorkeling at Dry Tortugas and that lemon shark approached us?" Enid asked. "We swam back to shore as quick as we could, but not you, Lori. You followed it fifty yards out into the ocean."

The mere thought made my heart race. "No way. I would never do that."

"Not when we first met, but at some point, my dear, you got sick of waiting. Waiting for your husband to pay you attention. Waiting for your dreams to materialize out of thin air. Waiting for life to come to you. You decided to chase life."

"You make me sound braver than I am."

Ruth held out a handful of stolen grapes. "I don't know if you were brave or just fed up. Either way, you were a lot of fun."

I took a single grape and popped it into my mouth, crushing the juice from the skin. The sweet taste tickled my memories. I knew this flavor at one point in time. My hand had held a glass in one hand and a dark bottle in the other. I'd been home, sitting on the couch alone.

I searched my purse for my notebook and pen to jot down

this slanted memory. As I replaced both in my handbag, my phone lit up. I withdrew it and discovered a text message.

Michael
I should've thought through this weekend more.

I stared hard at his words, not wanting to add more meaning than he intended, yet hoping still.

But I don't want to ruin your girls' trip. You deserve a chance to go and have fun. I just miss you.

◆

After our golf cart marauding, the night only got more interesting as I reacquainted myself with my friends. Throughout dinner, I realized Laney seemed to find fulfillment in being the smartest person in the room. Ruth had a comment about the looks of our server and every other man, as well as a prediction about their, let's say, prowess in certain arenas. How had I ever gotten past the blushing to enjoy this humor? Or had I been at the heart of it? Only time and memories would tell, I guess.

When I returned from a bathroom break that was more about needing quiet, I found Ruth holding my phone.

"Prince Charming texted." Ruth cleared her throat and read off my phone screen. "After ten months of sleeping in separate beds, you'd think I could handle a few nights away from you. Last night I realized I don't like not being able to roll over and touch you."

My cheeks burned, the anger flickering hotter than my bashfulness.

"Ruth, give her back the phone," Enid said.

I snatched it away from her.

Laney laughed. "I told my husband Michael's my hall pass if I ever have the opportunity."

Ruth held her glass of wine out and clinked it with Laney's.

The sweat on the back of my neck chilled, and I shivered. Michael was my husband. Was nothing sacred?

Enid shook her head, and I prayed she might say something, anything to put a stop to this talk. "Some things aren't worth the price you pay for them. I'd put Michael Mendenhall in that category." Her eyes met mine. "Amen?"

# *twelve*

**AVERY**

---
Hey.
---

I hit Send and waited. Goodness, I was breathing so hard the Jeep's windows got foggy. Why was I so worked up? It was Xander. Only Xander. I checked my phone again. No reply. With every second, hope dimmed. I folded my hands over the steering wheel and rested my forehead on them. All day, while every other student talked about their homecoming plans, I'd been consumed by yesterday's events. First, Courtney's hurtful accusations. Second, Xander's confirmation of those hurtful accusations. Self-absorbed. Conceited. Reckless. And what did I do? I proved him right with those terrible words I swore I'd never say to anyone ever again. I couldn't stop seeing the hurt in Xander's eyes.

*"Why are you meanest to the people who care about you most?"*

A ping interrupted my wallowing. I grabbed my phone.

---
Hey.
---
I'm outside your house. Can we talk?
---

92

I bounced my knee as those three dots on the phone screen indicated he was typing . . . and typing . . . and typing. Finally, his message appeared.

I'll be right out.

The two small windows touching the ground of the split-level home lit up. Xander still lived in our old neighborhood—far more modest than our current one. The homes were on the smaller side, with barely ten feet of grass separating one house from another. We used to live in the ranch with white vinyl siding three lots down.

It was quiet and peaceful on this street—something I didn't want to disturb by shutting my car door too hard, so I pressed it closed with my hip instead. I crossed the small yard and took a seat on his porch step. As I waited, a cool wind raised chill bumps on my arms. A jacket would have been a smart grab, but once I decided to head over here, I took off before I could change my mind.

Behind me, the door opened then shut before I saw anyone come out, leaving me wondering whether I'd actually be able to say what I came here to say. Fortunately, before my thoughts could send me running, the door reopened. Xander stepped out, carrying a knit blanket and wearing a frown.

He wrapped the blanket around my shoulders, and no amount of pride would keep me from accepting its warmth and sweet scent. Back in the day, when Xander and I were actual friends, Mrs. Dixon was always baking cookies and pies. The aroma of cinnamon seemed to live in the walls of his home. This blanket held that smell, and it reminded me of better days for us.

"It's late." Xander sank onto the step beside me.

"Only 11:45. I knew you'd be at the homecoming football game all night."

Xander simply nodded, his silence not helping my nerves. But I couldn't chicken out. Whatever needed to be said would be spoken here and now or not at all.

"Please don't stop coming over to my house. I didn't tell my parents you quit. Not yet . . . I wanted to ask you to reconsider first."

"Why should I?"

I shivered and pulled my legs into the blanket's protective covering. My thin pants weren't the wisest choice either. I really hadn't thought this through. "Because I need your help. Trigonometry is all new concepts for me, and videos on the internet have only confused me more. So will you keep coming over?"

He cocked his head and studied me. "You have to promise a few things first."

"Like what?"

"First, you have to stop cutting class. Anything we do is useless if you aren't even going to class."

"I can't promise that."

"Why not? Seems easy to me."

I chewed my lip. "Do you remember when we went to the school carnival in sixth grade, and you bet me a cotton candy that I was too scared to go into the fun house?"

"Yep."

"I took you up on that bet. Soon, I was standing in the room of mirrors, and everything was contorted and strange. Dreamlike—but not any dream I'd ever want to experience again. I couldn't find my way out even though I could hear Austin calling my name. Well, that's how I feel at school. I'm in a place I know, with people I know, but everything is contorted and mangled. The conversations, the scenery, even the air seems out of sorts, and no matter what perspective I take, I can't make it right."

What I didn't mention was how I'd had a panic attack in that fun house and collapsed to the floor, unable to move or speak.

By the time Austin found me, I was bathed in sweat and could hardly breathe. Austin wasn't here to save me anymore though.

Xander hesitated a moment. "I've always regretted not going in that fun house with you. Maybe I can make that up to you now. We don't have to be enemies." Perhaps he saw the hesitation gripping me because he added, "You can trust me."

Trust was a big word. "What about the Momentso post?"

"What Momentso post?" His blank face gave away nothing.

"The one that made everyone think I was ready and willing to do anything with anybody. The one that made guys think they could get me in their bed or the back of their car on the first date."

"The training wheels one," he said like the words tasted sour.

Above us a bat circled once, then disappeared into the dark sky. Xander jolted, and his eyes grew as wide as the moon above. "Wait. You don't think— You think I posted that?"

I remained as still as possible.

"You do." He slid a hand over his mouth. "I know I've teased you a lot, but I would never do something like that."

"Of course you would. You put gum in my hair, didn't you?"

"That's way different!" He glanced around, probably to see if he'd woken any neighbors. "And for the hundredth time, the gum was an accident."

"How could it possibly be an accident?"

"Fine." He sighed. "I was sitting behind you at a basketball game, right? And you were sitting with Sarah. She asked who you thought was the cutest boy in school and you said my name. My gum fell out of my mouth and landed in your hair."

"Okay, let me get this straight. You found out I liked you and it grossed you out so much that you accidently dropped gum in my hair. I feel a lot better. Thanks."

"Grossed out? Are you kidding? No, I'd liked you since the day we met, which is why my jaw dropped and the gum fell out of my mouth. I tried to get it out of your hair without you noticing, but I made it worse. The next day you came in with this short haircut, and I knew it was my fault. But you looked really pretty in this Jennifer Lawrence kind of way, and all the guys started noticing you. By the time I got the nerve up to apologize to you, I heard Kyle had asked you to the Valentine's Day dance and you said yes."

I stared at him, not blinking. Not breathing either apparently because my lungs suddenly made me gasp for air. Xander had liked me? For years? And he'd thought I was pretty, even after I chopped my hair? I gathered some courage. "Only because you didn't ask me."

Xander buried his head in his hands and groaned. "Why was I such an idiot?" He raised his chin and squeezed his eyes shut. "After Kyle, there was Andre. Then Dillon. Then that short kid."

"Colton."

"Ugh. Yes, Colton! Anyway, I was angry, mostly at myself, for missing my chance. You'd clearly moved on. In my immature way, I thought mistreating you was the best way for me to get over you."

"So you wrote that social media post?"

"No, I didn't. Avery, I was jealous. Not evil."

"But the day before, I overheard you with Austin. You said I was running out of guys to kiss and might have to turn to prairie dogs next."

A laugh burst out of him before he could squash it. Once he was back in control of himself, he looked sincerely at me. "I probably did say that. I'm not perfect. But I'd never post something mean about you on social media."

As much as I could in the moonlight, I searched his eyes. He seemed genuine. Not that I had a good read on people. That was Austin. And while he'd never liked Jake or Courtney, he'd trusted Xander Dixon.

"I never thanked you for that night—the night of the accident. I remember sitting on the floor of the emergency room while they tried to revive Austin. I felt so alone. Out of all the people I reached out to, you were the only one who showed up."

The moonlight cast a golden glow over half of his face, reflecting off his dark lashes and highlighting his perfectly formed lips.

"So, thank you. If there was a way to repay you, I would."

"How about you limit skipping school to once a week?" He smiled weakly. "Try to push through most days?"

"Fine. I'll try to limit it to one day a week." I added a groan for emphasis.

"Good. Second request." His grin faded a bit. "We stop being so mean to each other."

I thought this over for a minute, then stood, pulling the blanket off my shoulders and holding it out to him. "Deal."

He rose to his feet and accepted the blanket, both of his hands fitting over mine.

I didn't like how his touch made my stomach flip and my pulse race. So, what did I do? I froze in place, making the feeling last even longer. Even worse, it seemed to make all kinds of confessions bubble up. "I don't hate you."

Xander smiled, and not the sarcastic or teasing kind. An honest-to-goodness smile. "I don't hate you either."

Sweet Swayze, there might have been a twinkle in his eye when he said it too.

Dear Austin, I thought, go on ahead and roll over in your grave.

❖

**ONE YEAR AGO**

Startled by the knock on the door, I pierced the needle through the fabric and into my skin. I yanked my thumb to my mouth, tasting blood.

"Hey, sis, is this a bad time?" Austin asked, peering through the crack in the door. Before I could answer, Wynton clumsily barged in.

"Kind of. I'm trying to finish my homecoming dress and you made me poke myself with the needle. I just about bled all over the fabric."

Austin disappeared into my bathroom while Wynton watched the empty doorway, his tail slowing to a halt. When Austin reemerged with a small bandage, the dog circled him with more energy than usual—probably because he was expecting dinner soon. I wasn't the biggest fan of Wynton, starting with his name. After all, who names a dog after a jazz musician? Dog-Wynton was loud and messy and didn't understand that some people aren't dog people.

"Let me see your finger." Austin wrapped the bandage around my thumb, blocking the bead of red liquid from growing larger. He flashed that easygoing smile of his, and my annoyance fell away.

"Thanks."

He cupped a hand to his ear. "What's that? I can't hear you. My ears are bleeding from your horrendous music. Please tell me this whole 1980s love song phase will end soon." He perused the dress as it rested on the dress form. He grabbed a pair of scissors and snipped a loose thread off the shoulder. "You know who else likes terrible music?" He put the scissors back on the sewing desk and sat on the window seat.

"Don't say Xander," I warned, then pretended to gag.

"You know, I think he has a crush on you. And by the way you look at him sometimes, I think you might feel something too."

I scoffed.

"You were friends with him once. He's a nice guy under all that sarcasm, you know. Much nicer than Jock, anyway."

"Jake," I corrected him. I focused on the dress, hoping to

avoid one of his lectures about my relationship. Brotherly devotion, I'd learned, was a double-edged sword.

"Same difference. Anyway, Mom sent me up to tell you we need to leave at six if we want to get to the game on time."

I rolled my eyes. "Why do we all have to drive together? And how long do you think we have to hang out with them after the football game? Courtney's having a party. Do you think Mom will ever realize that we aren't six anymore?"

"I think it's hard on her, knowing she has less than two years before we graduate."

"Right. She's probably counting down the days until I leave."

Austin paused, chewing on his words carefully. "You know, it might be good for you to act a bit more like a kid. I hate hearing things about you. You deserve better than that."

I set the needle down and moved to the window seat opposite my brother. Those awful rumors. Sometimes I wondered if I should just do what everyone expected me to do. Be who they expected me to be. But that would mean disappointing Austin, and I hated disappointing him even more than I hated disappointing Mom.

"Come here." Austin scooted closer to me and offered his shoulder as a pillow. Of course I accepted. "I love you, sis."

I drew in a deep breath. In all the world, he was the only one I could count on to love me through anything. I was sure of it. "I love you too."

In front of us, Wynton lay down and released a loud whyhaven't-I-been-fed-yet sigh that made Austin and me laugh.

I sat up straight. "Hey, do you and Sarah want to come with me to Courtney's party after the game?"

"I could do without watching the popular kids get drunk and high and whatever else you all do. Nah, I like my simple life. Being popular seems like a lot of work. I watch you try to navigate it all day long. No thank you."

"Well, you may not be popular by school standards, but

everyone thinks the world of you. You don't even have to try. I'm jealous."

"Ah, you just wish Xander thought the world of you."

"Way to ruin a perfectly good moment, Austin." I shoved him off the window seat, and his butt hit the floor.

"That's it. I'm telling Mom." He jumped up and with a smile on his face, jogged to the door, trailed by Wynton. "But seriously, we've got to get ready so you can be crowned Junior Homecoming Princess. I'll be the one in the way far back cheering for you loudest."

# *thirteen*

## LORI

I wanted to remain buried in the covers the next morning to ponder love and loss, but the girls forced me to rise, shower, eat, and put on my golfing shoes. Like tee time could distract me from the anniversary of my son's death. I appreciated the intent but knew keeping my mind and body busy was not going to help. So, while they told stories about other moms in the PTO, I reminisced on the first time I held Austin in my arms. When they made crass jokes using common golf terms like *hole in one* and *gap wedge*, I recalled how Austin, though he learned to walk before Avery, wouldn't go anywhere without her.

Ruth tapped my shoulder. "Lori, it's your turn."

Enid handed me my driver, knowing I couldn't care less about my performance. I teed up and eyed the green. As I took my stance and addressed the ball, Laney whispered something to Ruth. Another crass joke? Or something about my husband's hotness level? Perhaps something about how I was no longer any fun? I swung through the ball, instinct informing my hips to turn. A solid hit. The ball climbed, a straight shot that bypassed the fairway and landed just short of the pin.

"Whoop!" Enid hollered. "You're looking at a birdie with that one, Lori."

"Birdie! Birdie!" I heard Austin say as he and Avery chased a duck at the park, their toddler feet clomping after the mallard.

"We lost her again," Laney said.

As the gloom gripped me in its claws, Enid steered me back to the golf cart, and I climbed on. A ping sounded from the pocket of my golf bag. Once we'd stopped next to the fairway so Ruth and Laney could take their second strokes, I retrieved my phone and found a text from Michael.

> Conference is going great. Here's a pic of me presenting on tax benefits for early retirees.

I zoomed in on the photo. Michael, handsome as ever in his business suit, stood to the side of a podium, casually addressing the audience like he was their best friend.

"What's that?" Enid asked.

I held out the phone so she could see the picture.

"You said that conference is in Texas?"

"Yeah. Dallas."

"Michael looks very professional. Wait." Using her thumb and forefinger, Enid zoomed out until the full stage came into view. "Is that her?"

"Who?" I asked. Two figures sat on stools stage left. A man and a woman.

Enid centered the photo on the woman. "Jade."

Sure enough, Jade Jessup, trimmed in head-to-toe navy blue, held a microphone in her lap as if she were on queue to speak next. Her attention, like everyone's in that conference room I was sure, was glued to my husband. A pleasant smile graced her pretty face. "How do you know about Michael's colleague?"

"Colleague. Really?" Enid caught her smile before it reached its full width. "Oh, you still don't remember, do you?"

"Remember what?"

Enid held quiet for some time, thumbing some dried mud off my seven iron. Finally, her eyes lifted to mine. "Michael's affair. With Jade."

## AVERY

"This way, sweet boy." I directed Wynton to a rock far from the mountain ledge in case the old dog decided to get some of that youthful energy back. From my duffel bag, I withdrew two blankets. One to serve as a comfy bed for Wynton and one to protect against the icy breeze stroking the mountainside. I settled beside Wynton and rested my back against the rock. From here, it seemed I could release all the pain and sorrow from the last year down into Coal Creek Canyon—letting it trickle down to the canyon floor and soak into the ground.

I shook my head, willing away the memory of my last conversation with Austin. It seemed to lodge itself behind my breastbone, expanding with every breath.

"Dear Austin, I didn't mean it."

At the sound of my voice, Wynton lifted his head. I leaned over and pressed my face into his side. Eventually, I placed my ear on Wynton's chest, allowing his heartbeat to lull me into a daze where there was no separation between heaven and earth.

"Avery?" a voice whispered.

"Austin, I didn't mean it."

"It's me. Xander."

Reality stung quick and fierce. I sat up, knocking Xander's hand off me. The cold centered on my cheeks, and I wiped the remnants of fallen tears away.

"Sorry to freak you out. I stopped by your house. Your grandma told me where you'd gone. I saw your Jeep at the trailhead. Can I join you?"

"Since you're already here." I straightened myself and scooched closer to Wynton. Not that it mattered. The divot in front of the boulder wasn't quite wide enough for two teens and a dog to share comfortably, so when Xander sat, we were pressed together, knee-to-knee, hip-to-hip, arm-to-arm.

"Why did you follow me up here?" I asked. "You aren't going to force me to talk about Austin, are you? I don't think I can handle that."

Xander stared straight ahead. "I didn't want you to be alone today."

"I'm not. Grandma's at the house, and I have Wynton here."

"You know what I mean."

And I did. We sat quietly. After a lick of wind caused Xander to rub the calf of one leg against the shin of the other, I stretched my quilt over his jeans. Purely selfish since I really wanted to trap his body heat close to mine.

"Xander, I have a question. Austin thought you still had a crush on me last year. Was he right?"

He angled his face away from me.

"Are you blushing, Xander Dixon?" I leaned to the side, jostling him a bit.

"Never. I thought you said you didn't want to talk about Austin today."

"I don't believe Austin was the most important player in that sentence."

Xander locked me in his gaze and something inside me melted, so I have no idea why my body chose that moment to shake with chills.

"You're freezing."

That was far less embarrassing than admitting that he had a physical effect on me. "Kind of."

"What else are you planning on doing today?"

"Whatever I can think of to keep me from dying of sadness . . . or hypothermia."

He placed his hand on mine. "You are going to make it through this day, Avery. I promise." Mischief danced across his brow. "If you are looking for something to do that doesn't include turning into an ice sculpture, I have an idea."

# *fourteen*

"Where on earth have you taken me?"

"The one place I know you can't be sad."

After I'd dropped Wynton off at my house, I hopped in Xander's Bronco and we drove down to Golden. He steered the car toward an open spot near JoJo's Pizzeria.

"What are we doing here?" I asked, somewhat afraid of the answer.

"Celebrating your birthday." Xander hopped out and jogged around the front. He opened my door and held out his hand.

"My birthday was in July."

"I know. We didn't celebrate it then, so we've got to now."

Anything was better than sitting at home and listening to Grandma complain about Dad. I accepted Xander's hand and stepped down to the pavement. He led us to the pizzeria's door and held it open for me. Joyful squeals mixed with the electronic sound effects of Skee-Ball, Whac-A-Mole, and dozens of other games.

We were greeted by a kid I thought might be a couple years younger than us. He stood by a velvet rope, holding a stamp in his hand to match parents to children as a safety measure. Xander put my hand on the podium flat next to his. The kid gave us a questioning look but stamped us with matching numbers, touching my hand unnecessarily and earning a questioning look from Xander.

The restaurant was filled with more kids than fans at a K-pop concert. The only open seats were at the end of a long table covered with Cocomelon tablecloths, half-eaten pizza slices, and puddles of spilled fruit punch. Nearby, on a stage, creepy animatronic animals sang a parody of "Welcome to the Jungle." At Xander's request, I took a seat and watched the show in horror while Xander got us cards to play the games. He returned with more than that though. He held a sign with "Reserved for Avery's party (2)" Sharpied on it and an inflatable pink crown that read "Birthday Girl."

"Oh no."

"Oh yes."

He attempted to place the crown on my head, but I jumped to my feet to fight him off, slapping his hands away and shaking my head in refusal. He managed to grab both my hands and hold them behind his back so I was practically hugging him. It wasn't the worst time I've ever had. I could get used to these flirty moments.

Someone cleared their throat. The awkward boy from the front door stood before us. "I'm your party planner, Josh. JoJo wants to wish you a hoppity boppity birthday," he recited rather hesitantly, no doubt questioning his choice of after-school jobs. "JoJo will be calling up all the birthday girls and boys for a special hoppity boppity birthday dance at the top of the hour. Take a turn in the ticket blaster, but don't forget to wear the special goggles so all the fun doesn't get in your eyes. I'll call your name when your pizza is ready."

As Josh trudged away, I looked at Xander. "You think you're so funny, don't you?"

"Funny? No. Charming? I hope. Now, let's go win some tickets."

We amassed as many tickets as possible. He teased me about my inability to play Skee-Ball. I ridiculed his attempt at Dance Dance Revolution. We cheated on Whac-A-Mole to get more tickets. After that, we ate pizza on borrowed Cocomelon plates and drank fruit punch. When the large rabbit mascot named JoJo called the birthday boys and girls up on stage, I donned my crown spectacularly and did my best to outshine a pair of three-year-olds, a five-year-old, and a set of six-year-old triplets when we were tasked with copying JoJo's Hoppity Boppity Birthday Dance.

I took a turn in the ticket blaster, and thanks to my competitive nature, scooped up three times the number of tickets as all the other kids. Xander congratulated me by lifting me off the ground in an embrace that lasted a bit too long for enemies or friends to share.

After we split a tiny cake, Xander said, "I have a gift in mind but I'm going to need all our tickets. Do you mind?"

I handed them over. He carried those and the backpack he'd picked up from his house on the way over here to the ticket counter. He displayed all the tickets we'd just won, then pulled out dozens of stacks of tickets wrapped in rubber bands. After Josh counted it all, Xander pointed to the display below. He returned with his hands behind his back.

"Do you remember the summer after sixth grade when Austin and I were really into Nerf guns?"

I nodded slowly, confused.

"Well," Xander continued, "we came here at least once a week in hopes of earning enough tickets to get this megablaster that cost 2,500 tickets. We were like, 200 shy of it. But once seventh grade started, we lost interest. For whatever reason, I never threw out the tickets. Think of this as a belated eighteenth birthday present from Austin and me. Give me your hand."

I obliged, and he slipped a bracelet with emerald green gems on my wrist.

"It's a good thing they had that or else you were getting a Nerf gun."

My vision blurred. I put my arms around his waist and rested my head on his shoulder, hoping he knew how much I treasured this gift and this day.

Afterward, he walked beside me to my front door.

"My grandma has bridge night with her friends, but my parents left me money to get food delivered," I told him. "We can do that and then maybe stream the new Marvel movie."

The smile slid from Xander's face, and he dropped his focus to our entwined hands. "Avery, I can't."

"What, are you a DC fan and can't break your allegiance?" I bumped him with my shoulder.

"No. I mean, I can't stay." Xander grimaced. "The home-coming dance is tonight, and I'm, uh, taking Sarah."

My arms grew heavy, and I dropped his hand.

"I'm sorry. Sarah wanted to do something to remember Austin today—"

"Something like moving in on his best friend?"

"It's not like that. Sarah and I are friends."

"If that's true, don't go."

"You know I can't do that to her."

The sun inched toward the mountains, but the land was still awash with its light—a stark contrast to the dark windows in my lonely house. At least I had Wynton. Who'd have thought that mutt would become my best friend and most loyal companion? I forced a laugh. Anything to push away what I was feeling. Why had I forced Mom to go away this weekend?

"You can still go to the dance with us," Xander said. "It'll be a group thing. Sarah will understand."

I crossed my arms over my stomach, the only hug I'd be getting tonight when the shadows descended.

"I don't want to leave you by yourself. Not today." Xander worked his jaw for a few moments. "I don't know what to do here, Avery."

An unseen weight pressed on my chest. I was slipping.

Then I was caught. Xander's arms surrounded me. I heaved, unable to find the air I so desperately needed. I clutched fistfuls of his T-shirt as he held me like he'd done a year ago. He'd been the only one who truly cared. Now he was leaving too.

My hands released his shirt, and my fingers clawed their way up and around his neck. I pulled his head down to me and pressed my lips against his. His body jerked, but I held tight.

He'd probably never kissed anyone before. Not if he had only ever liked me. I lifted up on my toes and crushed myself against him until his shock eased. Then, he began to kiss me back, clumsy and unsure. But where he was hesitant, I was not. Somehow I needed to convince him to stay. He stumbled back until the porch railing trapped him in place. My hands moved down his neck and chest until my arms surrounded his waist. I found the hem of his shirt and reached underneath until my desperate fingers dug into the skin on his back.

He winced, then took hold of my arms and pulled them away.

"Avery, Avery, slow down. This is a bit intense," he whispered, trying to catch his breath.

"So? Come inside with me. No one's home."

He stammered. "That's not a good idea."

"Don't you like me?"

"Yes, I do."

"And you want me?"

He shuddered. "Not like this. Not today."

I pushed off of him, rubbing my lip where it had gotten pinched in my efforts. "You would rather be with her? With Sarah?"

"No, it has nothing to do with her. It's you."

My cheeks burned and a tremble carried up my spine. "What's wrong with me?" I didn't need to hear his answer though. I'd messed everything up. I was acting just like everyone said I did.

"There's nothing wrong with you. You're perfect, and this is awesome. Really, really awesome. But this is an emotional day, and you aren't thinking straight. I do care about you—"

I stepped toward him, trying a new, gentler approach. "Then stay with me." I brushed my lips against his with every pleading syllable.

Still, he slipped from my embrace, touching only my wrist and thumbing the beads on the bracelet. "I don't want to leave you alone . . . but I have to. I can't do that to Sarah. She's expecting me."

Sarah. Sweet, innocent, would-never-hurt-anyone Sarah. Was I really asking Xander to stand her up? Was I doing to her what Courtney did to me? I slid my wrist free and wrapped my arms around myself. My chest hitched as I searched for breath, and I staggered back to my front door. My fumbling fingers punched in the keycode, but I messed up the numbers.

He stood close behind me, put his hands on my shoulders, and spoke tenderly into my hair. "Can I come over in the morning so we can talk about this? Or tonight even? After the dance?"

I couldn't speak. Not with the thickness pressing in on my throat. I couldn't look at him either. Breathing was taking all the effort I had. Finally, I unlocked the door and pushed it open, breaking away from his touch.

"Avery, please. I want to talk through this."

Turning slightly, but keeping my gaze fixed to the ground, I mouthed, "I can't." Then I shut the door, locking him out. Or, more accurately, locking myself in before I hurt anyone else.

# *fifteen*

## LORI

"Is there anything else you need, ladies?" the server asked as she took Ruth's empty dessert plate.

"Oh, no. The hot tub is calling our names," Enid said. "We're ready for the check."

The server nodded and disappeared. Lucky girl. If only I could come up with a reason to hightail it out of here. Not that I wanted to go home after Enid's revelation at the eighteenth hole.

"Do you think we can sneak a few bottles of wine into the hot tub?" Laney asked.

Ruth waved off the question. "Forget the wine. I want to sneak the bartender in with us." After spending the last thirty-six hours with Ruth, I wouldn't have been surprised if she'd already slipped him a key card to our hotel room.

The server returned with a sly look on her face. "Well, ladies, your bill has been paid already."

Laney guffawed, and Ruth cursed happily.

"By who?" Enid asked.

"The man over there in the gray suit."

I was the last to direct my attention toward the bar. When I spotted the dark-haired man wearing the wedding ring I'd given him eighteen years ago, my heart nearly stopped. "Michael?"

Ignoring Enid's groan, I rose hesitantly from my seat. He caught my eye and gave a small wave. He left his seat, and we came together in the center of the restaurant.

"What are you doing here?" It was the least of my questions for him, but the only one suitable for this public space.

Michael took my hand, brought it to his lips, and kissed it. A hint of mischief flickered in his eyes. "Isn't it obvious? I'm your knight in shining armor, come to rescue you from the dragons."

I blinked slowly. "What about your conference?"

"I skipped the gala. Being with you is more important." His face sobered. "Lori, I made a mistake. I shouldn't have said yes to the speaking gig. I should've stayed with you and Avery. Will you forgive me?"

I studied him. Was this the face of a man who could kiss another woman? Touch her? Sleep with her? No. Not my Michael. Enid had to be wrong. Or I was.

Before my tears could escape, I leaned into him and closed my eyes, feeling his arms around me but not answering his question.

"Can we go home?" I asked.

"There aren't any more flights to Denver tonight. I called Avery when I was at the airport to apologize to her. This was about two this afternoon. She was laughing when she answered. I guess she and Xander are spending the day together." Michael waggled his brows.

"That's what she told me too. There are worse things, I suppose."

"Right. She's a strong girl. We don't have to worry about her tonight." Michael drew in a chest-expanding breath. "I got myself a room here for the night. That doesn't mean you have to stay with me. If you want to stay with your friends—"

"I want to go with you."

His grin stretched wide, and I wished I could feel as happy as he seemed to be. Michael threaded our fingers together.

"Come on. There's something I want to show you." He led me through the dining room to the patio overlooking the vineyard. The sun dipped low on the horizon.

We settled onto a chaise lounge wide enough for two and watched the purples, oranges, and pinks feather across the sky. Michael curled his arm protectively around my shoulders and held me close. From where I lay, I glanced up at him and he kissed my nose—something he'd done to me and the kids in our early years as a family.

Warring emotions within me kept my breaths shallow and my lips dry. Grief over Enid's claim. Giddiness over Michael's visit. Sorrow from not speaking to my sweet boy for one whole year. Frustration over feeling like a stranger in my own life.

"Have you ever considered why God made sunsets so majestic?" Michael asked. "It makes you wish all of life's endings could be as beautiful." He was silent for some time, then he struggled to clear his throat. "I miss him, Lori. I thought that if I distracted myself enough, or if I wasn't home to notice his absence, the grief would never catch up to me. I wouldn't remember how I missed the caution lights and foolishly drove onto those tracks. But it hasn't worked, and I worry I've only added to your pain and Avery's." He squeezed his eyes closed and pinched the bridge of his nose. "God knows I miss our boy."

"I miss him too."

We remained just like that until the last of the sun's light surrendered to the deep blue of night. Together, for the second time in our lives, we were two broken people holding on to each other for dear life.

Down at the far end of the patio, a band began to play. The first few notes plucked my heartstrings. The singer crooned the first lyrics of Dolly Parton's "I Will Always Love You."

"Michael, it's our wedding song."

"Well, there's only one thing to do, then." He swung his legs off the chaise and stood. In that smooth way of his, he walked around to my side and held out his hand. "Dance with me?"

"Oh, I don't know if my legs are strong enough."

"I bet they are. And if not, I'll have you in my arms."

I straightened my new scarf and accepted Michael's hand. He led me to the stone banister separating the patio from the green space and rows of vines. He put one arm around my waist, then held our clasped hands out to the side the way fancy people danced, not us. Even though I'd grown up in dance studios, I'd never learned the waltz. We'd always been a "slowly shift your feet in a circle" type of couple. But now, Michael took coordinated steps and, miraculously, my muscle memory took over and followed him with ease.

"I know how to waltz?"

His soft laugh reached deep within me. "Austin wanted to learn before he took Sarah to the eighth-grade formal, so you hired Avery's old dance teacher to come over and give our family lessons."

"That sounds like the Austin I remember. Wanting to do something sweet for someone he cares about."

"He got that from you, babe."

Beyond my view and past the band, loud voices followed by laughter overshot the music. I recognized the perpetrators immediately. "It sounds like they found the hot tub." I nodded in that direction. "They are pretty wild. Why didn't you warn me about them?"

"I did."

"You said you didn't like Enid because she fills my head with . . . thoughts." An image of Jade flashed in my mind. "You said nothing about Laney and Ruth."

Michael squinted up at the sky. "Whenever I used to give my opinion on your friends, we'd end up fighting."

I filed through all the information Enid, Avery, and Mom had told me about the past few years. How it didn't align with my mind or my heart. "In my last memories, you and I were such a team. I always thought I was the most blessed woman in the world. To go from that to hardly seeing you and worrying about losing you to someone or something? No wonder I fought you."

Michael swallowed hard. "For anything that happened before the accident, I take total and complete blame. I'd give my very soul to put it all behind us and start fresh."

"Okay, then. Let's do it." I placed my hand on the side of his neck. "We'll start fresh."

"Lori, there's a lot you don't remember."

"I'm tired of waiting for my memories to return. I want to live now, with you and with Avery. I'll miss Austin every hour of my life, but my grief won't bring him back. Plus, I hate being a victim. What's past is in the past."

Michael pressed my body flush against his and touched his forehead to mine. He placed my hand against his chest and held it there as the weight of the world seemed to lift from his shoulders.

Likewise, the stress of this day, this trip, this life eased out of me on a breath. "Should we kiss on it?"

"I think it's only appropriate." Michael's lips swept over mine, side to side, bottom to top, just like our first kiss long ago. Knowing what would come next, I melted in his arms, a small moan escaping me. His hand left mine and slipped up my back until it reached the nape of my neck where the ends of my scarf came together in a bow. I felt the scarf loosen and slide down to my shoulders.

"Michael, no." I moved to cover my scar.

His fingers curled around mine, lowering my hand. And as I cowered in front of him, ashamed of my appearance, he dusted a kiss where my scar met my temple. "You're still the most beautiful woman I've ever seen," he spoke against my skin.

Before long, we stopped by the girls' room to gather my

possessions, then took the elevator to the top floor where he'd nabbed the only vacancy. The Marilyn Suite for fourteen hundred a night. Michael unlocked the door and ushered me in. To the left, double doors opened to a bedroom complete with a California King bed, its white bedspread sprinkled with rose petals. For a moment, I wondered if I'd stumbled onto the set of *The Bachelor*. To the right, in front of a sofa, a silver cart held a tray of hand-dipped chocolate-covered cherries and a bottle of milk on ice.

"I cannot believe you had a vineyard replace wine with milk."

Michael wrapped his arms around me. "I would challenge that you love your nightly glass of milk more than anyone loves their wine."

"That may be true. It's not very romantic though."

"Says who?" He placed a soft kiss on the side of my neck. Then another. And another. His kiss tickled the spot behind my ear, and a girlish giggle I hadn't heard in a long time let loose from my lips.

The invitation I'd waited months for. Maybe it had been his guilt over Jade that kept him from loving me in this way. Now, knowing all was forgiven, he was free. As much as my heart needed this, I was scared to death that at any second Michael might be jerked back to this reality where joy was fleeting and passion was saved for self-loathing.

I turned to him and, unwilling to waste any time, captured his lips with mine and felt the warmth of a thousand California sunsets spill over me. Long gone were the pert hello and goodbye pecks he'd been offering me. These were too-long-since-sunrise and too-long-till-moonrise, midday, side-of-the-mountain-highway swells of desire from our first year of marriage. Back then, we'd been innocent, craving something we'd never experienced and therefore couldn't comprehend. This was different. Like waltzing, my body remembered and demanded to dance in sync with Michael's.

After more hypnotic kisses, Michael pulled back. "Is this too soon?"

"No," I said, pleasantly out of breath. "I've wanted this."

"You should've told me."

"You didn't seem interested."

He studied me—my eyes, my mouth, perhaps the faint spray of freckles on my nose I'd yet to outgrow. "Lori, I've been interested since the day I saw you at freshman orientation. You in your Daisy Dukes and cowboy boots. My roommate was sure you were Jessica Simpson."

"Tripp. I'd nearly forgotten about that guy."

Michael traced circles on my collarbone. "I guarantee he hasn't forgotten about you."

"Why? Because I destroyed his ego when I turned him down."

His smile tilted in that flirty way of his. "And why'd you do that?"

"Your motorcycle might've had something to do with it. I was a sucker for tall, dark, and reckless."

Reckless. Something about that word made his expression fall. The glimmer in Michael's eyes dimmed. I'd chase it across the sky if I thought I might be able to capture it somehow and hold on to it forever.

Stay with me, I wanted to beg. Stay here. Stay now. Don't go back to that awful night where you drove past the caution lights. Don't go back to the reckless infidelity that tried to destroy us.

But it was no use. Michael positioned one last, good-night kiss on my lips. Just like that, he was gone.

# sixteen

## AVERY

As he walked toward our car, his shoulders sagged like he carried the whole Front Range on them. I adjusted my homecoming princess sash and hurried to catch up to him. Even in the dim light by the stadium's parking lot, I could tell my brother had been crying.

My spine stiffened. Did he hear about Jake's plans for us after tomorrow's dance? He wasn't my keeper. I didn't need him to save me, and I didn't need his approval. Not everyone had taken a vow of chastity like him and Sarah.

I blocked his path. "You know, don't you?"

Austin studied me. "Do *you* know?"

"Of course. Jake has been talking about the whole hotel room thing for a long time."

Confusion, then concern flickered over his expression.

"Your problem is you're too nice," I told him. "You don't understand what other guys are like. They beg and beg and beg. Jake's been waiting a long time, and if I don't . . ." I bit my lip hard enough to wince. "It's not like it could ruin my reputation or anything. People already assume they know everything about me."

After a shake of his head, Austin looked over my shoulder to where our parents stood by the car. "Ave, I didn't, uh . . . That's not—"

I grasped his hand and squeezed hard. "Are you going to tell them? They won't let me go to the dance if you do."

"Kids," Dad called out, his voice more strained than usual. "Time to go home."

Austin shook off my hold and walked straight past me without a word. He'd already told Dad. That must be why he wouldn't answer. He'd gone and betrayed me.

He opened the back passenger door for me. I glared at him, then hurried around the bumper to the seat behind Dad. As I climbed in the car, all I could hear was my blood throbbing in my ears. I blinked and we were already approaching the tracks. Not possible.

"I love our family too much to stay quiet about this," Austin said as our car breached the hill.

"Austin, don't."

We shared a glance, but all I could see were flashes of red as anger and fear cut through me. "I'm sorry, but this secret shouldn't be kept," he said.

"I hate you." The words echoed over and over in my mind as the crossing's signal blinked across his horrified eyes—the warning of an oncoming train. Why hadn't Dad seen it? What was wrong with him? I tried to yell, but my scream sounded like a horn blast. Austin's face went dark, and I was blinded by the light coming directly toward him. As time came to a near-halt, all the noise in the world was extracted. My head snapped the opposite direction of my body, then bobbled back the other way. The world spun and flipped on its axis. Finally, when the movement stopped, I found Austin's head resting on my shoulder. Not lightly. Heavy, very heavy.

Icy air cut through the fog of smoke and steam, but my neck was warm where Austin's blood streamed. "Austin?" I heard myself say. The only response was the slow strum of a guitar outside the car, playing a dirge for the dying.

I stretched my hand out to reach the musician but found only fur. My eyes were slow to open, but when they did, I was in my bed.

A nightmare. The same one I'd had countless times. But the guitar? That was new, and its strumming continued outside my window. Wynton, with his front paws on the window seat, growled at the late-night visitor. I checked my phone. Above all the ignored notifications from Xander, I saw the time. 11:27.

I got up and peeked around the curtain. Xander stood below my window with a guitar I'd never seen him play until now. I recognized the first lyrics he sang immediately. "Have a Little Faith in Me"—my favorite John Hiatt song. Each pleading line from Xander's lips burned like fire on my skin, reminding me how shamefully I'd acted earlier. How selfishly I'd tried to rip him away from Sarah, all for what? So I could use him as a comfort shield?

As the song neared its conclusion, a light flooded the back-yard. Grandma Anita's voice interrupted Xander's attempt at . . . at, I don't even know. She lectured him about good manners and appropriate calling hours before explaining that men must wait to be invited into a young woman's life or backyard.

Xander apologized profusely, then asked if he could speak to me for just a few minutes. That earned him a strict no. I thought about intervening and letting him say his piece, but as I sat there with my tears wetting Wynton's fur, I wasn't in a position to give or accept forgiveness.

---

"You better tell that Dixon boy that if I find him coming around after midnight again, calling your name outside the window, he's likely to find his head at the end of my baseball bat."

It wouldn't be a proper Sunday lunch if Grandma Anita wasn't pushing her way into someone's business. Most of the time, she saved it for the women in her Bible study. Although every few weeks, when the world's guardian angels took a Sabbath, she brought her talent for pestering to my table.

At least I got free Chipotle out of it.

"Well, Grandma, it's not like I invited him over. And it wasn't after midnight. It was 11:30. He's a random boy who thought he could get to me. That's all." I jutted out my chin and fixed my Avery-hates-the-world mask on my face. Maybe if I'd been able to find that mask last night, I could have confronted Xander and told him that I was foolish to think he could ever care about me.

Suddenly, Grandma reached out and pinched my chin, holding it tight. She stood and leaned over the table. Her blue eyes, dulled with age and sewn into a permanent glare by the wrinkled lines around them, drilled into mine.

"Avery Wheeler Mendenhall, you listen to me. No boy should ever make you cry, quit, or cower. No man either. Do you hear me?"

I might have nodded, but her hold on my chin was too strong. As quick as she'd assaulted me, she let go and went right back to eating her burrito bowl. I resisted the urge to check if she'd broken skin and took a sip of my Diet Coke instead.

"Your mother didn't pay me any mind. She shrugged off my advice as quickly as she dropped her pageant dress and sash on the floor by your father's bed."

There it was. The elephant in the room at every family gathering or birthday celebration. My parents' marriage was only four months older than I was. Just because I was failing Trigonometry didn't mean I was clueless in the math department.

I hadn't known that was out of the norm until we moved back to Mom's hometown in kindergarten and the older women at church told me to pray for my parents' trespasses. Even then, I just thought my parents loved sneaking into places they didn't belong.

Come to think of it, that's how I'd felt about church. When Mom brought me, I felt like I was sneaking into a place I didn't belong.

"Your mother had a very bright future ahead of her, as you do now. Don't let love or romance trip you up. No man should ever stop you from accomplishing your goals."

I finished the rest of my soda but kept sucking on the straw so it made that gurgling sound. It wasn't loud enough to drown out Grandma, but it sure was fun irritating her.

"Guard your heart." Grandma sat back in her chair. "That's what I always say. Guard your heart, and no one can break it."

I'd be lying if I said my ears didn't perk at that idea. Dad, Jake, Xander, even Austin in a way. I'd entrusted my heart to all of them. Dad neglected it. Jake betrayed it. Xander belittled it. And Austin abandoned it.

"How do I do that?"

"You keep your head up. Be the best version of yourself you can imagine. See the world as your stage and own it."

I'd always known Grandma Anita to be a bit . . . intense. It certainly hadn't done Mom much good, growing up in that competitive world of pageantry and perfection. Mom had only begun guarding her heart a few years ago. Before that she held it on an open palm, offering it to everyone. She must have finally taken Grandma's advice, and from what I could tell, she was better off for it, even if it meant she stopped putting up with my attitude. Now that she was back to her old self, I pitied her.

And refused to be like her. I gathered the remnants of our meals on the tray, carried it to the corner of the restaurant, and began sorting out the recyclables from the trash.

Grandma appeared at my side and tugged on a lock of my hair. "I gotta ask. What's your plan with this hair?"

"I don't have one. Just stopped getting it highlighted after the accident."

She tsked. "You can't take to the stage with your hair looking like this. Come with me. Time to shine up this diamond and sharpen its cuts."

# *seventeen*

## LORI

Words couldn't describe how great it felt when Dr. Klein cleared me to drive on Monday morning. Although hesitant at first, Michael came around to the idea after the doctor showed him all my tests. Physically, I had gained enough strength. Mentally, I was sharp. My reaction time was good. My latest CT scan showed increased brain activity in the injured lobes. So much that Dr. Klein couldn't understand why my memories weren't coming back faster.

We celebrated by picking out a car. It was surreal to walk into a dealership and point to the car I wanted, with only a moderate amount of price-negotiating. Where were the months of planning, saving, and searching? All that Michael seemed to care about was the safety rating.

The first place I went was Lake & Hearth, the local home decor store. Our living room needed a thick wool blanket for the couch. Something to soften it and make it feel warmer. The scent of lemon, rosemary, and vanilla welcomed me as I stepped inside.

In my mind, I saw a terra-cotta vase. My hands felt the brushed texture. *"That would look fab in your foyer."* Enid's voice. But I had disagreed. It was the perfect piece for the end of the hallway in the new house.

I took a deep breath and pulled up the latest text from Enid.

Sorry for how the weekend ended up. We
thought a fun trip might help get you through
the anniversary.

I thumbed a text back.

I think it was just too soon. Maybe we can try
again next year. Hey, do you remember when I
bought that terra-cotta vase at Lake & Hearth?

Staring at the phone screen didn't make Enid respond any quicker.

"Lori? Is that you?"

A woman in a Lake & Hearth apron approached. She opened her arms for what I suspected was a hug, but she stopped short of an embrace. Instead, she placed her fingertips on either side of my jaw and turned my head to the right, then the left. "Your hair is positively gorgeous, girl. When did you take the plunge?"

I sneaked a peek at her name tag. Kendra. And just beneath the name, Owner. She had a unique face with wide-set eyes and a narrow chin that had an elfin look to it. Pretty, but uncommon. But the best part? My soul whirred with vague recognition.

Was Kendra another friend I'd adopted in recent years? Perhaps, but what kind of friend wouldn't have known about my accident?

"Last October."

"Huh. Have you shared any recent pictures on Momentso? You look so chic, I know I would have remembered seeing them. Come to think of it, I haven't seen any posts from you in months."

Momentso? But Michael said I didn't have social media. Kendra must be mistaken. I mean, what reason could Michael possibly have to lie about something so silly? I shook my head.

"Did you delete your account?" Kendra's lips rounded. "Or did you unfriend me? Oh, this is awkward."

"I don't think so. Um, I was in an accident last October. I had a traumatic brain injury that required surgeries, hence the haircut. I have moderate retrograde amnesia so I can't remember the years leading up to that day. I don't remember being on that, uh, app or site."

Slowly, Kendra brought her hand up to cover her mouth. "I wish I had known. I feel awful that I didn't help you somehow. What kind of accident?"

"My family's car was hit by a train as we left a high school football game."

"That was your family? The one that lost the young boy?"

"Yes, that was my family. My son, Austin, was seventeen."

"Oh, Lori. I'm so sorry for your loss."

"Thank you." I breathed in deep, steadying myself on the exhale. "I apologize for not remembering, but did we meet on Momentso or . . ."

"No, we met here. You were my most frequent customer, and actually, you were the one who suggested we set up the store as rooms instead of shelves of items. We saw a vast increase in sales after that."

"Really?"

Kendra nodded. "I tried and tried to hire you as my curator."

"I wasn't interested?" That was hard to imagine. Working in this store would be a dream.

"If I remember correctly, you were quite interested. It was something about your husband not wanting you to work. Again, I'm not sure. I left you with the open invitation to join my team if anything ever changed."

So Michael forbade me from working? Why would he do that? He wouldn't have been threatened by my interest in something outside of our home and the kids' school, would he? No. Not Michael. That was about as likely as me signing up for social media. Kendra must be confused on both of those issues. Just like Enid had been confused about Michael and Jade. "Is that invitation still open?"

"Of course. All you have to do is reach out. I'd say you could message me on Momentso, but since you aren't using that right now, I'll give you my cell number."

After Kendra entered her contact information into my phone, she squeezed my hand and moved on to answer a customer's question about a lamp. I meandered through a bedroom, past an entryway, and into a living room. My eyes landed on a chunky knit blanket, more of a carmine red than vermillion, perfectly tossed over a faux suede chair. Ideal for the upcoming Christmas season.

My phone chimed.

> Yes! We found that vase at L&H about two and a half years ago. Please tell me you remember! If so, we need to celebrate by grabbing coffee sometime.

---

**AVERY**

When I walked into the cafeteria Monday afternoon, I knew Grandma had been right about everything. Shocking, I know. I had my first inkling when Mom and Dad came home yesterday, together surprisingly, and Mom was still a shadow. Now it was time for one of the Mendenhall girls to be the light.

I scanned the cafeteria. A table at the back had emptied and was being wiped down. I flicked my long curls behind my shoulder and headed toward the empty table. I'd barely sat down when Sarah slid onto the seat beside me.

"Oh my goodness, Avery. Your hair looks amazing!"

"Thanks." After being golden blond my whole life—first naturally as a kid, then artificially as a teen—this tawny ash-blond color I'd gotten at Grandma's salon was a refreshing switch back to my natural color.

"Are you doing okay? I was thinking about you all weekend."

My first challenge came quicker than I'd expected. Already, my confidence wavered, and my true emotions kicked and paddled wildly as they tried to surface. I would not, could not let them. "I appreciate you asking but I'm fine, Sarah. Truly."

Xander stood on the other side of the table, presenting himself as my next challenge. "Avery, can we talk?" For this, I needed to pull off my best Queen Elsa impression. Not that I was prepared to sing "Let It Go" at the top of my lungs, but that whole conceal and don't feel part? I had to try, otherwise my humiliation from Saturday would take me down.

"What about?" I asked, knowing he wouldn't bring up anything that might hurt or embarrass Sarah.

Trey Samuels took the seat right in front of where Xander stood. The guy was a walking meme. Hot, well dressed, and smoldering beneath the auburn curls falling over his forehead. He was a player, and not just in football. "Hey, girl," he said. "You look good."

Of course I did. I was actually wearing makeup for the first time all year. I'd stayed up late repurposing Austin's St. Patty's Day parade T-shirt, widening the neckline to hang off my shoulder and cinching in the waist. The emerald green color made my eyes pop. And my white jeans fit me like a Kardashian on a celebrity gossip blog.

Jake's best friend, Matt, joined us at the table as well. Before long, Jake and Courtney's whole table had come over to mine.

I pretended not to notice when Xander and Sarah finally slinked away, together. They'd make a good couple. It'd be best to stay out of their way.

The next day, Xander rang the doorbell promptly at 6:30 p.m., like always. Before I let him in, I checked my hair and makeup in the mirror next to the coatrack.

"Hi, Xander. Follow me." I made sure to add a joyful hint to my voice, and I smiled as I led the way to my room. I returned to my spot at the head of my bed and placed my laptop on my legs. "I have a history essay to write about fashion during the Cold War. I need you to help me."

Xander put his bag down by the desk and moved to sit on the bed. "Avery, I—"

"Can you grab that chair?" I pointed to the chair from my desk.

"Yeah, sure." He did as I asked and settled into the seat. "Can we please talk about—"

"Fashion during the Cold War? Yes, please. Let's talk about fashion during the Cold War."

He threw his hands up. "Fine."

We both pulled research about how style of dress was used to play political games between the two largest nuclear super-powers of the time, the United States and the Soviet Union. Then I left my laptop with Xander and moved to my sewing table where I began cutting apart a vintage floral tablecloth. As I pinned the pieces to my dress form, I spoke the sentences of my essay while Xander transcribed them onto the Word document.

"Two months after the Soviets put on their exhibition in New York, American fashion designers went to Moscow and showed off the leisure wear and dresses worn in the average American household." I paused, waiting for Xander's typing to catch up. "In a totally passive aggressive move, designers avoided the high-fashion styles of a wealthy, exploitative class. Rather, they presented the image of a classy and happy American housewife without a care in the world, thanks to her capitalist country."

I folded the fabric to form a lapel near the dress form's neckline. "In her floral dress, Second Lady Pat Nixon played the role of the sophisticated matron of Main Street in a photo op with Soviet president Nikita Khrushchev's wife, Nina." I glanced over my shoulder at my typist. "Add an in-text citation for Bartlett's book."

"What year was it published?"

"Two thousand and ten," I answered, then turned back to the dress form. The paper wasn't due until next week. How awesome would it be to have this replica of Pat Nixon's dress ready to wear when I turned in the paper? my hands stilled. I should've started a time-lapse of this project for a future video. I'd just have to start it after Xander left. After we finished, I stood, making it clear he could leave.

He didn't take the hint. Rather, he set my laptop on the bed and remained seated. "I'm seriously impressed. I don't know how you managed to make that topic interesting, but you did. And then to watch you re-create a dress from a used tablecloth with only a photo to guide you? You're amazing."

Don't fall for his flattery. Focus on your new agenda. The sooner you catch up on all your schoolwork, the sooner Xander Dixon will be out of your life.

"And your hair looks good. Is that your natural color?"

I ignored him. I climbed onto my bed and ran a spelling and grammar check on the essay. Xander touched my hand, but I yanked it away. This guy made about as much sense to me as comma rules. Everywhere one minute, nowhere the next, then randomly showing up in the places I least expected.

"I was hoping to sit with you at lunch today."

"Probably best that you didn't. I don't think Trey would have appreciated it."

"Yeah, he certainly jumped at the chance, didn't he?"

"That surprises you?" I asked.

"Honestly, yeah. Did you forget how that group treated you after the accident? You're going to let them cozy back up to you now that you look like you're back to Miss Popular? You're worth more than that. Besides"—Xander seemed to chew on his words—"I thought . . . that you liked me."

"Like you said, it was an emotional day. It's probably best to forget anything I said or did." I stared straight ahead at my closet door, hoping I was pulling off the whole icy glare thing. Come on, Elsa. I need your help here. Maybe a fabulous blue dress would help.

"But you kissed me."

Guard your heart. "Here's the truth. I was sad and lonely and desperate to feel something, anything."

He stood, releasing the world's heaviest sigh. He slipped his backpack over his shoulder and reached into his pocket for his keys. "You know what, Avery? I don't believe you." Great. He'd found his smirk again.

"I guess I'll just have to prove it to you, then."

# *eighteen*

## LORI

I slid the plate of eggs and toast in front of Michael and took my seat across the table. The coffee I poured prior to starting his breakfast had cooled considerably with the chill in the air. Still, I swallowed a gulp. "Hey, Michael, do I have any other email addresses?"

Without looking up from his phone screen, Michael shook his head. "Why do you ask?"

"I stopped by Lake & Hearth the other day and spoke to Kendra, the owner. She said I did have a Momentso account, but I checked and I didn't register it under my normal email."

He met my eye. "No, you didn't. That Kendra must be confused."

"Enid said I had one too. If I can get into that account, the posts may jog more memories."

Michael slathered butter on his toast. Sweat glistened on his forehead—the result of hurrying through a shower after his morning run. "I thought we'd agreed to keep the past in the past."

I froze, holding my mug to my lips. I inhaled a breath of French vanilla–scented air. "I think we both know that was a naive agreement, although I do understand that it would be easier for one of us to just pretend nothing happened."

Michael was quiet for several long moments. "You have lori
.stowe@prexmail.net. You could try that."

"My maiden name? Why did I use that?"

"I don't know. I thought you'd abandoned it years ago. I ran
across it while you were in the ICU."

Good grief. Hidden emails and secret social media accounts.
What on earth was going on between us back then? One thing
was clear: Michael wouldn't tell me anything. "Why do I feel
like you don't want me to remember the past?"

"That's ridiculous."

I set my mug on the table, a bit too hard, making the coffee
slosh up the sides. "Michael, did you have an affair with Jade?"

His eyes found mine. I didn't like the blaze that overtook
them as his face grew redder and redder. He placed his hands
on the table's edge, pushed his chair back, and stood abruptly.
"Did Enid tell you that?"

An ache filled my chest until it got so big it burst into a
thousand aches that traveled to every part of me. "So it's true?"

"No. It's not. Enid thinks that because . . ." He trailed off
without finishing.

"Because why?"

"Because you thought that before the accident. But it wasn't
true then, and it sure as the mountains isn't true now."

"Why did I think that?"

"I don't know. Paranoia. Insecurity. Your friends' gossip
about other husbands who have cheated. I have no idea." Michael pulled his jacket off the back of his chair and slipped his
arms into the sleeves. "Lori, I can't get into this right now. I
have to meet with a lot of clients today. I can't be late."

"Of course. You don't want them to feel like their needs
aren't important."

Michael closed his eyes and exhaled long and slow. When
he looked at me once again, the fire in his eyes had been extin-
guished. He rounded the table and gently lifted my chin with

his knuckle. "I may be a lot of things, but I'm not an adulterer. I love you. I love us. I wouldn't do anything to jeopardize that."

I didn't respond. Instead, I remained in place until he left and the garage door closed again. Then I grabbed my phone and clicked on the Momentso app. I typed the Prexmail email address in as the username and entered the same password I'd used for years, MissCoTeen_01.

No username found.

# *nineteen*

## AVERY

I still struggled to believe it, but Grandma Anita had been right. After four weeks of acting like no one could hurt me, I was on top again. On the second Saturday in November, our football team was in the district semifinals. The whole school came to cheer them on.

While I may not have been the head cheerleader anymore, I was front and center of the student section, wearing Trey Samuels's away jersey. The only thing better than being the quarterback's girlfriend was being the all-American running back's girlfriend. Trey wasn't the smartest guy or the nicest. In fact, he was kind of the guy version of who I was pretending to be. But he sure was a great kisser, unlike someone else I knew.

Xander stood in the back of the band with the other drummers as they waited behind the end zone for their halftime performance, which meant he was only five yards in front of me. You'd think I was competing, considering how many times he tossed a glance at me over his shoulder. It was almost as many times as Sarah, a flutist in the section next to the drummers, sneaked a peek at him.

Down by six points, the Cougars had time for one more play before halftime. Jake handed the ball to Trey, who then juked and spun past the defensive line and sprinted thirty-eight yards to the end zone. While the student section went wild, Trey outran the end zone and hopped up the wall to the student section. He pulled off his helmet and kissed me. It should've been sweet, but gross was the word that came to mind. He was sweaty and took the kiss way deeper than I was expecting. So maybe he wasn't always a great kisser. But it sure did solidify our power couple status. After the team disappeared into the locker room, the band performed a Journey medley, ending with "Don't Stop Believing." It was kind of fantastic, and I found myself swaying and clapping to the drumbeat. Soon, the students behind me were doing the same. Austin would have loved this.

◆

"Austin would have loved this." Sarah squeezed my hand and Xander's after their halftime show ended and they'd been given the go-ahead to take a break. "But you know what? What Austin experiences in heaven is a million times greater than this."

I wanted to tease her over the cheesy talk, but I couldn't, thanks to my stinging eyes. Xander, however, was serious as a car accident, and his eyes bore straight into me. When Sarah bopped over to Margot Lowry to share a soft pretzel, Xander and I remained.

"Nice jersey," he said. "I guess you and Trey are a thing now?"

"Yep."

"Do you even know him?"

"Do you?"

"I know what he shares online. You find that attractive?"

"Why do you care? There's a great girl over there, and she seems to like you. Why don't you go talk to her? Plus, she has a soft pretzel, which I know you love. You used to eat all of ours before I ever had the chance to grab one."

"First, stop with the Sarah stuff, okay? Second, you snooze, you lose when it comes to soft pretzels. Third, that guy's not good for you, especially after the year you've had."

"My dad isn't paying you to badger me about my schoolwork *and* my relationship."

"No, I offer that free of charge, but the working conditions suck." He raised a brow and bared a lopsided grin.

"Your life must be incredibly boring."

"Or maybe I promised Austin—" Xander mashed his lips into a straight line. Even though temps were in the forties, tiny beads of sweat appeared above those lips. How on earth had we gotten close enough for me to see that anyway?

"What? What did you promise Austin?"

Xander leaned in. "I don't want you to get hurt. Or used. Or humiliated."

"Not possible. I'm untouchable." My father's daughter.

Around us, fans cheered. Trey and his teammates jogged back into the stadium. He pointed at me, and I blew him a kiss. "You should go find a seat," I told Xander. "My boyfriend's about to put on a good show."

"Yeah, I'm pretty sure he already is."

In the second half, the lead changed hands several times. After a bad snap caused a fumble, the Mustangs scored again. Down by eight, with three seconds on the clock, Jake used a quarterback sneak to score six points. They needed to complete a two-point conversion to tie the game and send them to overtime. Jake faked a handoff to Trey. Even he seemed confused. Jake ran for the corner of the end zone, but he was tackled at the four-yard line. With zero time left, the game was over. The Mustangs celebrated while the Cougars trudged back to the bench. All except Trey and Jake. Amid the cheers of the Mustang fans and the collective sigh of the home team fans, Trey and Jake pushed each other until the coach stepped in between them. I left the game without speaking to Trey. Anything to avoid seeing Xander's face.

So much for the show.

# twenty

**LORI**

"Mom, please don't make us do the thing where we all go around the table and say what we're thankful for." Avery held a turkey leg in her hand and drummed it on her mound of mashed potatoes. Maybe, like me, she'd noticed that the other leg—the one Austin would've customarily gotten—was still attached to the bird on the center platter.

"I think we should," Michael said. "It's tradition."

"Don't you think our traditions have been shot to pieces at this point?" Avery asked.

"I'll go first." My mother, although she'd never supported my marriage to Michael, somehow always ended up at our table on holidays. I suspected it was because she had nowhere else to go. Even the hardest hearts need love sometimes. "I'm thankful you pulled through, Lori. And you now have a second chance at life and at making your dreams come true. And I'm thankful for Avery's independence and empowerment. She makes me proud."

Michael raised his glass of water toward my mother. "Anita, I'm thankful for all your help this year. You kept things running when I couldn't. Avery, I'm thankful for how you've persevered. Not many teenagers have dealt with so much loss, but you're fighting to get back on track. And my wife"—Michael stared out the window—"I'm thankful every day I still have you." He said it like he expected me to walk out the door any minute. Strange.

Avery pulled a chunk of meat off the turkey leg and fed it to Wynton under the table. "I'm glad I have this guy."

All eyes were on me. I took my memory notebook off the buffet table and opened to the bookmarked page. "I appreciate each one of you for your patience with me. With every recovered memory, I get to relive blessed moments in my life. Memories like Avery's last dance recital. The cruise you and I took, Michael, and that beach in St. Thomas. The banana pudding cake you made for my thirty-fourth birthday, Mom. When Austin asked if I could drive him and Sarah to get ice cream for their first date. And finally, I'm thankful for opportunities to get back to what I love."

We dove into the meal, and for a couple of minutes, no one spoke. Michael was the one to break the silence. "What opportunities were you referring to?"

I swallowed a bite of stuffing and placed my fork on my plate. "Yesterday, I picked up an application for Lake & Hearth. Kendra needs some extra help for the holidays."

"You want to work retail for twelve sixty-five an hour?"

"I wouldn't be doing it for the money. It's my passion. Maybe my purpose."

"Lori, if you want to get back into interior design, that's something we should talk through and plan. But standing on your feet for hours each day, taking orders from a boss?"

I locked eyes with him. "Isn't that what I do already?"

Time may as well have stood still. Avery glanced between us. Michael didn't look at me at all. The small part of me that instantly regretted my words dissolved when Michael continued eating. No apology. No clarification. Just more turkey.

Mom, however, trained her gaze on me, a proud grin on her face.

The remainder of the meal was painfully quiet, save my

mother's rundown of small-town gossip. After his bites slowed to a stop, Michael stood. "Thank you for the delicious meal, Anita. I'll handle the dishes."

"I'm sorry I made that awkward," I said after Michael left the dining room. "It slipped out."

"Don't you dare apologize for standing up for yourself." My mother reached over and clasped my hand. "Change happens when we shove people out of their comfort zone."

"I don't want to shove anyone anywhere." I stood and carried my plate and silverware into the kitchen, where Michael was already wrist-deep in soapy water. "Michael, I'm sorry—"

"There's no need to apologize. I understand."

"Well, I don't. Is it that you don't want me working for Kendra, or you don't want me working?"

He turned the hot water off and peered at me. "You're sound asleep by 8:30 every night after a day at home. Can you imagine how exhausted you'd be if you stood on your feet and moved furniture all day?"

I lifted my shoulders in a half shrug. He wasn't wrong.

"Contrary to what your mother believes, I'm trying to look out for you."

I leaned my hip against the cabinet. "What about before the accident? Why didn't you want me working then?"

"I don't know, Lor. Maybe because you'd always wanted to stay home with the kids. To be there when they got off the bus. It was my job to make the money. If or when that changed, you didn't tell me."

"Or it could be that I did tell you and you weren't listening."

Michael winced slightly before nodding. "Could be." He dried his hands on a dish towel and placed them on my upper arms. "You've always supported my career. I want to do the same for you. Just take it slow. Please."

He returned his focus to the soaked roasting pan. My focus landed on his forearms, where his muscles strained with the circular scrubbing motions. Back in the day, such a sight might have led to a midday "How you doin'?" Not anymore though, so I needed to tamp down the hormones whirling within me.

Avery dashed through the kitchen with her purse over her shoulder. "Mom, Dad, I'm going to Trey's. Bye."

"Who—" The door to the garage shut before I could get the question out. "Where is she going?"

"I have no idea." Michael dunked the pan again. "At least she's getting out."

"Michael, I'm not trying to do anything other than work ten, maybe fifteen hours at a home decor store. I can't sit around thinking about what I can't remember anymore. If I don't work with Kendra, I'll probably start volunteering at the PTO again. I have to do something, especially through the Christmas season, as I'm missing Austin." I caressed his bicep with my knuckle.

His gaze trailed my touch. "If the choice is working, volunteering for the PTO, or being sad, I hope you'll choose to work."

# *twenty-one*

## AVERY

"Trey, this is my tutor, Xander. Xander, this is my boyfriend, Trey."

Xander stood on the welcome mat that still said "Harvest Blessings" even though Thanksgiving was, like, three weeks ago. Hesitantly, he stepped inside, looked into the family room, and lifted his chin in a nod. "Hey."

"Sup." Trey welcomed me back to the couch by pulling me down onto his lap. "I've seen you around," he said to Xander. "Thanks for helping my girl. I hope you don't mind me hanging out."

"Not at all," Xander replied coolly, averting his eyes from us entirely. "What do you want to work on today? Want to study for the Chem midterm?"

"I already did that and finished my Trig homework. What I need help with is my English essay. It's on *Of Mice and Men*." I pulled myself off of Trey. Although I didn't care about offending or hurting Xander, I didn't want to be trashy. "Can you help?"

"Hundred percent," Xander said. "I read that last year. What's the prompt?" He took the seat on the other side of me, not quite as close as Trey, but close enough for it to be uncomfortable, especially with my current emotional state.

I bent the fingers of my left hand backward until it hurt.

"How is George and Lennie's relationship like that of siblings?" I read. "How was George's final decision to end Lennie's life an act of love? What do you think George's life was like after losing Lennie?"

A curse slipped out beneath Xander's breath. "It's ridiculous that your teacher would make you write on this topic. Email her. She'll understand. And if she doesn't, I'll take this to Principal Wright and—"

"It's due tomorrow."

"Avery . . ." Ugh. I hated his dad tone.

"I would've started it earlier, but every time I sat down to work on it . . ." I chewed my lip.

"Don't write it, then," Trey said. "It's senior year. No one expects us to work."

"That's not an option for her," Xander argued.

Trey puffed out his chest. "Sure it is."

I needed to step in before they started circling each other. "It's not that easy. I don't have a football scholarship to a major university and an entire booster club making sure I graduate."

"Well, hurry up so we can be alone." Trey put in his earbuds and started listening to music.

I shook my head and turned to Xander. "I can't write this." The emotions were taking over, jutting out my bottom lip and puckering my chin in that ugly way. I might have been embarrassed if anyone else could see my face, but this was Xander.

"Yes, you can because I'm here to help you. We're a team." The way he looked at me, with his eyes the color of the ocean on a calm day, made me believe him.

We started working, and after a few minutes, Trey reclined for a nap. Soon, his socked feet pressed against my hip. Xander's scowl said it all. I used my elbow to nudge Trey's feet away, but they returned.

"Kitchen table?" Xander asked.

"Yeah."

After we set up at the table, Xander helped me brainstorm the essay. Each time the thoughts merged too close to my reality, I'd close my eyes and focus on my breathing. And each time, Xander waited for me to steady myself. Through it all, he never touched me but kept his hand on the back of my chair, his body angled toward me.

Halfway through the writing, I buried my head in my hands and let the tears fall. Tears for Austin and me. Tears for George and Lennie. A hand grazed my back, combing the ends of my hair. I couldn't help myself. I leaned into Xander and allowed myself to be comforted.

"Thanks, man. I've got this." Trey lifted me to my feet by my elbows and led me into the hallway, out of Xander's sight. Then he covered me. My mouth with his, my body with his. For all the talents this guy had, tact wasn't one of them. He must have taken my shoves against his chest as calls of "kiss me harder" because that's just what he did when all I wanted to do was cry over my dead twin.

In my periphery, I saw Xander head to the front door. It slammed before I finally heaved Trey hard enough for him to get the point. He laughed as I followed Xander outside. The dusting of snow on the walkway bit into my bare feet as I jogged down to his truck and yanked open the driver's door.

He scrubbed both hands over his face. "I can't do this. I thought I could, but I can't. It's torture."

"I'm sorry. This isn't how I want it either."

"What do you want?" Xander stared at the wheel, breathing hard.

"I want peace."

"Does Trey give you peace? You know his reputation. He's using you for his own . . . pleasure. He doesn't care about you or your future."

"He can't hurt me."

Xander scoffed as he stared through the windshield. "I guess there's one good thing that's come out of this. I now know where I stand with you."

"What does that mean?"

"You said you'd prove you didn't like me. Well, I believe it now. You don't care about me at all. Not as a friend, certainly not as anything more. Because you know this is tearing me apart, and you don't care if I'm collateral damage."

The frostbitten soles of my feet burned, forcing me to balance on one foot, then the other. "What about my essay? It isn't finished."

"You're gonna have to finish it on your own. I'm out."

After I kicked Trey out of my house, I peeked into my parents' bedroom. Mom had gone to bed early, exhausted after a few hours at work. Every time she came home from the store, she was tired but happy. She slept on her side, looking angelic as always and facing the lamp on Dad's bedside table. She always kept that light on, waiting for him to come home. It was sad. She didn't deserve Dad's neglect. As a matter of fact, I didn't either. Back in the kitchen, my laptop had fallen asleep with the Steinbeck essay three-fourths completed. I found the glass dish of brownies Grandma had dropped off earlier and cut a square from the middle where it was doughiest. That's what Dad deserved for his years of late hours and work commitments: the overcooked brownie edges.

I returned to my inhumane writing task with a glass of skim milk and my plate of delicious brownie sludge.

The cursor flashed after the last words I'd written on the screen.

"For George, life without Lennie was sure to be—"

I held down the backspace button and retyped.

"For George, life without Lennie was destined to be—"

Sad. Lonely. Painful. Agonizing. Desolate. Unbearable.

Wynton lifted his head and stared at the door to the garage. It opened a second later, and Dad, holding his phone to his ear, walked in. When he saw me at the table, he cocked his head in either confusion, concern, or frustration. The last one was most likely.

"I'm home now. Gotta go. See you tomorrow," he said, ending the call. "It's after eleven. Why are you still up?"

"It's after eleven. Who were you talking to?"

"A coworker."

"Jade?"

Dad slipped his phone into his pocket. "What are you doing up? Homework still?"

I clenched my jaw to keep from laying into Dad about his sus coworker only because Grandma's words still rang in my ears. No man should ever stop you from accomplishing your goals. To get everyone off my back, I needed to graduate. To graduate, I needed to pass English. To pass English, I needed to finish this dumb essay. "I need help with my English assignment."

"What happened to Xander helping you?"

"He did help me, but then he, uh, quit."

"Avery!"

"Michael!" I combatted. "Please. I'm too tired to deal with the Xander mess tonight. I'll fix that later."

"Your mom couldn't help?"

"With her brain trauma? I don't think so."

"Okay. I'll do it." He saw the brownie pan and sighed. "Did you cut a brownie out of the middle?"

"Yeah. So?"

"Wasn't that inconvenient?"

"Yeah, but it's the only good one. You can have the rest." I didn't expect him to grab the whole dish and a fork, but he did, then settled himself next to me. I explained the assignment and read what Xander and I had written so far.

Dad put his fork down after only one bite. "Which teacher

asked you to write this? How could they not offer an alternate question or assignment? I'm calling the school tomorrow—"

"As much as I appreciate your crusade, can we just finish the thing? My face looks weird if I don't get enough sleep." That's what I said, but a big part of me wanted to put my arms around his neck and thank him for, I don't know, seeing my hurt?

"All right. It still ticks me off though. The caliber of teaching has gone down since I left." He cleared his throat. "When you write a paper, you start by telling them what you will tell them. Then you tell them. Finally, you tell them what you told them. Make sense? You've already told them what you wanted to tell them, now bring it home. I heard you say that George and Lennie were linked because of a shared history—working together on farms. And shared hopes for the future—having a farm of their own. And their decision to look out for one another is what made them brothers."

"Yep."

"And George took Lennie's life into his own hands because Lennie would face the exact opposite of their hopes if the law got involved. Instead of hope, he'd face fear. Instead of freedom, imprisonment. Instead of joy, he'd feel hatred and pain. Lennie's last moments were spent inside their pipe dream. He ended this life happy and loved."

I downed the rest of my milk, half expecting it to spill out of my middle because I felt truly gutted. Lennie's last moments were nothing like Austin's. Not at all.

"So, let's go back to this first sentence you've written of the conclusion. For George, life without Lennie was destined to be . . . What?"

"I typed 'filled with envy.'" I didn't wait for Dad's commentary. I continued typing.

Even if George ended up fulfilling their dream of owning a farm, he'd carry with him all that he'd saved Lennie from:

fear of the truth being found out, self-hatred because he hadn't done enough to protect Lennie from harm, pain at missing his brother. Those would hold him prisoner for the rest of his life. Likewise, he'd envy Lennie for feeling wholly loved in his final moments while George would never feel loved again.

Looking over my shoulder, Dad asked, "Why wouldn't he feel loved?"

"He'd distance himself from people so he could never feel that kind of loss again."

"And so no one would ever count on him to keep them safe again," Dad added.

"Right." I chanced a glimpse at him. Typically, the guy was pretty blank faced, but he sported a frown at that moment. "Is that why you are the way you are?"

"I could ask you the same question."

"But you won't because of the distance. I know how it is."

"Avery, you don't understand. It's a father's job to provide and protect. I've already failed at one of those."

"I'm pretty sure you've failed at both. Providing involves more than making money."

"Yeah, it's providing a home, cars, food, clothes, opportunities, college."

"How 'bout love and affection? Read a psychology book or watch some Dr. Phil, Dad."

"It's late, Avery."

"Yeah, it is, but soon it's going to be too late. The best thing that ever happened to this family was Mom losing her memory."

"Don't start—"

"You lucked out because she can't remember what you drove her to. She had a life and friends, and she wasn't going to put up with you working late. And, oh yeah, the Jade thing wasn't helping."

His face darkened with a rosy hue. I wasn't sure if he was

mad or embarrassed. Honestly, I didn't care. Somebody had to say it.

"Jade has nothing to do with this."

"Look, Dad. Mom once said that I'm exactly like you. She's right in a lot of ways. We're both hardheaded, stubborn, and self-absorbed."

"Does this have a point?"

"The point is, you and I might be a lot of things, but we aren't cheaters. So why are you doing everything a cheater does? Late nights and late phone calls? You're old. You should know better. If you don't change your ways, Mom will once again realize what a bum you can be in the husband department. She's already seeing it. Isn't our family broken enough without you driving Mom away again?"

Dad leaned back, never taking his eyes off mine. Finally, he nodded. "Understood. I'll do better."

"Good. I'm glad I could be of assistance," I said with a proud grin.

"Now, time for bed." Dad rose from his chair but paused above me. "Also, I'm not that old."

I scrunched my nose. "Eh, you're kinda old."

Dad knuckled the top of my head, then kissed it. "Agree to disagree."

# twenty-two

**LORI**

"Holy smokes, Mom. Babe alert. You look amazing!" Avery tossed her clutch on my bed and hugged me from behind. Luckily, she hadn't fought us too hard when we told her we'd be attending Michael's office Christmas party as a family.

"Thanks, honey, but you don't have to say that."

"Uh, yeah, I do, because you need to hear it, and I don't know if Dad will say it." Avery stepped away and looked me up and down. "That dress . . . where did you get it?"

"The mall. Don't judge me," I said with a teasing glare. Both Avery's fashion sense and her recent environmental consciousness far surpassed my own. To her, the mall was akin to a fur factory.

"I think I can put my protest on hold for a minute to celebrate your hotness."

"Oh, Avery. You look beautiful too. Tell me about this outfit."

She stepped up to the mirror and ran her hands down the front of her sleek and sparkly champagne-toned dress. "I found this at Goodwill. It was a total Grandma dress, but I took my shears to it and restyled it to fit better. Still doesn't mean I'm excited about this party though."

"You still have time to bring a friend. What about that Trey boy you've been seeing?"

"Meh." Avery turned to check out the dress's profile. "He's not exactly the parents' office party type."

"You could bring Xander."

"And make this party even more torturous for me? I don't think so."

"Are you girls ready to leave?" Michael peeked his head into the room. His gaze took a lazy jaunt down to my toes before climbing back to my face.

The past few months had taught me not to expect too many words of affirmation from Michael, so this small look of appreciation would have to be enough. I slipped into my ballet flats instead of the sexier black heels I'd briefly considered. Even though my legs seemed to be back to full strength, I couldn't chance a fall.

Michael outstretched his hand to me, and I accepted it.

"Dad, isn't Mom gorgeous?" Avery asked before borrowing my lipstick and applying it in the mirror.

He nodded and smiled at me. "That dress looks nice. Yours too, Avery."

She groaned loud enough to make Wynton bark from another part of the house. "Nice isn't a compliment. You're hopeless."

The party started with cocktails, followed by a formal dinner. Whoever had planned this party had spared no expense. Full glitz, as they said in the pageant world. After dinner, the dancing began.

Avery rushed up to me in between songs. "Mom, save me. Dad is making me dance with his coworker's son, and his breath smells like a wrestling mat." Avery kneeled beside my chair, her expression drawn into a snarl. "And he keeps smelling my hair. It's so weird."

"So, you've already danced with him once?"

"Twice. And if I'm forced to dance with him a third time, I'm afraid of what he'll try."

"You don't have to dance with him. Tell him your mother is trying to guard your virtue."

"Ew. I don't want him even thinking about my virtue." Avery scanned the area around us. With no awkward teenage boys around, she slid into her chair. "How are you holding up? This is way past your bedtime."

Her comment triggered a yawn that I tried to cover with my napkin. "I'm doing my best. The conversations have been trying."

"Just imagine how exhausted Dad must be. He's chatted up every person in this room, I think. Have you guys gotten to dance yet?"

"Uh, no."

"You know, if Austin were here, he'd have you out there on the dance floor with him." Avery's eyes went glassy. "He was always good with that kind of stuff. He'd know what I was feeling even before I did."

"Yes, he had a gift for that, even when he was little."

"He would have loved all these decorations. Christmas was his favorite holiday. Do you remember when he and I would dress like elves for Christmas Eve? My first solo sewing project was making a reindeer costume for Wynton."

"I do remember that. Wynton hated it! Tore it to pieces."

"And I cried and cried," Avery said.

"Then Austin wrote you an apology letter from Wynton with the excuse that he just really liked venison."

Laughter felt good. I dabbed the corner of my eyes with my napkin.

"You know," Avery said after the silliness subsided, "Dad and I didn't decorate for Christmas last year. It didn't feel right with Austin gone and you in the hospital. I couldn't handle seeing all those dumb arts and crafts ornaments Austin forced us to do."

"I know the feeling." Although this venue was drenched

in holiday spirit, with each table decked out in red and silver and centerpieces featuring white lights, holly, and bells, our home remained sterile and cold. Although Christmas was only eight days away, the only hint of a season change was the chunky knit blanket I'd purchased from Lake & Hearth. No one had mentioned getting a tree or hanging lights. There weren't any letters addressed to the North Pole with requests for particular presents. While I was desperate to gain the full breadth of my memories, the Christmas ones were too raw. I was all-too-happy yesterday when Michael surprised Avery and me with tickets for a Caribbean cruise that started on Christmas Day.

Still, I felt guilty that Avery wouldn't have one last childhood Christmas before she went on to college or wherever she planned to run after school ended.

"Avery, you ready to dance again?" A lanky boy with the hygiene of a middle school gym blushed red as he stared at my daughter.

"I can't. I have a strong moral stance against the messaging in this song."

It was a good try but "Baby, It's Cold Outside" was on its last few notes. It bled into the familiar first lyrics of "Frosty the Snowman."

"This song too. I don't like how it objectifies snowpeople."

"Oh." The boy shifted on his feet, unsure how to proceed.

"Hey, Tim." Michael appeared at the boy's side and patted him on the back a bit too hard, as the kid lost his balance and grabbed the closest chair for support. "Princess, how about a dance with Dad?"

Avery jumped out of her seat at the offer. "Yes, please."

"What about the snowpeople?" Tim asked.

She curved her hand into a C around her ear, pretending not to hear him.

The kid and I watched Michael and Avery take a spot on

the dance floor. After a moment, Tim turned back to me. "Do you like to dance?"

"Not as much as I like eggnog." I downed the remainder in my glass, then held it up. "Excuse me." Before Tim could say anything else, I left the table and headed to the bar. I bypassed laughing couples, a few of whom I vaguely recollected, and offered nods and smiles. The bartender wearing a Santa hat greeted me as I neared.

"What can I get you?"

"Eggnog, please. No rum though."

"No rum, no fun," he joked.

I shrugged. Maybe he should join Laney, Ruth, and Enid on their next trip.

"Merry Christmas, Lori." Jade was dressed modestly compared to many of the other women in the room. A simple green turtleneck that matched her eyes and a taupe pencil skirt. Unlike me, she'd opted for the heels, making her legs look even longer.

"Merry Christmas, Jade," I said. For the thousandth time, I reminded myself that Enid had been wrong. My former self had been wrong. Michael said so. "Are you having a nice time?" It had become my go-to question this evening. In every other conversation, I'd honestly wanted to know the answer. With Jade, I wanted her to say no. Maybe she'd take off early that way.

"Yes. Well, except for the teenager who keeps asking me to dance."

"Ah, I believe I met him as well."

"If I'd known he'd be here, I would've nixed dancing from the plans completely."

"Oh, you planned this?" I asked.

"Every detail."

"How about that? It's beautiful," I said honestly. I bet everything Jade did was beautiful. When she burned toast, the scorch marks probably formed a portrait of the Virgin Mary.

"Thank you." She took my hand. "Hey, Lori, I know we don't know each other well, but I wanted to tell you that I really feel for what you and your family have endured. You especially, with your injury. Believe it or not, I know what it's like to return to a life that doesn't always make sense. And I know trauma. If you ever need someone to talk to—"

"Jade, do you have any children?"

She inched back, dropping my hand. "No."

"Then you can't possibly fathom what it's like to lose one. And more than that, to lose your memories of him as well. You don't know what it's like to see your daughter come apart at the seams because she's lost her twin. I honestly pray you don't know that level of trauma. And even if you do, there's nothing you could say to make anything easier or better for me or my family."

Jade's long, dark lashes flittered, and she clasped her hands at her narrow waist. "You're right. I'm sorry. Sincerely. I won't bother you again."

I focused on the bartender, who was grating nutmeg on my drink. By the time I accepted it from him and took the first sip—which didn't taste as good as I'd hoped—Jade was nowhere to be found. I kept to the outskirts of the room, watching the happy interactions between Michael's employees and clients who'd all had a prosperous year, thanks to the bull market. I reached into my handbag to check the time on my phone. I found a text from Michael waiting for me, sent only two minutes before.

> Meet me in the room next to the coat closet
> marked Guest Services. One kiss. That's all I
> need from you.

I pressed my lips together. This was exactly the type of text I would've expected in those first years of our marriage, when Michael and I burned for each other. We'd always tricked our-

154

selves into thinking that a little kiss or touch would tide us over until we got home. But it never failed to do the exact opposite.

I noticed two couples slipping into winter coats in the foyer and headed that way.

As I neared the room where Michael waited, I checked behind me, to the left and to the right. A small twinge of excitement, of danger, sent tingles up my spine. Michael wanted me, not Jade. While I waited for an older man to disappear into the men's room, I leaned against the wall. Faint sounds caught my ear. No. Hushed sounds. Voices. From the other side of the coat closet's door. Michael's door. I wrapped my fingers around the cold handle.

Woozy, I held it tight and closed my eyes, the back of my lids burning bright white as my ears gathered a piercing noise. A train horn? No, that couldn't be. I willed my mind to focus, to find Michael. The door opened without action on my part, and I stood face-to-face with Jade, her eyes watery and impossibly green. Upon seeing me, she rushed past, leaving only Michael in the coat closet, and he didn't look happy.

"Lori, what did you say to Jade?" The accusation, the anger in his voice, hurt the most. He'd been the one breaking his vow, and he was angry at me?

"How could you?" I asked.

"Not this again. Lori, this is not the time. I'm not okay with this nonsense anymore. You've been through a lot, but that is no excuse for treating Jade this way."

"We, Michael. We've been through a lot. Isn't that what you meant to say?"

Michael hung his head and tossed his hands like he was giving up or something.

"Give me the keys," I said. "Avery and I are leaving. I'm sure Jade would be happy to give you a ride home."

# twenty-three

**AVERY**

Principal Wright wore serious as well as he wore a reindeer tie. "Your teachers are a little worried about your progress, Avery. But they said if you buckle down and work hard, you could still potentially graduate without attending summer school. How is tutoring going?"

I'd hoped to get through this meeting without saying a single word, but Mom and Dad sat in the chairs beside me with vacant expressions, waiting for me to answer. Those expressions had been ever-present for them both since Dad's work party last weekend. They weren't the ones who had to dance with Tim, so it made no sense. "Tutoring hasn't always gone well."

"Should we find you a different tutor?" Principal Wright asked.

"No. It's not Xander's fault. He's a great tutor. It's my fault. I was resistant at first, and recently I've been a little distracted."

"Because of Trey?" Mom had already told me Trey gave her creeper vibes. It was part of why I'd called it quits with him a few days ago.

"Who's Trey?" Dad asked.

"Way to keep up with my life, Daddio." I straightened my spine and fixed a serious expression on my face. "Yes, I was distracted with Trey, but I broke up with him already. I'm done with boys and distractions. I will graduate on time. I promise."

We agreed that nothing else needed to be said, then stood to leave. The principal ushered us to his office door, except he'd changed his mind about being finished with us because he held the door handle hostage. "Lori, this may be out of line, but I've fallen behind on buying my mother Christmas presents this year. I'd like to redecorate her front room. Could I get some suggestions from you? I know you work at that Hearth store."

My parents answered simultaneously—a cute party trick if they'd actually agreed and weren't eyeing each other with frustration.

"Michael, that is something I could easily do."

Dad's flaring nostrils were persuasive because Mom ended up giving the principal Kendra's name and number, using the excuse that she was busy preparing for our trip on Sunday. Outside in the hall, I paused to squeeze Mom's hand. "I'm proud of all you're doing for your career, Mom. You've got my support, at least." And just in case Dad missed that dig, I pinned him with a glare. I watched them walk out the front doors. Dad, like always, held the door for Mom. However, they walked one too many paces apart to pull off the happy couple.

I tapped my fingertips against the side of my leg, asking myself, What would Austin do?

Xander emerged from behind a pillar. "How'd the meeting go?" The senior class had lunch period right now, so knowing he'd chosen to skip his lunch with friends to wait on the results of my meeting meant a lot. Of course, he'd given up a lot more than that this semester. Hours out of his busy week, including the ones he didn't get paid for, where he'd send me articles, videos, and ideas to supplement my lessons. Not to mention his self-respect. I'd been a total jerk to him—ignoring him, insulting him, assaulting him the day of the dance, and the latest offense, making out with Trey in front of him.

Some might say I did it to make him jealous, and they'd be right one hundred percent.

"He said I need to pick up the pace if I want to graduate in May."

"And what was your response to that? I mean, other than that glare of yours?"

"This may shock you, but I told him I have an awesome tutor, and I'm ready to put everything I have toward this." I headed toward the cafeteria. If I hurried, I'd have ten minutes to scarf down the lunch Mom packed me.

Xander remained by my side. "Hey, I heard a rumor about you."

"That's never good."

"Did you break up with Trey?"

"Oh. Yeah, I did."

Xander couldn't have been quieter if he'd traded his voice for a pair of legs, Ariel-style. I'd be lying if I said my heart wasn't a little tickled by his interest in this rumor.

"To answer the question I know you and everyone else in this school are asking, I broke up with him because he was in the way. Not to be mean. He was nice and everything but—"

Xander coughed up a laugh. "He was not nice."

"Okay, he wasn't nice. He only cared about one thing. I know I'm worth more than that. Plus, I know where my focus needs to be."

"Good for you."

"From now on, no boy will get in my way."

Xander stumbled on the threshold heading into the cafeteria. Coolly, though, he saved himself from falling. I grabbed his arm. "Are you okay?"

Eyes pinched, he nodded his head. "Fine. I'm fine."

I glanced around the dozen mostly full tables. "Lucky for you, no one saw that." Further inspection showed why. Everyone was looking at the center aisle where Trey, smiling, spoke to Jake. Whatever he was saying had turned Jake's face as red as the ketchup splattered on the floor. Jake stepped up to Trey, bumping him with his chest so they were talking nose to nose. His fist was clenched tight at his side while Courtney tugged on his other arm.

"Better listen to your girlfriend and step away," Trey said.

"Erase the pics." Jake seethed.

"Aww, you're just mad I sent them to everyone on the team but you. You wanna see what Avery's been up to? Or should I say down to?"

Jake lunged at Trey, slamming him into a table and sending girls squealing. Students jumped to their feet to see the fight.

"What's he talking about, Xander?" I asked, sensing the walls closing in.

"I don't know."

While all the students closed in on the fight, one person fled the scene, straight toward us. Sarah. "Oh, Avery . . ."

"What?" I asked.

Sarah's words caught on her tongue for several seconds.

"Sarah, tell us," Xander demanded.

"Trey sent pictures of you and him. Ones he took in his bedroom, I guess. He sent them to all the guys on the football team. A lot of people have seen them now."

My lunch bag slipped from my hand, then my lungs reacted, sending all my breath out in one single cry that was quickly overtaken by the sound of a train's horn in my head, its light speeding toward me as my surroundings shook.

Xander shoved his way through the cheering students. Sarah grabbed my arm, but I pulled free and followed Xander. We broke through the tight circle, where Trey was on top of Jake, pinning his shoulders to the ground. A slew of curses sprayed from Jake's mouth, followed by a thick serving of spit that hit Trey's face. In the struggle that followed, Jake kicked Trey's phone, sending it spinning toward us. Xander picked it up, wincing and turning away from the image on the screen, before handing it to me.

The picture showed no face, just body parts I'd certainly never let Trey see.

"It's not me," I said in disgust. "This isn't me."

No one was listening. Trey landed a solid punch to Jake's cheekbone. With Jake reeling on his back, Trey stood triumphant, licking at the blood on his lip and grinning. Xander sprang forward, hooking his arm around Trey's neck and yanking him backward until Trey was the one on the ground.

Words I didn't know Xander Dixon knew spilled from his lips. Jake rallied and threw himself on top of Trey as soon as Xander let go.

No more. No more. I backed away, bumping into students in the process. I turned and shoved my way through just as the janitor and Principal Wright entered the cafeteria in a full sprint. Not able to feel my feet, I lumbered back into the hallway and toward the front door. Realizing I was still holding Trey's phone, I veered to the right and dropped it into the janitor's abandoned bucket of gray mop water. I pushed my way through the main door and welcomed the icy wind on my bare arms and face. Had I driven to school? Where had I parked? Was this what Mom felt like? Locked outside her mind, unable to piece simple moments together? I felt for my purse and found it hanging across my waist. My keys. I needed my keys. And the car. The wind whipped that morning's snow into twisters around me until I couldn't see anything.

I heard my name. Faintly first, then louder. In the next shallow breath, warmth found me in the form of Xander. His cologne offered a strange comfort, as did his sweatshirt as he held my cheek to his chest. I crossed my arms over my chest, tucking them into the shelter he provided. "It's not me. I promise it's not me." My body shook, and I realized I was sobbing.

Xander's voice purred over my hair. "I'm here. I'm here." Not "it's okay" or "don't cry." Just "I'm here." The simple reminder that once again, he'd shown up right when I needed him.

"Do you believe me?" I asked, pulling back to peer into his eyes.

He inhaled sharply. "I-I . . ."

The sides of my mouth pulled down painfully. "Of course you don't. Nobody will."

"I do believe you. I just don't know what else to say. Want me to take you home?"

"I don't want my mom to see me like this."

"Then I'll take you to my house. We'll be alone. You won't have to pretend you're okay."

# twenty-four

Xander led the way into his home. It had been years since I'd been inside. Seventh grade, maybe. Before the gum incident. It wasn't much to look at. It had been in desperate need of a remodel back then, but it had survived his parents' divorce and years of his mother raising him on her own. In that way, it was more of a home than my own.

I followed him down the basement steps but paused on the stairs to peruse his family pictures. In the largest one, Xander stood in between his stepbrothers, who were sitting on top of a fence. On either side of them stood his mother and stepfather. Everything I knew about them painted the image of a happy family. The way my family once was. Several more photos filled cheap frames, including one I knew well.

"This was your sixth-grade school picture, right?"

Xander returned to the stair below me. "Yeah, it is."

"I shouldn't tell you this, but there isn't much about me that's a secret anymore," I said, wondering if skin could grow used to embarrassment enough to no longer blush. If so, I should be close. "I had a wallet-size picture of this that I kept in my diary for years."

His familiar smirk appeared, and he grabbed my hand, pulling me down the stairs behind him. He brought me to a bookshelf and pulled out a worn copy of *Gregor the Overlander*.

He opened the book and pulled out my sixth-grade picture. "You weren't the only one with a crush, remember?"

"No wonder Austin was always teasing us about each other. He knew all along." I readjusted our handhold so I could make it last a bit longer. I should've let go, but after this afternoon, I wasn't in a place to turn down any form of security.

That's when I saw it. A folded piece of computer paper tented for display and featuring a drawing of two birds in black ink, facing each other on a thin wire. The handmade card I'd given him the day his dad moved out for good.

With my free hand, I touched the edge of the paper, careful not to make it fall. "You kept this?"

"I did. Pathetic, huh?"

My heart swelled. "Not at all."

His thumb grazed my knuckle. At least I wasn't the only one clinging to this handhold. Across from the desk, there was a neatly made bed. Anchoring the far wall, a leather loveseat faced a TV and video game system. Finally, underneath the only window, which dropped twelve inches from the ceiling, sat a drum kit, multiple guitars on stands, and a speaker.

"You get the whole basement to yourself?"

"When Joe and the boys moved in, my mom felt bad for me, so she gave me the whole floor—not that it's much to brag about."

"I love it." I focused on a framed picture of him and Austin standing in a stadium before a band competition. They had their arms around each other and were laughing. I couldn't help but think how Austin wouldn't be laughing if he'd been in the cafeteria today. "Xander, I'm so embarrassed about stupid Trey and those pictures. Even though that wasn't me, everyone will think it is. No matter how much I deny it."

He released my hand and faced me. Compassion lit his expression. "We'll still try."

I nodded slowly. "I'm sorry for parading that jerk in front

of you when, really, you were the one I wanted. Xander, you're the one I should've been with."

He placed one hand on my hip and the other loosely on my neck. With a feather-soft touch, he swept his thumb along my jaw. "We're here now."

"How do I get through this?"

"I'm not sure. But if you're game, I can show you how I try to cope. Music has the power to lift our spirits when we go through hard times. That's why I enjoy performing."

"You know, before you came to my house after the dance, I had no idea you could do more than play the drums."

He dropped his hands and puffed out his chest. "Yep. I can even play a little clarinet."

"No way you are as good as I was."

"You're probably right," he said, laughing. "I never did understand why you quit. You were good."

I groaned. "When I became friends with Courtney and that whole group, they told me band wasn't cool. So I quit." I shook my head. "Remind me never to do anything just to look cool again. Oh, and my band teacher told me I was perfect for the clarinet because I had long, fat fingers. That did it. I'm insecure about my hands thanks to her."

Xander grasped my hands and held them out for his review. "She was right."

I tried to rescue my sausage fingers from his ridicule, but he held them tight.

"I'm kidding. They are slender and delicate." He studied them again before threading our fingers together. "And I don't know if you noticed, but they fit perfectly with mine."

Yeah. I noticed. In any other situation I'd swear I was being fed lines, but it was different with Xander. When he stood this close to me, I felt safe. I felt cherished.

"Also, you don't have to do anything to be cool. You just are. Have you noticed how many girls have gone back to their natural hair color since you did? It's astounding the effect you have on people."

"Does that include you?"

He rolled his eyes. "Girl, you have no idea the effect you have on me. Now come over here and sit down. We're going to make some music." He guided me to the stool behind the drum kit, even as I reminded him I couldn't play. Before I knew it, Xander, braced against my back, his arms reaching around me, held my hands which held the drumsticks. With his guidance, I drummed a simple steady beat.

He lifted his electric guitar off the stand and placed the strap over his head. He turned on the amp and grabbed a guitar pick. Then he strummed along with my beat. Once we found a rhythm, he began to sing the opening line to "Summer of '69"—one of my all-time favorites.

Oh, but he didn't just sing it. He rocked it. His voice was smoother than Bryan Adams and a touch deeper, but just as strong. And the way his tone wrapped around certain words and hugged them to my chest? Sweet Swayze.

When the song ended, I did an earsplitting drum solo.

"Nice. I always thought that song needed a trash can ending."

After announcing my retirement, I placed the drumsticks on the stool and moved to the couch. "You're so talented. I could listen to you sing all day."

"I'm, uh, glad you like it." He grinned bigger than I'd ever seen and glanced everywhere but at me. Xander wore bashfulness as well as he wore his jeans.

I fumbled to remove my sweatshirt. His sweatshirt, actually. He'd offered me his after we got in my car at school. By the time I'd succeeded, he'd replaced his guitar and joined me on the couch.

"Can I tell you a secret?" he asked.

I nodded.

"I'm hoping to study music at Belmont University next year.

That way, I can try to play some gigs in Nashville, get my name out there. It's kind of stupid."

"It's not stupid. You're talented. I can absolutely see you being a musician like your dad."

"Not like my dad." The jagged edge of his voice pricked me. My parents may not have been perfect, but they were still here, still trying. They hadn't rejected me the way Mack Dixon had rejected his family. And where had it gotten the man? Nowhere. He was still a no-name musician trying to break into the world of country music. I'd heard Austin lament about it to our parents all the time.

A sorrowful realization settled over me. I'd rejected this boy the same way his father had. Yet he'd still been faithful to me. I leaned toward him and kissed his cheek.

He turned Santa Claus red. "Um, how about a Christmas movie to celebrate the start of break?"

"That's perfect. I keep forgetting it's Christmastime. My parents aren't exactly filled with the holiday spirit these days. For the second year, we don't have a tree."

"That's not right. You always loved Christmas. You and Austin both."

I shrugged. "It's fine."

After scrolling through the options on a few different streaming services, we decided on the live-action *Grinch*. A few minutes in, I broke the silence between us. "I've gotta ask. You're squeaky clean. With my reputation what it is, doesn't it embarrass you to be seen with me? After that picture, it's only going to get worse."

He shifted, squaring his shoulders to me and raising his honest blue eyes to meet mine. "I like you. Nothing you've done and nothing that you haven't done can change that. After all, you were my first kiss."

I pressed my palm to my forehead and closed my eyes. "I was afraid of that. I'm so sorry."

He removed my hand and waited until our gazes locked. "I'm not. Even if it was a bit . . . more than I imagined, I'm glad it was with you. I wanted it to be with you."

I chewed my lip. "I'll make it up to you someday. I promise."

"Sounds like a plan. But just so I'm clear, where does that leave us? First, we were friends, then enemies. Then I was your tutor, then we were friends again, then whatever we were at JoJo's—"

"That was my favorite phase, by the way," I interrupted.

He chuckled. "Mine too. What now?"

I thought for a moment. "Friends," I said. "I like you too. But I think I need to get myself and my future sorted out first. Am I a brat to ask you to wait for me a little longer?"

He laughed. "I sort of like when you're a brat. Of course, I'll wait for you. As long as it takes."

"Thank you."

We watched another minute or so of the movie, but something still pressed on me. "You know, it has been kind of a rough day. For only today, can we pretend that friends hold hands?"

"Only if you pretend not to notice if my palm gets sweaty."

"Deal." I leaned against him, coiling our arms, and weaved my long, fat fingers with his.

# twenty-five

## LORI

"What is taking that girl so long? The Christmas Eve service is always busting at the seams. If we're any later, we'll be standing against the back wall the whole time." Michael drummed his fingers on the steering wheel to match the tune of Bruce Springsteen's "Santa Claus is Comin' to Town" playing on the radio.

It took all my self-control not to silence it. Christmas didn't feel like Christmas anymore. December in the Mendenhall home was merely another month. No Christmas decorations, no festive music or frosted cookies. Just more refrigerated dinners and nights spent with Michael's back to me.

To be honest, I had no desire to attend church, but Xander had invited Avery, and I didn't have the heart to let her go by herself. I have no earthly idea why Michael decided to come along.

"This feels like a sham, going to church together," I said quietly. "Be honest with me. Did you mean to send that text to Jade? Is that why you two were in the coat closet together?"

"Lori, for the thousandth time, nothing is going on between Jade and me. She followed me into that room to tell me about your conversation."

"What did she say?"

"She warned me that she'd upset you. She felt awful." Michael thunked the back of his head on the headrest. "Why is it so hard to believe I'd want to sneak away for a few minutes and kiss my wife in the middle of a party?"

"Because I've been home for four months and kissing me seems to be the last thing on your mind."

"The last thing on my mind, huh?" He huffed and shook his head.

Finally, Avery left the house, wearing the faux suede coat she'd found at a secondhand store a few weeks ago, slacks she stole from my closet, and her brand-new Nomasei vegetable-tanned leather booties—an early Christmas present from us. I was more than happy to let her open them after Peter called to tell me what happened at school. Even after she informed us it wasn't her in the pictures, we promised to make sure Trey got the punishment he deserved—a hill that Michael swore he'd die on if the school didn't act appropriately.

Avery climbed in the back of the Lexus. "Sorry. I couldn't decide what went best with these boots."

Michael backed down the driveway cautiously. "It's fine. One question, Ave. Will those boots still be considered eco-friendly after we stomp Trey into slush?"

I tried to shoot him a look but Avery laughed.

"Um, he'd have to be considered a valuable resource to make them lose that status. We're in the clear." There was a strange peace about her, even now, upon mention of the event with Trey. She'd gone over to Xander's immediately after school on Wednesday. This I knew. But what had he said or done to make her shine pretty now?

As much as the seat belt would allow, I twisted my body and caught her eye. "Is something going on between you and Xander?"

"Momm, please."

I held my hands up in surrender.

We arrived at the church at the same time as the rest of the town so we were fortunate to find seats. Sitting two rows up with his family, Xander looked back over his shoulder, searching until he noticed Avery. She gave a small wave. He whispered something to his mom, then exited his row and entered ours, squeezing into the spot next to Avery.

It felt good to be back here. In the past, church had been a thing for Austin and me. Michael attended but often responded to emails on his phone during the sermon. Avery went because one, Austin invited her, and two, it was another place to show off her fashion choices. I went for the messages, the worship, and the midweek Bible studies.

However, today's message felt more like a knife than a salve. Young Mary carried a babe who would be sacrificed for the sins of others. Yet, knowing this, she still loved wholeheartedly as a mother should. So when Michael reached for my hand, I let him take it.

I stole a peek at Avery seated next to me. She wore a pleasant, almost angelic expression. The reason was clear, considering the way Xander's knee kept bumping hers and how he kept whispering to her. I knew how this story went. I'd lived it once.

Michael noticed too. At one point, his gaze passed over Avery and Xander's grazing knees and then landed on me. He lifted one corner of his lips into a knowing grin. Then, as the pastor asked us to bow our heads to pray, Michael shifted and leaned his knee against mine, making me wonder if I was still living this story, puzzling as it may be.

◆

The soft sounds of a guitar gentled me awake. I rolled toward the music, bumping into Michael's shoulder. He'd crossed our invisible barrier at some point, surely in his unconsciousness. The room had cooled considerably, and Michael's body exuded a warmth I would gladly crawl into if I thought he'd let me.

The clock on his bedside table read 12:01. Why would someone be playing music outside our window at 12:01 on Christmas morning?

"Michael, what's happening?"

"It's fine, babe. Go back to sleep."

Beyond our bedroom door, quick footsteps swished against the carpet in the hall.

"Avery." Still too sleepy to know what I was informing Michael of regarding our daughter, I sat up in bed.

"It's Xander."

"Xander?" I yanked the covers aside and scrambled off the bed. A quick slide of the curtains revealed the scene. Down below, Christmas lights had been strewn around the blue spruce near the center of our backyard. A fire in our never-used firepit provided the only other light, but it was enough to show little Xander Dixon holding a guitar and playing "O Holy Night." Wynton ran to Xander as fast as his old bones would let him. He was followed by Avery, stepping gingerly through the snow, shrouded in that red Lake & Hearth blanket.

"He's going to wake the neighbors," I said.

"They're fine with it. I cleared it with them yesterday."

"You knew about this?"

Michael roused himself from the bed and joined me at the window. "He asked if he could do something special for Avery. I thought it would be good for her to experience a bit of Christmas, so I agreed. Who do you think strung the lights and prepped the firepit?"

"When?"

"This morning—I guess yesterday morning now—when you and Ave went to buy toiletries for the cruise."

"Michael, why didn't you tell me?"

"Because we've barely spoken all week." The fact was tinged with shame for both of us, I imagined. And on Christmas, no less.

Outside, Xander ended his song and motioned for Avery

to sit in a camping chair by the fire. He'd even placed something—a blanket or a towel—on the ground for Wynton to lie on, which he did obediently. I was beginning to think that boy was a miracle worker. He picked up a thermos, poured its contents into a mug, then handed it to Avery before taking his place by the tree. The next song was "The First Noel," and he urged her to sing along. I shook my head again. They were caroling. First church, now this. We'd tried our best to shun Christmas, but Christmas found us, thanks to not-so-little Xander Dixon.

"He's good for her, I think," Michael said.

I nodded my agreement. "He looks at her the way you used to look at me."

The weight of Michael's stare pressed down on my shoulders, threatening to make me shirk away. But I was done with being weak. If my husband no longer loved me, if he no longer found me attractive, if my marriage were to fail, I would know I'd done all I could to preserve this family and keep my vows. I'd loved him, cherished him, honored him for richer and for poorer, through sickness, health, and even amnesia. If only—

Michael stepped behind me and placed his arms around my middle, holding me in our family picture pose. His breath, warm and deep, fanned through my hair, tickling the top of my ear.

"Is this okay?" he asked. Still asking for permission, after all these years of marriage. My instincts betrayed me, and I leaned into him until I felt his lips place a kiss where his breath had just been. Chills raced over my arms, which I bared in my cotton nightdress. Michael's hands left my waist, found my shoulders, then drifted down slowly to my wrists. His mouth settled on the spot where my neck met my collarbone, long enough for a sweet kiss to change into a sweltering one. A slight moan escaped my lips, permitting him to dismiss any distance between us.

Slowly, afraid that any sudden movement might frighten him away from the intimacy I'd been craving from my beloved, I turned to face him, poising my body the best I could to make my desires known.

The faint light from the outdoor scene reflected in his eyes, a flicker of the flame I felt wherever he touched me and beyond. "Is this what you want?" His robust voice reached the deepest part of me.

When I said yes, he drew the curtains closed.

# *twenty-six*

**AVERY**

Avery

I'm in the Twilight Zone. Did you ever see that show with the monster on the wing of the plane? I keep expecting to see that out my window.

Xander

Why?

Because my parents are acting so so so weird. They're being all touchy-feely and cutesy with each other.

Isn't that a good thing?

Maybe but we've been stuck on the tarmac for over 90 minutes, so I'm totally grossed out.

It could be worse. Santa brought my brothers both recorders. I can promise it is more pleasant on the plane than in my house.

Looks like we're finally taking off. Text later?

Of course.

8:12 PM

I'm on a boat! It's so cool. Austin would love
it. My dad won't pay extra for me to text
when we're out at sea, so I'll text when I get to
Mexico. I just wanted to thank you again for last
night. You're kind of dreamy when you want to
be.

Happy to do it. Merry Christmas!

Merry Christmas

MONDAY 10:42 AM

Greetings from Mexico! Last night there was a
teen dance party. I was one of the oldest people
there. A guy asked me to dance. I said no and
told him I have a boyfriend named Xander. So
you are officially my imaginary boyfriend for the
rest of the week. I hope you don't mind.

I'm going to be the best imaginary boyfriend
ever

Btw my parents are still being gross. Like, I'll
come back to the room and their bedsheets are
all wrinkled and the little towel animal is dead
on the ground.

Imagine what his last moments were like

Ew.

TUESDAY 4:17 PM

I'm sunburned. And I ran into the guy from the
dance party again. He wouldn't accept that I
have a boyfriend so I found a place that did
temporary henna tattoos. Here's a picture of
my arm.

I know a heart with your name in it is so cliché, but I don't care what people think is cool anymore, right? The girl told me after that it won't disappear for three weeks! This imaginary relationship is going to last longer than I thought.

Thanks to a Sharpie, I now have a matching Avery tattoo on my arm. Here's the pic.

WEDNESDAY 7:20 PM

I'm watching a movie with Hayden, Margot, and Sarah. I keep thinking about how great your laugh would sound in the theater. Even though you're a thousand miles away, you're still distracting me.

Good distraction or a bad distraction?

Definitely good.

THURSDAY 9:08 PM

I spent the day in Grand Cayman. I'm so sorry to say it but I cheated on you, Imaginary Boyfriend.

Say what?????

His name is Azul and he's a bottlenose dolphin. Here is a picture of me kissing him.

Isn't he cute?

How can I compete with a guy that good-looking? Now I feel like I have no porpoise in living.

I really sea a future for Azul and I.

Water you doing to me?

FRIDAY 10:39 AM

Another day at sea. My parents are still all over each other. I'm starting to get used to it. I don't mind so much. Anyway, I wanted to tell you that I kind of miss you.

Kind of?

I miss you. Okay?

I miss you too. No one's been a brat to me all week. ;)

SATURDAY 11:15 PM

I'm guessing you're celebrating New Year's Eve in a hot tub with Azul right now.

He left me for an octopus. He said she had better legs. We're at a hotel in Miami. Our flight takes off in the morning. Are you doing anything fun for New Year's?

Hayden had people over for games and to watch the ball drop. I came outside to text you.

Are you going to kiss anyone at midnight?

I don't think my imaginary girlfriend would like that.

No, she wouldn't. It's probably good that we aren't in the same place. I may be tempted to mess up this whole friendship plan.

I may be tempted to let you. Happy New Year.

Happy New Year to you too.

# *twenty-seven*

## LORI

I lay tangled in the sheets, searching the ceiling for an excuse to get my husband back in bed. Unfortunately, Michael's company was an unforgiving foreman, and he its dedicated worker. Like clockwork, he'd wake at 5:30 for a morning workout, step in the shower at 6:30, eat breakfast at 7:05, and be out the door at 7:25. Three or four times since we'd returned from the cruise, I'd convinced him that more creative workouts could occur outside of our basement gym. This had been one of those mornings.

The steam from his shower found its way into the bedroom, tingling my arms with warmth on this cold January morning. Life was good. My husband loved me, my daughter was happy even after returning to school and facing the crowd, and I had finally settled into a job for the first time since college.

"I forgot to tell you," Michael called out from the bathroom, "one of my clients' brother-in-law's the bursar for South Georgia State. She heard about Trey Samuels's suspension and told him that the star running back their school signed is a PR nightmare. It looks like he may not be playing ball there after all."

"That's fantastic. There should be repercussions for what he did." I pulled my satin robe from the foot of the bed and slipped my arms into it. I stood, still slightly wobbling from sleep and whatnot, and walked into the bathroom where Michael had wrapped himself in a towel and was now prepping for a shave. "I have news too. On Tuesday, Kendra promoted me to assistant manager. After less than a month."

Michael's hand paused mid–shaving cream swirl on his cheek. "That's great, babe."

"I'll pick up more hours as a result."

He exhaled loudly, his reflection staring at me. "I think it's excellent. Maybe not the exact way I pictured you returning to the field, but I'm here to support you any way I can."

Now it was my turn to release a breath. "I'm going to make sure Avery's awake." I headed downstairs, pausing at Avery's door for a wake-up knock. Wynton whined from the other side, so I opened it to offer an escape. "Avery, honey. Time to get up."

"Make me coffee?" The grumble came from the unmoving bundle of blankets in the middle of the bed.

"Extra creamer?"

"Please."

After I'd made coffee for Avery and me and had two sips settling in my stomach, I sat down at the table and checked my email on my phone. Once I'd sorted out the junk, I found not one but two unopened emails. One from Peter with the subject line "PTO minutes." And a second from the Momentso Support Team with the subject line "Re: Locked out of account."

I'd sent my request for help accessing my old account so long ago, I'd given up hope of ever hearing back. I clicked on it.

Lori,

We're sorry to hear about your recent health problems. We'd be happy to help you unlock your Momentso account so you can get back to sharing all the moments that make life worth living. Please answer the following security questions. Upon completion of these questions, we will send messages to four of your Momentso friends

and ask them to verify your identity. Please provide the usernames
of four friends on Momentso.

I chewed my lip. Michael and I were happy again. What
if something about this account rocked the boat we'd just
climbed on? No. It wasn't worth it. I set down my phone just
as Michael, dressed in a crisp white button-up and navy slacks,
strolled into the kitchen.

"Do you want me to make breakfast?" I asked.

"No, I need to head into the office early. You know. Client
problems." Michael's brow furrowed.

"Of course."

He poured himself a travel mug of coffee and screwed on
the lid. His heavy steps plodded across the tile as he gathered
all his things: his laptop bag from the counter stool, car keys
from the drawer, protein bar from the pantry, and finally, a
kiss from me.

After his lips left mine, he spoke. "As you pick up hours,
do me a favor. Pay attention to your health. Nothing is worth
a setback."

"I'll be mindful. I appreciate your support on this."

"It's the least I can do." Coffee in hand, he left.

I glanced down at Wynton. Using my foot as his pillow, he
snored lightly in his sleep. The perfect image for my Momentso
debate. I would let sleeping dogs lie. A vibration lifted my focus
to the table. Behind my mug, Michael's cell phone lit up. Oy.
He'd be mad at himself for forgetting that. Reaching for it, I
tried to come up with a playful ransom for him to get his phone
back. A full body massage, maybe? Or a night out dancing—

Jade Jessup
I'm afraid what will happen if people find out. I'll
lose any respect I've gained in this job. No one
will trust me again.

The text's preview went away as the screen went dark.

The door to the garage opened. "Forgot my phone." Michael jogged inside, searching all the flat surfaces.

"It's here," I said, holding it out.

"Thanks, babe. I don't know what I'd do without you." After another rushed peck on the lips, he was gone, and I shifted my focus back to my phone. In the mail app, I copied and pasted the security questions into my reply message.

Question 1: What is the name of your favorite pet?

I typed "Wynton Marsalis Mendenhall."

Question 2: What is the name of the school where you attended for sixth grade?

There was a character limit so I couldn't write that my mother didn't trust the public school system to provide the proper material to educate me according to her beliefs, yet she didn't want to take the time to educate me herself, so while she prepped my next pageant dress, I taught myself via books from the library. Instead, I wrote "Homeschool."

Question 3: What is your favorite song?

"'Dreams' by the Cranberries."

Now, four friends' usernames. Kendra and Enid's usernames were easy to find in a public search. I typed in Avery Mendenhall. Two options appeared. One, ModernCher, hadn't been active for a while, so I chose the second. Immediately I recognized some of Avery's clothing creations. Is this what she does in her room? Upload videos and pictures to Momentso as TheCompassionateCloset? I entered her username into the email.

Who now? Laney and Ruth? Would they take the time to respond? We'd hardly spoken since our girls' trip. I searched my mom's name and found nothing. Peter? I had to scroll through quite a few Peter Wrights before I saw his picture. He resembled *The Princess Bride*'s Wesley—a look that might have been attractive in his younger years, but now that his blond hair was salted with gray, that side part and floppy swoop of bangs left a lot to be desired.

Or maybe he'd used one of those filters that made you look younger. Would I have been friends with Wright_Go_Cougars though? Unlikely. Still, I put his name down. I took a breath and hit Send. With any luck, I'd finally be able to see just who I'd become the final year of Austin's life.

# *twenty-eight*

**AVERY**

"Activities," Xander read off the online college application. "Do you think insult-slinging is a hobby? Or maybe that's considered a skill for you."

"Oh, you're one to talk," I said, nudging him. Halfway through our session of filling out my Common Application, we'd abandoned the couch for the rug. Laying on our stomachs and propping up on our forearms with my laptop in front of us, we had the perfect posture for sharing the screen—and flirting.

As if reading my mind, he nudged me right back. "Okay, we've gotta get this filled out. Be serious, Avery Wheeler Mendenhall."

"I'll be serious when you stop making fun of my middle name."

"Wheeler is a last name, not a middle name."

"When your mother's idol is Society of Decorative Art founder Candace Wheeler, it becomes a middle name. Austin Alan Mendenhall? Dad named him after—"

"Wait." Xander pressed his fingertips to his temples in concentration. "It has to be a financial wizard or something."

"Don't hurt yourself."

"Alan Greenspan?"

"You're such a smarty-pants." I tapped Xander's socked foot with mine.

"I know, I know." After a little foot wrestling, Xander demanded we get back to work. "We can list up to ten activities that show interests, extracurriculars, volunteerism, community participation."

"Ten?"

"You can list up to ten. I heard the average number students write is six."

"Xander, I spent a third of my time in high school alone in my bedroom. Even six will be tough."

"Well, you're good at whatever you set your mind to, so whatever you do have will count double."

"Okay, write cheerleading. For the first time in school history, the title of captain went to a junior. It was only for two months though."

"Extenuating circumstances." Xander typed away, making me sound far more successful and talented than I was.

"Student council member, fashion club president, dance team freshman year. That's about it."

"What about your online presence—ModernCher? You had some following. How should we describe your videos? Offering high school students insight on how to dress their best? Or something about following trends? Ooh. What about encouraging healthy self-esteem through fashion?"

"I don't know. That isn't me anymore." I rolled onto my side, facing him, and propped my head up on my hand. "When I stayed home from school last year, I learned about fast fashion and the abundance of clothes the world mass-produces so we can keep up with all the trends. A ton of those new clothes along with excessive amounts of donated clothes are causing an environmental disaster." My words tumbled over one another as I spoke faster and faster. "Those clothes get sent to African countries and fill up their landfills. To make matters worse, the synthetic material these manufacturers use gets into the ocean and poisons aquatic wildlife."

Xander began to laugh.

"You're making fun of me."

"I promise I'm not. I knew you loved fashion, but I had no clue you were so passionate about the environment. It's awesome. Was that the video you were making that day we worked on your essay? The upcycled dress? And why you created Pat Nixon's dress out of a tablecloth? All your trips to thrift stores make sense now."

With a deep breath in then out, I relaxed. I knew this guy could rile me up. The surprise came in how he could settle me.

"You never cease to amaze me." He placed his hand over mine. "It makes me proud to be your imaginary boyfriend. What's your account name?"

"The Compassionate Closet." I rolled back to my stomach and opened a new tab on the browser. I pulled up Momentso and tried to keep my focus while Xander tucked a loose strand of my hair behind my ear, then began finger-combing other locks down my back. My account popped up. "Here it is."

"Fifty-seven thousand followers? And this account is less than a year old?"

"Yep." I clicked on one of the first videos I'd made, in which I taught folks how to mimic one of Zendaya's red-carpet outfits by modifying a standard white button-down into a cropped blouse. After it was over, I rolled back to my side and allowed Xander to retake my hand. "I would love to get dual degrees. One in fashion design and merchandising and another in environmental science so I can do my part to end fast fashion and make a difference for our world."

"I could kiss you right now," Xander said. And he meant it. Less than eight inches separated our lips.

Goodness knows I wanted to kiss him. His desires weren't exactly a mystery either. I noticed them every time his gaze dipped to my mouth in conversation or whenever he'd find small ways to touch me. Tapping my shoulder in the school hallway only to appear on the other side of me. Placing his hand on the small of my back when we walked into the lunchroom. Suddenly, all those reasons we needed to remain only friends were as fleeting as those trends I used to chase to feel good about myself.

I swallowed hard and sat up. He followed my lead, sitting cross-legged with our knees touching. Refusing to think of possible consequences, I placed my hand on the side of his neck. My fingertips tingled from the heat of his skin. I trailed my hand down past the collar of his T-shirt and clutched some cotton in my fist. Slowly, I drew him toward me until our breath mingled.

The door leading to the garage opened, and my father's voice put a kibosh on whatever step Xander and I were about to take. I released his shirt, and we both sat up straight. I pulled my computer onto my lap and began typing random words I'd have to erase later.

*Kiss. Boyfriend. Love. Dream. Dad. Has. Terrible. Timing.*

## twenty-nine

**LORI**

"Mom, what do you think about this one?" Avery said, holding a maxi dress against her body. "I think it has potential. A jumper, maybe."

I tilted my head one way, then the other. I still couldn't see anything good coming out of the pumpkin-orange frock. "You're the one with the expert eye in fashion. All I know is I wouldn't make a throw pillow out of it."

Satisfied with my answer, Avery placed the dress back on the rack. Her fingers walked across the tops of the hangers as she perused each garment. After I'd discovered TheCompassionate Closet in my Momentso friend search, I'd asked her about it. Although she was a bit sheepish at first, her passion got the better of her. Soon she was telling me about the effects of apparel mass production and scheduling our first thrifting trip.

So there we were, one hour in, and Avery was still going strong in her mission to do something to make the world a better place. How could she ever have believed I wasn't proud of her?

My baby girl glanced at me and I smiled.

Minutes later, Avery disappeared into a dressing room, and I found a chair nearby. Considering the armload of clothes she'd held, I had some time to pass. I retrieved my phone and pulled up my email. Still nothing from Momentso after almost two weeks. Could it have been marked as spam? I clicked on the junk mail folder and scrolled past store ads and bogus offers for free money. My heart stuttered when I saw a message from "Momentso Help Desk," dated eight days ago.

> Lori,
>
> Your account has been restored. Please use the following username and password to sign in at the link below. You'll be able to change your password to something of your choosing in Account Settings>Change Password. Unfortunately, no reason was given for your initial deactivation. Welcome back and thanks for sharing your life's moments with us.

Not wasting a moment, I logged in. My profile page loaded on my screen, and the picture made me gasp. Reclining on a beach in front of turquoise water, I looked happy. I looked free. In my (ironically) pumpkin-orange sundress, my skin was golden. Glimmering, even. My face was lifted to the sky, welcoming the sun's kiss, and my hair—my long, glorious curtain of vanity—flowed down to the sand behind me.

I resisted the urge to toggle the ends of my current style, which, at long last, reached my clavicle, and instead, I scrolled to the About Me section.

> To live is the rarest thing in the world. Most people exist, that is all.
>
> Oscar Wilde

> Mother, Friend, Lover of life, Adventure-seeker & PTO President

Below that, I found a list of groups I'd joined: EndeavHer More Travel, Bold Betties, FRHS Band Boosters, Inspired by

Tarry & Dwell Magazine, Sanna Bristow Readers (Royal Flush in stores NOW!!), VoiceFinders, Battleax Beauty Queens.

I nearly swallowed my tongue. Not only did I not recognize this woman, but I was intimidated by her. Still puzzled by what a "battleax beauty queen" was, I scrolled to the latest post.

Only a fool is surprised when the bough he's been neglecting for years finally breaks.

Dated October 15, the morning of the accident.

"Can you hold these?" Avery dumped a load of clothes onto my lap, jolting me back to the present. "I just met a girl who follows me on The Compassionate Closet. I offered to show her what she could do with the stuff she found." Her eyes lit with a joy I hadn't seen in years. At least, I didn't remember seeing.

"Of course. Take your time," I said, thankful for a chance to learn more about who I'd been.

It took only a few minutes to realize Momentso Lori had two sides. Empowered Lori promoted social justice initiatives, encouraged self-love, and cheered for others on their victories, both big and small. My heart swelled with pride with each of these posts. I liked this Lori. I admired her.

But then there was the other Lori. The Lori who seemed lost, bitter, and let's just say, unfulfilled. I cringed as I read through comments I'd made on a shared article about famous actor Hunter Dean Lawrence. Things about what I'd do if I ever met him in real life. And my comments about the plumber in Sanna Bristow's fan group? Whoa.

I couldn't get over how out of character it was for me.

The funny thing was, my Momentso friends—all nine thousand of them—didn't seem to mind. Weren't any of them concerned for me? For my marriage? Then again, how many had been concerned for me as I lay in a coma for two months? Probably not many since I only recognized a few.

But that wasn't what concerned me most. Clearly I was active on the site, posting and commenting several times a day. How did Michael not know I'd had an account? Did I keep it hidden from him? If so, what reason would I have to do that? And lastly, why and when had I deactivated it?

Avery approached a moment later, but she wasn't alone. "Mom, this is Jenna and her little boy, Karson."

I nodded to the girl towering over Avery. She was thin— too thin—with terrible posture and acne that could easily be cleared up with a visit to a dermatologist. That was a luxury not everyone could afford though. My gaze traveled down to the towheaded toddler in the umbrella stroller who was currently sucking on his cheeks to make a fish face. Must be teething, I thought. Austin did the same thing.

"Hello, Jenna. Hi, Karson," I said, lifting the pitch of my voice to grab the little boy's attention. It worked. Karson smiled big and bounced his stuffed dog on his thighs.

Soon, the four of us were eating Mexican food at a nearby restaurant—something Avery had insisted upon. I tore up pieces of tortilla for Karson as Jenna lay bare the story of her life. She hadn't had an easy go of it. She and Karson had recently run out on the baby's father and currently lived at a women and children's shelter on the north side of Denver. The name of the shelter, Felicity Ridge, conjured a memory. Michael and I, dressed to the nines, at a fundraiser. He'd stood on the stage and delivered the ask, encouraging attendees to donate to the worthy cause.

"You know, Jenna," Avery said, "I have an extra sewing machine if you don't have one. And if you want, I could come over and show you how to use it to alter the clothes you got."

Jenna's face flushed and she sank in her seat a bit. "I couldn't ask you to do that."

"You don't have to. I offered." Avery signaled to me with a pointed look.

"Jenna, nothing would make Avery happier. Maybe I could come over too, and keep this sweet angel busy while you two work." I held out my finger, and Karson wrapped his spitty fist around it.

Two baskets of chips and salsa later, Jenna agreed, and plans were made.

---

"Felicity Ridge is a great organization. I joined their board of directors two years ago." Michael flipped a chicken breast on the grill pan, then checked the asparagus in the oven. "I think it's a fantastic idea for Avery to volunteer there."

I swirled the milk in my wineglass like a real dairy connoisseur. "How did you get connected with it?"

As the meat sizzled, Michael searched the spice cabinet. For what, I wasn't sure since he'd already seasoned every dish. "Uh, Jade, actually. She knows the owner. I got involved because you have a heart for women who have been through what those residents have."

After downing the rest of my milk, I wiped the corners of my mouth with a napkin. "So you did it for me?" I hadn't meant for it to sound sarcastic, but the edge was there.

Michael's focus remained on the spices. "Anything else happen on your girls' day out?"

"Yeah. I got my Momentso account unlocked."

He kept his back to me and said nothing.

I hopped off my stool, then crossed the kitchen to shut the spice cabinet he was still absently staring into. "Did you really not know I had an account? I seemed to be on there a lot. I get that you worked long hours, but it's like you and I didn't know each other at all." I ran my hand down the back of his bicep. It being Saturday, he'd left his suit on the hanger and opted for jeans and a T-shirt that had a picture of Clark Griswold and the words "World's Best Dad" on it. My only problem was how great his arms looked. I didn't want to be attracted to him right now.

"I did know about it. I'm sorry I didn't tell you."

I'd had an inkling and yet this still took me aback. "Why didn't you tell me?"

"I-I don't know."

"Even though we talked about how it could jog my memory?"

He turned my way, a pained expression on his face. "Has it?"

"A little. Not as much as I'd hoped." My breath spilled from my lips. "I learned a lot about who I'd become though, even if I don't recognize myself in that woman. It makes me wonder if I'll ever become her again."

Michael studied my face until the smoke from the grill pan rose between us.

## thirty

**AVERY**

*Dear Austin,*

*This letter will be as painful for you to read as it is for me to write. Don't say I didn't warn you. Last night, Xander dragged me next door to Margot's house with all your friends. I can't say I wanted to attend a murder-mystery dinner, but Xander wanted me there. I told you we were just friends until I got my life together, but it's been getting tougher. I know when a guy wants to be more than friends. Hard swallows, sweaty palms, lingering glances. And Xander has another tell. His left eyebrow arches when he wants to kiss me. And lately, his brow has more arch game than McDonald's.*

*I'm sure this all grosses you out, but I warned you.*

*The game was actually fun. It was set in 1970s Los Angeles. My character was Delancey Herald, investigative reporter, and Sarah was a reformed go-go dancer turned nun. Xander played the part of Diggs Pardee, the owner of Studio 72, the hottest dance club in the city.*

*After several courses, I admitted to murdering crime boss Richie Valentine because he had my husband buried beneath the dance floor of Studio 72. Or something like that. I couldn't stop laughing long enough to fully put the story together.*

Then we played sardines. All the lights were turned off. One person was named It. That person would hide somewhere, and whenever another partygoer discovered It's hiding place, they'd join them in the spot. During the round, more people would find the person and pack themselves into the hiding spot, like sardines. The last person to find the group was the next It.

Several rounds in, I searched the formal dining room for the spot where Sarah picked to hide. Sarah, as you know, is petite enough to squeeze into tiny places, which made her great at this game. But I was Delancey Herald. Nothing got past me. I got on the floor, lifted the tablecloth, and searched the seats of the chairs. A pair of white Skechers caught my eye. I crawled under the table and climbed onto the row of chairs opposite Sarah.

Then it happened. She asked me if you'd be okay if she dated someone.

I didn't know what to say. You loved her more than anything. You were "engaged to be engaged." Isn't that what you said after you gave her that promise ring? But knowing you, you'd do anything for her, even if that meant letting her be with someone else.

I told her that. I hope you don't mind. Honestly, I thought she meant Matt Vermillion. Remember him? The really nice football player I hung out with? He totally has a thing for Sarah.

But it wasn't Matt. She asked me if Xander ever talked about her to me.

Worst-case scenario. Like, ever. Sarah is the perfect girl. Kind, cute, talented, smart, hardworking. And she's been through so much this past year but she managed to hold herself together. She was there for Xander after you died, and he was there for her. Meanwhile I locked myself away.

And yes, Xander talks about her sometimes. "Sarah got into Princeton." "Sarah got a full ride to UC Berkeley." "Sarah gave me this cool guitar pick she found at a store." What does he tell others about me? "Avery may not graduate." "Avery can be a real brat." "Avery thinks she can save the world by sewing clothes together."

When it was my turn to hide, I went to the back of a costume closet in the garage. That's where the Lowrys keep all the stuff for their killer Halloween parties.

Before I was able to wrap my head around Sarah liking Xander, someone opened the closet door, paused, then shuffled through the rack of clothes. From the cologne, I knew it was Xander.

"Found you," he said. You probably don't think Xander can be smooth, but let me tell you, he can be, sweaty palms and all. But all I could think about was Sarah, even when I saw the infamous arched eyebrow. So all I did was move in for a hug, keeping my face turned away from him. A nice, platonic hug.

But if it was so nice, Austin, why did it hurt so much? I told you this letter would be painful, and I'm sorry. I feel really alone, though, and I could sure use some advice down here.

Your sis,
Avery

# *thirty-one*

## LORI

"Lori Mendenhall?" a nurse called from the other side of the waiting room.

I slipped my phone in my purse, gathered my coat, and made my way to the open door. After I settled onto the couch, I stared at the poster of the brain's anatomy. Right in the center, the hippocampus sat all plump and happy to keep record of all of life's memories, unless a closed brain injury caused swelling to compact it.

Dr. Klein soon arrived and took a seat across from me. "Hi, Lori. How are you doing?"

"I'm okay."

"Still having headaches?"

"Only one or two a week."

The doctor jotted a note on his tablet. "That's good. That's real good. And how is your memory progression?"

"My memories are returning. Not in order, but they are coming back. And getting back into my social media account has helped."

His attention lifted from his tablet to my face. "I thought you said you had no social media."

"I did say that. I guess I, uh, forgot." I released a short laugh and shrugged. "But the memories I've had haven't all been happy."

"Talk to me more about that."

I bit my lip. He can't help unless I'm honest, I guess. "Some memories were about my marital struggles. Michael, by trying to provide for me and the kids, ended up neglecting us completely. It turned me into a person I didn't like."

Dr. Klein's expression didn't waver as he listened. "How does it feel to remember that?"

"Not good. To know I felt unhappy and unloved? It makes me wonder if I did something. Like, what if I did something that led to the accident?"

"What do you mean?"

"I think Michael blames himself for missing the flashing lights. What if I said or did something that made that happen?" Like calling him out for cheating on me with his protégé, I considered saying.

"The accident wasn't your fault. It wasn't Michael's either. Remember what the, uh . . ." Dr. Klein scrolled through what I assumed was my electronic chart. "Here it is. The National Highway Traffic Safety Administration discovered that the crossing was supposed to have gates added when they built the high school, and the westbound train was driving too fast for that area as well. It could have happened to anyone."

"I know." I twisted my fingers in my lap. "I still don't remember much from the time before the accident, but there's this feeling that hits me whenever I try. This bitter sadness, knowing all that I lost."

"Have you been to the crossing since that day?"

I shook my head quickly.

"They reconstructed it," he said. "There's a bridge for the trains, a tunnel for the cars. It looks completely different. Maybe if you visited it—"

"No!" I yelled, my sharp voice rising from my clenched stomach. "You think because it looks different, I can visit the spot where my son died? Is it supposed to make me feel better that no one else will go through what I did because they made it safer? I'm sorry if I don't fit into your handbook of grieving parents, but I don't get any closure knowing they fixed it. None of that erases the pain I feel every time I walk by his room and every time I wonder who I am." I sucked in a deep breath to stop the room from whirling. What good would passing out do me? And why was I so worked up? My anger wasn't with Dr. Klein or anyone else here. They'd merely tried to help. No, my anger was soul-deep, and my digging was only exposing more of it.

Dr. Klein remained silent and still.

With no box of tissues in sight, I fumbled in my purse for my travel pack, finally giving up and letting the tears fall un-hindered. "The thing is, Dr. Klein, I've been trying so hard to remember, I never thought about the repercussions when I do. Will it all be worth it?"

"I can't answer that, Lori. I don't think you can either. Not until it's all said and done."

# *thirty-two*

## AVERY

Xander Dixon's confidence seemed to be shaken for the first time in his life. Ever since I'd rejected him by turning away from his kiss at Margot's party two weeks ago, he'd been quiet. But not just quiet—the sad kind of quiet. I never would've thought I'd miss his smirks and smart-alecky comments, but I did. I'd give anything for him to tease me again or even call me a brat.

But I knew how it felt to have the boy you like give his attention to someone else. Thanks for that, Jake. I couldn't do that to Sarah. Not after she already lost Austin.

Valentine's Day made the situation even worse. At lunch, Sarah handed Xander a heart-shaped box of chocolates and a small teddy bear, then said something cute about not wanting him to feel too lonely. Xander accepted the gifts with an unenthusiastic hug and proceeded to eat half the chocolates in one sitting. Once Sarah left for class, he offered the remaining chocolates to friends, avoiding me, of course. Then he tossed the box and tucked the bear into his sweatshirt, so his face stuck out above the zipper.

Sweet Swayze, he looked cuter than ever.

At our tutoring session that night, he'd helped me with my Biology presentation on ornithology: the study of birds. I'd chosen the mourning dove. It seemed only fitting after my year. At exactly 8:30, Xander packed his things into his book bag and started to head out. But instead of leaving, he halted at my bedroom door. "I don't get it. What changed between us?" He turned to face me. "I thought we were waiting for you to catch up with your schoolwork. Now that you're just about there, you don't like me anymore?"

I closed my laptop and moved it to the end of my bed. "I know that's how it seems, but it's complicated."

Xander dropped his bag and paced at the foot of my bed. "I don't think it is. You liked me. Now you don't. Did I wear unfashionable clothes or not style my hair the way you like it?"

I climbed off my bed and blocked his path. "Is that what you think of me? That I'm that shallow?"

He rubbed his forehead. "I don't know. Sometimes I wonder if I know you at all."

"How can you say that? Xander, with Austin gone, you're the only one left who knows me. Besides, you said you'd be patient with me. Now you're acting like every guy I've dated, wanting and needing more than I'm able to give." I picked at my nails. They were longer now that I'd stopped biting them—a gross, nervous habit for sure, but still probably my healthiest coping mechanism after the accident.

He squeezed his eyes shut and lifted his face toward the ceiling. "You're right. I'm sorry." After a moment, he let out a breath and returned his gaze to mine. "Please be honest with me." He stepped forward and clasped both of my hands between his. "What happened?"

I didn't want to be honest. To do so would betray Sarah's confidence. But if I told him about her feelings, maybe he'd finally see her as more than a friend. As hard as it would be for me to witness, they could be happy together. Prom, graduation, summer. They'd be able to build a solid relationship before they had to do the long-distance thing for college.

"Avery." My name spoken in the lowest register of his voice was unnerving, to say the least.

"Sarah happened. That's what."

That must have shocked him because he dropped my hands. "What do you mean?"

I met his gaze. "Sarah likes you."

Xander didn't look too surprised. "She told you that?"

"Not in those exact words. She wanted to know if Austin would be okay if she dated someone new, then she asked if you ever talked about her. She likes you."

"Okay," he dragged the word out for an entire stanza. "I don't like her in that way."

"Why not? She has everything you need in a girlfriend. She's smart, cute, into music—"

"She's not you." Xander lowered his head so we were eye to eye. "You're all I can think about. You're all I dream about. When I think about my future, I see all these possibilities of what life might look like, but the one thing that's always there, always, is you." He was breathing so fast, I was tempted to place my hand over his heart to calm him. "For me, there's no one else. You're it."

"I don't want her to get hurt. This"—I motioned between us—"would hurt her."

"I love Sarah, and I'd hate to hurt her too, but she's tougher than you think. This is nothing compared to what she's endured. You have to know that."

The lump in my throat grew. "And what would Austin say? He'd be devastated if he knew I hurt her."

"He'd be devastated if you hurt yourself. Austin wanted this for us. He saw it way before we did."

"I know, but—"

"Please. For the sake of greeting cards and 1980s love songs. . . . For the sake of John Cusack, give us a chance. It's Valentine's Day, after all." He placed his hands on my hips and touched his forehead to mine.

My resolve was fading fast. Why did he have to smell so good? I backed out of his grasp. "I can't."

He frowned. A little disappointment now would protect him from a lot of disappointment later, so I stood firm. "It shouldn't be this hard."

"I'm sorry."

Xander put the strap of his bag over his shoulder. "So am I." Then he was gone.

---

When Dad came home from work, I was sitting at the kitchen table slapping my ice cream with the back of my spoon. Even peanut butter and chocolate weren't enough to absorb the pain of losing Xander. Wasn't there a limit to the amount of ache one heart could endure?

"Uh-oh. What happened to you?" Dad asked. "Wait. Was it me? Should I send myself to my room?"

"No, it wasn't you. Not this time, anyway."

Dad grabbed a spoon out of the silverware drawer and then seated himself next to me. "Give it to me."

I pushed the bowl of ice cream over to him.

"Not the ice cream, goof." But that didn't stop him from taking a spoonful. "What's going on?"

"I'm sad."

"What reason do you have to be sad?"

I considered naming all the obvious reasons but chose to keep to the one within my control at the moment. "Sarah and I both like Xander."

"Austin's Sarah?"

I exhaled dramatically. "Yep."

"I thought you and Xander were already together. The way you two sit so close during tutoring? I was about ready to give him my talk, man to man."

I smiled. "What talk is that?"

"You know . . ." Dad rubbed the back of his reddening neck. "About boundaries and respect and . . . stuff."

"You never had that talk with other guys I've dated."

He pushed the bowl back in front of me. "Which is why I want to have this talk with Xander."

I stabbed the ice cream with my spoon. "Don't worry. You won't have to have that talk. We aren't together. I've been trying to take care of myself the past few months. When I thought I was ready, Sarah told me she liked him. I don't want to hurt her, so I told Xander to forget about us."

"What did Xander say to that?" Dad's phone buzzed. He reached into his back pocket, silenced it, then placed it face-down on the table.

"Don't you need to get that?" I asked.

"Whoever it is, they aren't as important as you."

I rolled my eyes and shook my head, but my heart squeezed just the same. Maybe there was hope for Dad after all.

"Go on," he said. "What did Xander say about Sarah?"

"He got annoyed. He said he doesn't like her like that."

"Okay, then. What's the problem?"

Was this really so difficult for others to understand? "He should like Sarah like that. She's a better person than me—"

Dad straightened in his seat. "Hold on a minute. How can you say that?"

"She just is." I was getting pretty tired of explaining this to everyone.

"She's a different person than you, but no better. If Xander likes you, then you should take him at his word."

"And hurt Sarah?"

"No, I'm not saying that," he said. "But consider this. She and Austin had a wonderful, healthy relationship for years. That's something she'll always carry with her. Don't you deserve that same opportunity?"

I shrugged. "Having a healthy relationship didn't benefit you and Mom, did it? You guys were happy once. Now you're miserable."

"Not true." Dad helped himself to another bite of chocolate peanut butter. Did he think silence between a married couple meant happiness? Because I remembered how Mom and Dad acted when they were happy, and it wasn't circling without speaking and never acknowledging each other.

"Dad, be real."

"Ave, if I knew how to fix things between your mom and me, I would. I'd do just about anything."

"It's the 'just about' part of that sentence that speaks the loudest. I know it. Mom knows it."

"What do you suggest I do?"

"Whatever it takes."

"Like quit my job?"

"If it would make you a better husband. If it would separate you from the woman Mom thinks you're sleeping with?"

"I'm not."

"The woman Mom *thinks* you're sleeping with?"

"I need that job to provide for you and your mother."

"I know, I know. Provide and protect. You've been saying that my whole life, but the job you have that provides for us hasn't exactly protected us, has it?"

Now it was Dad's turn to spoon-slap the ice cream. "I can't just quit my job."

"Fine. But do everything else. Show her how much you love her. Pursue her the way you did when you were young. Come on, Dad," I teased. "Wouldn't that be so much fun?"

"I guess it would."

"Good! For starters, what have you done for Valentine's Day?"

"Ave, when you've been married for nearly nineteen years, Valentine's Day is—"

I cut him off. "Don't give me that. You need to do something for her."

"All right. But what about you and Xander? You're my daughter. If there's something you want, then go get it. Do you honestly think Sarah would be happy knowing you and Xander stayed apart for her?"

I set my spoon on my napkin. "I didn't think about it like that."

Dad squeezed my hand. "Xander's a good guy. There aren't many teenage boys I would trust with my only daughter. If you want him, go get him. Don't let anything stop you."

"That's great advice for both of us."

Dad nodded lazily.

"I think I'll drive over to Xander's to talk to him. Is it all right if I'm out till 10:30ish?"

"Yes, but no later. It's a school night."

Leaving my ice cream for Dad to finish, I leaped from the table and hugged his neck. "Thanks for listening to me."

"Happy to help. Go get him."

---

Here goes nothing. I hit Play on my phone and turned the volume up on the connected speaker. Piano notes sounded along with what might be one of those triangle instruments. As far as I knew, the original song had no clarinet, but hey, there's a first time for everything. And if I wanted Xander after all the drama I'd put him through, I had to enact all kinds of idioms: eat humble pie, go above and beyond, take desperate measures, and so on.

Standing a few yards away from his front door and near his room's ground-level windows, I rested the mouthpiece of the clarinet between my lips and blocked the airhole with my tongue exactly how Ms. Talley taught me in fifth grade. My fingers covered each of the holes, and I played a note. What note, I wasn't sure. It definitely didn't pair well with the first syllable Peter Gabriel sang. Oh well. I played four beats. Then I lifted my right hand's ring and pinkie fingers for four beats of some other note. Then back to four more of the all-holes-covered one. Man, I'd really lost all my music knowledge. What would Ms. Talley say?

The good news was I had cranked up the speaker loud enough that my clarinet only mostly butchered the song. The lyrics to "In Your Eyes" still rang out for Xander, and probably his entire street, to hear.

The front door opened, and Julius, the younger of Xander's stepbrothers, stood in the doorway. After a few seconds, Xander came up from behind and shooed him back in the house. Just as Xander came out onto the front stoop and shut the door, I paused my four-beat rhythm to take a deep breath. When I started my notes again, he flinched, but kept up his slow approach. His lips formed the smallest of smiles, making me lose count.

He reached for the speaker, then turned down the song. Stopping in front of me, he gently took the clarinet from my hands. "Welp, I think I now know what Prince was talking about."

"What do you mean?"

"The sound when doves cry."

"Was it that bad?"

"Noo," he said. Then he tossed the clarinet into a bush.

"I didn't want to be lame and hold the speaker over my head. Besides, you appreciate a good serenade."

He cocked his head. "Define good."

I wanted to laugh. Any other time I might have. But I'd come here for a reason. "I did some thinking."

"And?"

"When mourning doves meet their mate, they do a bonding ritual where they gently nibble each other's necks."

"Okay, not what I expected you to say, but go on."

"And then, once they're bonded, they grasp beaks and kind of bob their heads up and down."

"This is getting weird. Where are you going with this?"

I placed my right hand on his cheek. "You're my dove, and I'm yours. We're meant for each other and no one else. Do you agree?"

His left eyebrow arched as he nodded slightly.

"Then what are we waiting for?" I moved slowly, giving him time to prepare himself for his second first kiss. His breath stuttered, making me smile. I caressed the side of his nose with mine, then positioned my lips, barely parted, in a slight misalignment with his and waited for him to take charge of what came next. Cautiously, he did, kissing me soft as a feather and holding still for a handful of seconds. Instead of releasing me, he captured my lips with more confidence, and I melted into him.

I'm not sure when I fell for him. Maybe it was the day I first met him on the kindergarten swing set or when he held me the night my world upturned. Maybe it was a slow progression over the past few months. I shared with him the kind of love that surpassed high school hallways and ice cream dates. It was a love I could trust—a healing kind of love.

For the next hour leading up to curfew, I allowed Xander to practice kissing in a splendid—and sometimes awkward— ritual of trial and error. By the time I whispered good night to my boyfriend, I had found something to be thankful for.

# *thirty-three*

**LORI**

On a stool behind the cash register, I checked my watch. 5:15. I pulled out the invitation from my purse for the fifth time that day. Handwritten in Michael's best penmanship, he'd invited me to celebrate our nineteenth anniversary at The Fort restaurant. Because it was a drive, I needed to head out as soon as Kendra returned from the phone call she'd taken.

Mixed emotions fueled thoughts of all kinds regarding tonight. That it could be a sort of restart for us. Ever since Valentine's Day, he'd been acting strange, but in a good way. That day, after getting no acknowledgment from him at all, he'd sent me the sweetest email. Sure, it was an email—not the most romantic form of communication—yet he'd taken the time to remind me of how we'd spent each Valentine's Day during our relationship. Unlike myself, he had an impeccable memory. It was sweet that he remembered small things I hadn't, like what dress I'd worn on February 14, 2004—an old pink pageant dress. Or what song the twins sang at their preschool Valentine's Day performance in 2009—Stevie Wonder's "Signed, Sealed, Delivered."

Almost every day since I'd received that email, Michael had done something to show me he still loved me. My latte of choice was delivered to the store during my shift. Texts and phone calls wanting to chat. Movie tickets to a showing of my favorite classic, *On the Waterfront*, followed by Michael performing Marlon Brando's most famous lines in his spot-on impersonation.

"Do you have any more of these ceramic bowls?" An older woman in an unapologetically chartreuse dress pointed out a chip on the bowl's lip.

"Let me check in the back room." I weaved my way between the displays and opened the door to the back. Kendra sat sideways on the chaise lounge I'd unwrapped a few hours earlier. Her arms held her stomach, and she rocked forward and back in time with her sobs.

"What's wrong?" I sat next to her and placed my hand on her shoulder.

"That was my momma. Daddy was diagnosed with end-stage colon cancer."

"Oh, Kendra, I'm sorry." As someone who never had a father, I could see how important her father was to her. She'd often lamented opening the store here instead of back home in South Carolina.

"I need to go home to Charleston. I need to be with him."

"You should. You'll feel better being close."

"What about the store?"

"I can go full-time if you want. Andrew and I can handle it until you get back."

She blew her nose into a tissue. "I don't want it to be too much for you."

"Psh. I love being here. And why are you worrying about me right now? Go on home and do whatever you have to do. I can close up."

"What about your anniversary dinner?"

I waved my hand like doing so could make this sudden crummy feeling disappear. "Michael will understand."

It was nearly ten when I pulled into the driveway. Michael had been disappointed on the phone, and after I'd sent Kendra home, disappointment settled in me. I wanted to see him. It was still our anniversary, after all.

I'd grown accustomed to seeing Xander's truck in the driveway ever since he and Avery made things official last month. They were cute together.

The house was primarily dark with sounds of warfare bouncing off walls. The only thing welcoming was the smell of popcorn. Michael sat on one end of the sectional with a bowl of popcorn and Wynton's head on his lap. On the opposite end, Avery leaned back against Xander's chest, their arms tangled around her stomach.

"Hey, Mom," Avery said.

"Hey, Mrs. M." Xander offered a quick nod, which I returned.

"What movie are you watching?"

"Dad's trying to convince us that the best Batman movie is the one from 2000," Avery said.

"2005," he corrected her.

"It's so boring. Nowhere near as good as the one from 1989. Every time we make fun of it, Dad throws popcorn at us. Come join us." Avery stood and, grabbing me by the hands, led me to Michael. She then returned to Xander and gave him a peck on the lips.

"Hey. No kissing during Batman." Michael threw a kernel, and it bounced off Avery's back onto the floor where Wynton played cleanup. "You behave, or I'll make you watch the sequel next."

"Ooh, the one with Heath Ledger as the Joker? I love that one," I said. Not wholly sure Michael wanted me here after I stood him up, I remained standing.

"Happy anniversary," Xander said after welcoming Avery back into his arms.

"Thank you." I turned to Michael. "Happy anniversary."

Michael placed the bowl on the arm of the couch and got up. What followed was an unconvincing hug. "Happy anniversary. Are you too tired to join us for the second half?"

"Not too tired. It sounds like fun, as long as you don't start talking about how pretty Katie Holmes is."

"Fair enough." Michael waited for me to choose my seat, then sat a couple of inches away. Close but not touching.

For the rest of the movie, Christian Bale's Batman brooded around Gotham City. Avery and Xander held hands, whispered to each other, cracked jokes with us, and snuck short kisses. They were certainly more affectionate than Michael and me. We didn't touch until the very end, when Michael began playing with the ends of my hair at the base of my neck.

After the movie ended, Avery walked Xander to his car, lingering quite a while. Michael and I angled ourselves to face each other to have whatever conversation was to come.

He started. "How's Kendra doing?"

"Not good. She and her father are close."

"That's tough. It reminds me of when we went through that with my dad," Michael said, referring to his father's ALS diagnosis back in 2013. A year later, he passed away. Not too long after, Michael lost his mother to heart failure. She'd literally died of a broken heart. "It makes you rethink things."

"It seems most people rethink their life and make relationships their priority. You decided to start a business."

"A business of relationships. And a business that would help me ensure you and the kids would always be taken care of. I wasn't able to do that as a teacher. Not without moving to a place with a lower cost of living."

"Was it worth it?"

An unfamiliar sheen appeared in Michael's eyes, reflecting the light from the frozen blue television screen. "How can

I answer that? I don't regret removing the worry from your mind about finances. I don't regret giving Austin and Avery everything they needed."

"They needed you. I needed you."

His gaze met mine. "Tonight, I think I got a taste of what you felt the past few years. Coming in second to your work."

"I won't feel guilty about helping Kendra out."

"I'm not asking you to. I'm thankful, actually. Years of that? No wonder you grew to hate me."

I couldn't refute that. The more I scrolled my old Momentso posts and comments, the more resentment I remembered. Resentment that had seeped back into my heart with every recall of missed dinners, canceled plans, distant looks, distracted presence, interrupting phone calls, and on and on.

"A woman can only cry to her husband's blank stare so many times. I never understood how you could be so harsh and uncaring when I was in obvious pain."

Michael hung his head. "Every time you would cry, all I wanted to do was fix it. Only I didn't know how. The only option I saw was to give up the business, but that would mean giving up my ability to provide for our family. That's what I vowed to do that day in the ultrasound room. I promised to do anything I could to keep you all safe and sound." He took my hand and kissed my knuckles. "I'm sorry I wasn't smart enough to know how to do that without pushing you away at the same time."

The front door opened and closed. Avery bounced in, humming what I think was "Summer of '69."

"I'm going to bed now," she declared with a singsong lilt to her voice. She approached us for a group hug, putting one arm around my neck and one around Michael's and drawing us together. "Happy anniversary. I'm glad you guys did the whole shotgun wedding thing."

"Don't let that give you and Xander any ideas."

"Are you kidding? Xander won't even try to get to second base."

"Oh, Avery," I said.

Her laugh gave my heart a squeeze. "Good night."

After Avery danced her way up the stairs, Michael and I were left to stare at each other. A stalemate.

# *thirty-four*

**AVERY**

April 3

Dear Austin,

A few days ago, I turned in the last of my junior year assignments while staying on track with my senior year schoolwork. Principal Wright said the teachers would have two weeks to make the final determination over whether I've done well enough to graduate next month.

It didn't feel like much of a celebration with Xander and Sarah sitting in the front of his Bronco as we drove to Moab, Utah. I never should have come on this spring break trip. Sarah still has no clue Xander and I are together. Why? I knew you'd ask. Basically, neither one of us could figure out how to break the news to her. It was one thing to play it cool at school—our relationship doesn't need schoolwide attention to exist—but a week exploring, hiking, and sitting around campfires under starlit skies?

It's been hard enough trying to force a friendship with your friends. Whenever I try to talk to Margot and Ellie, I get the feeling they don't even hear me. The opposite is true with Hayden and Nico. They ogle over me to the point of awkwardness. The only guy who doesn't is Matt. He's too busy ogling over Sarah.

But honestly, I need a break from our house. Dad has been

214

*trying so hard the past few weeks. Mom has taken over as
the work-obsessed parent. As acting manager at the store, she
rarely comes home before ten. When she's home, she's exhausted,
distracted, or a bundle of nerves. Too many times I've had to
interpret for them so they could communicate at all. What will
happen this week without me there? I can't worry about that
now.*

*Our campsite is the coolest. The Conestoga wagons make
us feel like pioneers—if pioneers carried iPhones and wore
Birkenstocks. Both the girl wagon and the boy wagon have
double bunk beds and a small kitchenette. Each cabin has a designated restroom in the single building near the wagons. Then
again, we aren't exactly roughing it since the restrooms include
a jacuzzi tub and mints. Why someone would want to eat a
bathroom mint goes beyond my comprehension but whatever.*

"What are you doing over here all by yourself?"

I slammed the notebook closed before Xander could see
what I was writing. I squinted, trying to avoid the late afternoon
sun that shone behind him. "Writing."

He plunked down next to me on the red dirt. "I have to ask.
Why do you have a notebook with aliens on it?"

"None of your business," I said, holding the cover against
my chest.

"Are you writing a letter? To Austin?"

"How did you know that?"

"I've seen it in your room."

My throat released a squeak, but before a full-blown panic
could set in, Xander continued. "I've never read it. What kind
of person do you think I am?"

"The kind of person who would read a seventh-grade girl's
diary."

He rolled his eyes. "Give me some credit. I have matured
slightly since then."

"Credit supplied." I showed him the cover, then thumbed through the pages quickly. "This is how Austin and I liked to keep in touch when we were apart or busy or whatever. We'd write letters to each other and keep them in here. I still keep him up-to-date on life. Not that I expect him to come down and read it. It tricks my mind into thinking he's across the state instead of across the heavens."

Xander raised his hand and marked an invisible tally mark in the sky.

"What was that?"

"One more thing I love about you."

◆

As the sun set over the red rocks to the west that night, washing part of the blue sky with brilliant orange, I devoured my chicken kebob. Xander's stepdad was a chef and had taught him how to turn chicken from bland to delish. After dinner was cleaned up, we sat around the campfire chatting. Well, everyone else chatted. I lay my head back in my Adirondack chair and lost myself in the sea of stars above, thinking how much better this would be if it were only Xander and me.

We headed into Arches National Park the next morning to hike the popular Delicate Arch Trail. Although it was only a mile-and-a-half climb, it took us all morning to reach our destination. It felt even longer though. Austin had always been good at making conversation with people he didn't know well. I preferred to keep my mouth shut and simply observe, but as I'd overheard Margot tell Ellie, it made me seem like a snob. The Delicate Arch is the ultimate photo backdrop, and everyone got pictures together, except for Xander and me. When Sarah asked me to take a picture of her and Xander, I said yes, not realizing she would hop on his back, piggyback-style, for the shot.

With that image frozen in my mind, I led the group back down the trail. A few minutes in, Sarah caught up with me.

"Thanks for taking that picture. It came out cute."

"No problem."

"I'm thinking about telling Xander how I feel. I wanted to get your advice because you are way more 'I am woman, hear me roar' than I am. I'm a little nervous about being the one that brings it up to him, but he's not doing it so . . ."

The sun beat down on me, and I took a sip of water from my CamelBak. It didn't help make my queasiness go away. "Uh, Sarah, there's something I should've told you before."

Sarah's wide eyes pinned me with guilt.

"You know that Xander and I have been spending a lot of time together this year while he tutored me—"

"Austin would be ecstatic to know you guys are friends now."

"That's the thing, Sarah. Xander and I, we're, uh, more than friends. He's kind of my boyfriend."

Shifting her focus to her feet, Sarah heaved a few breaths. "Kind of?"

"He is my boyfriend," I said with more confidence. "Neither of us knew how to tell you. We never meant to hurt you."

"You've . . . you've talked to him about this? About me?"

A heaviness filled my chest. "Yeah."

Sarah glanced over her shoulder, then worked her jaw a bit. "Did you get together after you knew I liked him?"

"Um, that's kind of complicated. But yes."

Her brows knit together, deepening the shadow in her eyes. With a shake of her head, she grunted quietly. "You could have any guy in school. Why did you have to go after him?"

"It wasn't like that." I reached for her hand, but she slapped me away.

"You know, I always defended you. When people at school gossiped about you or made fun of you, I told them to mind their own business. When Courtney was bragging to everyone that Jake had always liked her more than you, I called her out for being an awful friend to you. And when Austin called you conceited or self-absorbed or a brat—"

I slipped on the slide-rock, landing hard on my tailbone. Yet even that couldn't compare to the pain tearing at my chest. After Sarah's initial shock over my fall, she pushed forward down the trail, an apparent sign to Margot and Ellie that she was the one hurt and in need of care. They hurried past me to get to her.

Xander and Matt were the first to come to my aid. I gave Xander a knowing glance, and he seemed to understand. He told Matt to go on ahead of us, then turned the full breadth of his attention to me. "You sure you're okay?"

I shrugged.

"It should've been me. I should've stepped up and told her about us. I was a coward, and I'm sorry." He toed a pebble with his shoe. "Do you want a hug?"

"Not when she can see us. Rain check?"

"You got it."

For the record, I'd rather be cussed out than ignored. Apparently, Margot, Ellie, and Sarah knew this because their "pretend Avery doesn't exist" game was strong the rest of the day. Even having Xander next to me wasn't enough to soothe me.

"How about a little story time?" Margot asked. Across the circle from me, on the far side of the campfire, Margot held a book flat on her lap. Wearing a half sneer, half smile, she cleared her throat. "'I know you say God doesn't hate anyone, but I think he might hate me. Why else would he take you away?'"

Ice slid up my spine. My journal. Margot was reading my journal. She'd gone through my bag and taken the most personal possession I had.

"'Why else would he force me to spend time with Xander? Or give me such messed up parents?'"

"Is that— Margot, where did you get that?" Xander asked.

"Wait, there's more." She flipped to another page. "'I kissed Xander today. In my temporary insanity, I tried to get him to do a lot more than that. I immediately regretted it. He's so clumsy and awkward. Plus, he likes Sarah—your Sarah.'"

"Give that to me," I warned her.

A few more pages. "'You should have been the one to survive the accident. You could keep Mom and Dad together. Everyone would rather you have survived. Probably even Xander.'" Margot raised her bottled water. "Hear! Hear!"

Finding my legs, I leaped up from the chair and rounded the fire, but I wasn't quick enough. Margot tossed the journal into the flames.

Even before I finished my gasp, the pages singed and curled. I reached for the journal, but arms grabbed me around the waist and pulled me away just as the heat seared my fingers.

"Avery, let it go," Xander said against my ear.

"Austin! It's Austin." I bucked my body, swung my arms, and kicked my legs. Anything to get free of his grasp. Something snapped against my wrist. My bracelet—the one Xander had given me on my birthday as a gift from him and Austin. It was gone. Small green beads scattered across the dirt as Matt tried and failed to retrieve my journal from the fire with a skewer.

I didn't recognize the wails coming from my mouth. My legs gave out, and Xander and I sank to the ground. He alternated between stroking my hair and wiping my tears. Soon, he led me to the passenger seat of his Bronco. He disappeared for a while, eventually returning with my suitcase and his duffel bag. The last thing I remember was watching headlights gleam over curving roads as Xander held my hand.

# *thirty-five*

## LORI

"Let's bring that tan-and-white gingham chair over and stick it in the corner of the display, right above the vent." I drummed my fingers on my thigh. "Let's not toss a blanket on the arm," I told Andrew as we stood in the living room area of Lake & Hearth. "People will sit in the chair and imagine curling up with a book, but they'll feel the chill from the air below. We'll place the display of blankets directly in their line of sight. Even if they can't splurge on the chair, they'll buy the blanket to give them that warm and cozy feeling." I turned to him. "What do you think?"

Andrew clucked his tongue. "I think it's brilliant. I'll set it up. When Kendra returns, I hope she lets you implement more of your ideas. From the looks of it, she won't be back for a few more months. Just imagine what you can do."

"You too! When she sees the shelves you built in the back room, she will cry tears of joy."

"Aw shucks." Andrew's smile reached ear to ear.

I shooed him off and spun on my heel, nearly colliding with a body. "Enid. Hello."

"Lori. I figured you were here after no one answered your door." Enid squeezed my middle with her hug.

"Is something wrong?"

"Yes. No. I don't know, but I wanted to talk to you. I'm so sorry about spring break."

"What do you mean?"

She looked as confused as I felt. "You haven't spoken to Avery?"

My hand clutched at my heart. "Is she okay?"

"Oh! No, she's safe. I mean what happened between her and the girls."

I released my held breath and smoothed my hair. "I've been here since eight this morning. And I haven't checked my phone."

"Well, I guess Avery stole Xander from Sarah. Margot tried to defend Sarah and some journal of Avery's got destroyed. I'm not sure exactly, but Avery and Xander left Moab last night."

I leaned in, wondering if I'd heard her incorrectly. "Wait, she left to come home?"

"Margot heard they spent the night at Xander's aunt's house. Maybe in Grand Junction? I'm not sure."

"I need to check my phone," I said, searching my pockets before I remembered that it was in my purse. "But Avery didn't steal Xander from Sarah, for the record. Margot has incorrect information. If you need anything, Andrew would be glad to help. Excuse me." I hightailed it to the back room where I stored my purse during work hours.

I gripped the door handle. It turned easily enough, but the door, I'd noticed, liked to stick in the jamb. Perhaps Andrew could fix it before Kendra returned. I pushed my weight against the door with no luck. Giving myself some space, I rammed my shoulder into it hard enough to rattle my brain against my skull. Immediately, I regretted the move as a dull pain bloomed inside my head, but at least the door opened. I caught a whiff of the raw, freshly cut wood from Andrew's shelves, yet when I opened my eyes, there were no wooden shelves. No purse or Lake & Hearth inventory in sight. Only office supplies lining

221

metal shelves. Most surprising were the two figures locked in a heated embrace against the back wall.

I froze in place. "I'm sorry. I—"

The man, whose face had been buried in the woman's neck, looked up, and as his walnut eyes went black, I stopped breathing. Shock registered on Michael's face but not quite regret. No, he seemed to be frustrated that I had the nerve to interrupt his infidelity. His mistress wore a yellow sweaterdress, belted at the waist where my husband's hands clutched fistfuls of it. Her glossy obsidian hair cascaded down her back. Michael loved long hair on women, a fact that made my scalp burn, along with my face, ears, and eyes. Every part of me flamed with humiliation, anger, and betrayal. I was sure I'd stumbled into hell on earth.

"Mom?" At my side, Austin stood with his arms hanging loose, his band uniform starched, crisp and neat—a stark contrast to the mangled remains of our family.

"I shouldn't be here," I said, feeling sawdust inside my throat. It scratched more with every attempt to swallow it down. No one seemed to hear me. Austin spoke my name again, and I grasped for him, only to find my fingers incapable of making contact. My hands sliced through him. Was I invisible? A spirit? Dear Jesus, why can't I reach my son when he is right next to me?

Jade pushed off Michael and stared, not at me, but Austin. "I'm sorry, Austin. I'm so sorry. Please don't tell."

Austin's chin trembled, and heavy tears pulled at the brim of his eyes. "If you don't, I will."

Michael didn't move, except to grab for Jade. My chest began to cave due to the weight of it all, and my legs began to wobble. Jade came for Austin then, with her hands outstretched. He backed away, and although my strength was waning, I pooled the last of it to step in Jade's way, slamming into the closet door in the process. I immediately fell to the floor, a puddle of arms, legs, tears, and sales tags.

"Lori! Oh no, Lori!" Enid flung herself down beside me. "What happened? How did you fall?"

Looking past her face, I no longer saw an office supply closet, Michael, or Jade. I didn't have to search for Austin. He was long gone, but the memory of what he and I witnessed was here to stay.

Hands shaking, I sat on my bed next to the packed suitcase. This would be easier if I simply left before Michael came home from work. At least Avery wasn't home yet, so she wouldn't have to witness what came next. I'd called but got her voice mail.

The suitcase I'd packed with her things stood upright in the hallway within sight. A pang of guilt rattled my spine. I was about to leave my husband alone, without his wife, daughter, or son. At least he'd have Wynton. My mother hated dogs, so when I called her after I left work, she told me to keep the old boy home.

Home.

Home.

God, I don't want to leave, but how can I stay after recalling that memory?

Downstairs, a door shut. Pockets emptied onto the kitchen island like always—car key fob, office keys, phone, wallet. Footsteps that I felt more than I heard.

"Lori?" A pause. "Babe?"

My bottom lip jutted out, and my chin began to quiver. Only in a cruel world would those we love the most have the ability to hurt us the worst. I heard him climb the stairs, and my heartbeat quickened. He paused by the suitcase and gave it a long study. "I thought Avery took Austin's suitcase. Did she come back—" His eyes locked on the luggage next to me.

"Are you going somewhere?" Concerned, he stared me down. "Lori?"

"I remember what happened. In the closet." My voice, although broken and cracked, held firm.

His expression fell. His lips moved but made no sound. After a hard swallow, he finally spoke. "Babe, whatever you think you remember happened a long time ago. We can get past it."

Was he serious? "Whatever I think I remember? Michael, I know what happened. It's clear as day in my mind. The kiss?"

Michael dropped onto the occasional chair in the corner of the room. He kicked his legs out and raked his hands through his thick hair. "I hoped you'd never remember. As much as I want you to get better, I didn't want you to remember that."

I wanted so badly to be mad, to spit fury and make him rue the day. But sadness and grief overwhelmed all the anger. "How could you, Michael? And how could you lie to me after I saw you with her at the Christmas party? You swore nothing ever happened between you two."

He looked taken aback. "Hold on. What exactly did you remember?"

"It was at your office. I opened the door to the supply closet and caught you kissing Jade."

He bolted to his feet. "That never happened!" He paced a few feet, stopping in front of me.

"I know what I saw. I know what you did. You lied to me about Jade before, and you're lying about her now."

Michael blew out a breath. "Lori, I love you. I wouldn't chance losing you with some fling at work. What happened in that closet, it's not what you think."

I couldn't let him make me give in. "But you do admit that something happened."

# thirty-six

**AVERY**

As I stood in the hallway, my heart unraveled into tufts of fabric and thread. Xander pulled me into Austin's room, whispering about how I shouldn't hear this. Didn't he understand? I couldn't walk away now. Not after what I'd overheard. My nose began to itch, and my eyes burned as angry tears threatened. A cry rumbled up from where that dread had settled a few minutes ago. I muffled its release by jamming my mouth against Xander's shoulder.

Wynton appeared in the doorway. He brushed past our legs and jumped onto Austin's bed. I left Xander's arms to comfort Wynton, stroking him behind the ears and down his neck again and again. Poor guy wasn't used to yelling. I had the hottest temper in the house, and I much preferred death glares to screams. Xander joined us on the bed. While he also ran his hand along Wynton's fur, his focus remained on me, making me wonder if it was really the dog he was trying to comfort.

Mom's voice carried from the other room. "I know what you're doing. You're trying to make me think I'm crazy."

"Lori, I love you." Dad's tone was softer now. "Since I first saw you, you are the only woman I've ever kissed or wanted to kiss. Why is that so hard for you to believe?"

"Because believing you means I don't believe me. I'm going to stay with my mom. I'm bringing Avery too."

That temper of mine burst. Before Xander could grab my hand, I shot up, into the hallway and then my parents' room. On the bed, next to a filled suitcase, Dad sat, holding his head in his hands. Mom stood with her back pressed to the wall. An easy target that I found quickly. "You're leaving Dad? Even though he swears he's never kissed that lady?"

"When did you get home?" Dad asked.

"It doesn't matter. But I'm glad I did, because someone needs to act like an adult here. Dad, maybe if you'd chosen us even once over your job in the past four years, she'd be able to believe you. And, Mom, I'm sorry, but your brain is broken, so how do you know your memory was just that—a memory? What if it was a dream?"

"Avery . . ." Such a weak warning from Dad. Why on earth was I the only one strong enough to fight for this family?

"I thought we were supposed to be bringing our family to-gether. Why are you guys trying to tear it further apart? I don't want to live with Grandma. Without Wynton? Without Dad? No way. Nope, nope, nope."

"It's not a question, Avery," Mom said. "You're my daughter and—"

"I'm Dad's daughter too. Besides, I'm eighteen. Don't I get a choice in this?" I crossed my arms. "I'm staying right here. This is my home. This is where our family belongs, and it's really frustrating that I'm the only one that sees that. Oh, and by the way, I hope Austin isn't looking down on us, because he would be so ashamed of you both, just like I am. Now, until you start acting more like adults"—I paused, attempting to catch my breath—"you're grounded to your room. You let me know once you've worked it all out."

◆

Shocker, they didn't work it out. They didn't listen to my instructions about staying put either. Mom left. I stayed. Dad locked himself in his room. And Xander? He let his T-shirt become my tissue as we sat on the couch that night.

Blessed be the tear catchers.

Fortunately, Xander didn't seem to mind his shirt getting soaked through. Over the past hour, he'd heard me cry, fuss, yell, curse, and hyperventilate. He'd done everything he was supposed to: nodded when appropriate, stroked my hair, hand, or back, and kissed my forehead. Such a good boyfriend.

He went to the kitchen to get me a glass of water and returned with a pen. On his left hand, halfway between his wrist and the base of his thumb, he drew the simple profile of a dove with a line underneath. Then he took my right hand and drew a symmetrical dove in the same place. After he capped the pen and placed it on the coffee table, he laced our fingers and pressed his palm to mine. Our doves now faced each other, sharing a single wire, just like in that picture I'd drawn for him when his dad left.

"Avery, I know I played it cool that day in my bedroom, but that drawing meant the world to me. I can't tell you how many times I've gone back to it." Xander stared hard at our joined hands. "I knew that even if you weren't able to understand what I was feeling, you were willing to go through it with me."

"Which is exactly what you've done for me after Austin's death."

"I tried."

"No, you did. Thanks to you, I haven't felt alone in a long time." I rolled my hand slightly toward his, making my dove kiss his dove on the beak. "You know, I might be tempted to believe that love is a complete sham after all the examples I've seen if I didn't have you."

A slow smile stretched his lips wide. "What are you saying?"

"I'm saying that maybe we could be the one example of love that makes it." My cheeks grew hot as I searched his eyes, afraid such words might scare him off. But Xander wasn't like most eighteen-year-old guys.

"Are you saying you looove me?" He dug the fingers of his free hand into my underarm, and I squirmed under the tickling.

"Not if you're going to respond like this," I warned, somehow finding my way even closer to him.

He released a soft laugh. "You don't have to say it. I know you love me. I know because you and I are pretty similar." He took a deep breath and secured both arms around me. "And I love you. To be honest, I've loved you since the first day I met you. But back then, I loved you for the way you would pick dandelions at recess and the way you laughed at all my jokes—even during my knock-knock phase. In middle school, when you wouldn't speak to me anymore, I loved you for the way you would stand confidently in a crowded room in a hideous feathered skirt you made."

I bit my lip to hide my smile, but I don't think it worked.

"Now I love you for how you've been able to triumph over everything that's happened. I love you for how you care for Wynton and your parents too. I love you for the look in your eyes after you kiss me. I love you, Avery."

I thought I'd run out of tears, but perhaps happy tears came from somewhere else in the body. Like the same place that tells your lips to smile and your feet to dance. I nuzzled my nose against his. "I love you too. Let's show them all that love can last."

"I like that challenge."

## *thirty-seven*

**LORI**

If "I told you so" had a smell, it would be my mom's homemade brownies, topped with walnuts. I had made difficult choices in my life, but nothing—nothing—compared to the decision I made to leave Michael that night. When I got to her house, my mother welcomed me with open arms.

She practically handed the brownies to me as I came through the door. As I laid in the guest bed that night, my mind played tricks on me. My memory of that kiss was still clear and unchanging. It killed me to replay it over and over in my mind. No one wanted it to dissolve into nothing more than me.

If Michael would simply admit he'd made a mistake, even if it had been more than a kiss, I could forgive him. It would break my heart in pieces, of course, but we could make it through. I'd known marriages that had been shaken by adultery, and yet, after years of dedication and hard work, their relationship was stronger than ever. That would be Michael and me, I was sure. If he would only admit it.

But that was four days ago. Walking into church alone on Easter Sunday after separating from my husband was like entering a bear's den with an open wound. Fortunately, no one knew what had happened between Michael and me yet, so the condemnation I felt was likely imagined. But it was Easter, and if I ever needed to hear about resurrection, it was now.

229

In the sanctuary, I found Michael and Avery seated in our usual section, with one seat separating them. Xander sat on Avery's left, holding her hand. As she glared unswervingly toward the front of the church, Xander's gaze moved from her to me, then back to her. Even when seething with anger, she was beautiful—so much like a modern-day Scarlett O'Hara that I wondered if she'd upcycled my curtains to make her Easter dress.

Michael, on the other hand, wore a tailored suit with a splash of sorrow. His eyes, perched between pinched brows and dark circles, met mine, which probably weren't in any better shape thanks to all those long days and sleepless nights. People say there's no rest for the wicked, but the wicked's victims don't exactly slumber in peace either.

He stood to let me squeeze by, but when I was directly in front of him, he stopped me with a hand on my hip.

"Thanks for coming," he said. He placed a gentle kiss on my cheek, and I waited for God to strike him dead. Would he confess his sin to the pastor at the end of the sermon? Maybe he already had, and that's why he would dare offer this affection. He might've thought he'd fixed the problem and could now move forward with his life. There was no lightning though. And the only thunderous sound was from the speakers above us that played Chris Tomlin's "Your Grace is Enough."

"Happy Easter, Lori," Xander's mother said from the row behind us. Her husband repeated the greeting, then turned his focus to the tween boys jostling each other at his side.

"Happy Easter, everyone." I sat pageant-style, hoping to display some dignity. On a day when there should be an abundance of warmth, my seat chilled my backside and legs.

In the aisle, a familiar face paused at our row. Sarah's suntinged skin looked quite pink against her white dress. She worried her lip, carrying more shame than the twins when they'd been caught giving their pet roly-polies a bath.

Avery released Xander's hand, but he took it back and held it protectively. Sarah smiled politely before taking a seat next to her family.

"Have you and Sarah made up yet?" I asked Avery.

"I don't want to talk about it while we're sitting at church. Maybe if you were actually home . . ."

"I can come over. Or you can come to Grandma's. You're welcome anytime."

"Look, Mom. I'm super proud of you for pursuing your dreams, working at the store and all that, but career women can be married too. You don't need to leave Dad."

"Please keep it down," I said.

She frowned. "I don't want you to divorce—"

"Honey," I interrupted her, "we haven't said that word at all."

Suddenly a hand clasped onto my knee. Michael leaned across me. "We're a family. We've survived worse than this. But getting angry at each other won't help. Austin wouldn't want that."

Avery rolled her eyes. "Austin wouldn't have wanted a lot of things, Dad."

---

**AVERY**

Never in the history of the world had there been a more awkward Easter dinner. Not only did I have to pass the cheesy potatoes from Grandma to Dad and the green beans from Dad to Mom, but as I finished and stood, finally free to leave, Sarah came to the door.

"Avery, can I talk to you, please?" Her voice was barely audible above the sound of the birds chirping in the trees.

I nodded, and the two of us sat on the top porch step.

She straightened the skirt of her dress, smoothing it over her knees. "I'm sorry for everything. I'm sorry I reacted so bad when you told me about you and Xander. I should have seen it all happening."

"We never wanted to hurt you, Sarah."

"I know. I think I just miss having someone who's always there for me." She twisted the ring on her finger one direction, then the other. Not just any ring. Austin's promise ring. A tear dripped off her lower lashes, leaving a starburst pattern on the white cotton of her dress. "That's not true. I miss Austin. But now, I realize that you and Xander have what I had with Austin. Who am I to get in the way of that?"

I swallowed the lump in my throat. "That's a huge compliment, Sarah. I always admired your relationship. Austin loved you so much."

"After you left Moab, I was more upset that you had thought so little of me. Like I would be selfish and not support the relationship Austin used to pray would happen."

"Austin prayed for us to get together?" I asked. I'd known he'd hoped for it, but praying? That's a whole 'nother level of commitment. And soo Austin. I glanced up at the cottontail clouds hovering in the sky and pictured Austin high-fiving Jesus right now.

"And I'm sorry about your journal" Sarah said. "If I'd known Margot found it, I would've taken it from her. I never would've let her burn it."

"I know."

"We let her know what we thought of her actions."

"Sarah, you don't have to—"

"It was wrong. Evil, really. I think she sees that now." Sarah hugged her knees. "Um, Avery, I know there isn't much time left in the school year, but if you want, I'd really like us to spend time together."

I looked at Sarah's red-rimmed eyes and remembered how she used to look at Austin with such love. I thought back to all the trouble Xander and I had gone through so she wouldn't feel this kind of sadness. Who was I to deny her request? "I'd love that. There's actually this thing I've been doing. A couple times a month I go to this women and children's shelter called Felicity Ridge and teach them how to redesign thrift store clothes to fit their size and style on a budget. Would you ever want to go with me?"

Sarah shrank in place.

"If you aren't comfortable in that environment, we could get coffee or something," I offered.

"It's not that," Sarah said shyly. "It's only, well, I can't sew."

I laughed, probably too loud for this situation. "I can teach you."

"Then I'm in. Also, there's something else. I have news."

"What's that?"

"Matt asked me on a date, and I said yes."

I covered my mouth with my hand, faking surprise, before revealing a grin. I had known he liked her. "Love that! Matt's a great guy. He'll treat you right."

"I think so. We're going to see a movie tonight."

"That's awesome, Sarah. I'm happy for you guys. And I know Austin would be too."

# thirty-eight

One week later, the school was abuzz with recent prom pairings. With the dance three weeks away, there were new ones every day. But I had bigger and better things on my mind.

I burst through the cafeteria doors and ran to the lunch table where I normally sat with Xander, Sarah, and the others. I found Sarah, but Xander's spot was empty.

"Where is he?" I asked, jogging my feet in place.

"Xander?" Sarah glanced around innocently. "I have no idea where he is."

Behind me, someone whistled, and I turned to see Xander standing in the center aisle, holding his guitar. I recognized the beginning melody of "When I See You Smile" as he plucked the strings. Before he sang the first line, tears were already washing away my makeup. The sweet lyrics cradled my heart. Without Xander, who knows when I may have smiled again? He'd made it his mission. If this moment was any proof, sweet Swayze, he'd accomplished it.

Xander carefully laid his guitar on a lunch table. He pulled a single white rose from his back pocket and handed it to me. On instinct, I buried my nose in its petals, a far better scent than everything else in that cafeteria.

"Avery Wheeler Mendenhall, will you go to prom with me?"

I let my kiss answer for me. Before I got too swept away, I broke the kiss. "I have a surprise too. I'm graduating!"

"Are you serious? That is the best news I've ever heard." He lifted me off my feet, hugging me breathless. "What do you say we cut out early? I'm not ready to let go of you."

"Are you kidding? I'm not throwing away my future for some boy!" I pushed him away playfully.

We were the last to leave the lunchroom, but when we got to the hallway, Jake stepped in our path.

"Hey, Avery, can I talk to you for a minute?" Jake asked. He cast a glare at our clasped hands. If that bothered him, he must have hated to see us kiss. For a moment, I worried he might try something with Xander, but fortunately, as if he could read my mind, Jake pocketed his hands.

"Jake?" Courtney walked up behind him and gripped his arm. Her gaze flitted past mine before landing on Jake. "What's going on?"

While Jake stood speechless, I stepped around him, tugging Xander with me. "Nothing I want to be a part of. You'll have to excuse us. We have some celebrating to do."

---

## LORI

My mother's house was much more peaceful when she wasn't there. I did love her, but I was quickly learning I was a magnet for toxic personalities.

I was more than ready to cast off that tendency.

Without a computer, I had to rely on my phone for nearly everything. Not ideal. Would Michael mind if I stopped by the electronics store and picked out a laptop of my own? Wait . . . why did I need his permission? I was making my own money now. But enough to buy a new laptop? What about an apartment? Or a car without his name on the title? Who was I kidding? I couldn't survive without Michael.

Jesus, I—

Guilt pressed in on me. Would God hear the prayers of a woman who walked out on her husband?

"Why do you look like you ate a rotten egg?" Mom asked.

Lucky me, she'd rearranged her social calendar to align with my evenings off, which left me pinned with a target for her negativity and criticism.

"It's chilly in here, that's all." I pulled an old, crocheted blanket out of the chest that served as my mother's coffee table and wrapped it around my shoulders like a cape. I settled onto the corner cushion of the couch.

"Jesus Take the Wheel," my mother shouted from her recliner. On the television, the *Wheel of Fortune* contestant chose not to solve the puzzle about chart-toppers. She spun the wheel instead. It slowed as it neared the five-thousand-dollar marker, and the crowd noise grew in excitement only to fall as the wheel ticked one more time and landed on the bankrupt marker. The woman's total dropped back to zero, and my mother snickered. "Dummy."

A contestant named Doug asked for a *k*, then easily solved the puzzle.

My mom grimaced. "Of course he got it right. He's a worship pastor! She should've solved it when she had the chance."

"Maybe she thought it was worth the risk to go for it. One less tick mark and she could have added five thousand dollars to her total and won the game."

"After what you've been through, I wouldn't think you'd ever suggest someone take foolish risks again."

My attempted sigh sounded more like a groan. "Mom, I'm drained. If there's something you want to say to me, say it."

"I don't have to. You've already discovered what happens when you hop in bed with the first guy who gives you attention. It took nineteen years longer than it should've, but at least you know now."

I pulled the blanket higher up my neck. I'd pull it over my

head completely if I didn't think my mother would yank it off. "Michael was never a risk. I chose him. And he chose me."

"You're still taking his side? After you left him?"

"I'm not taking his side. Yes, he's made mistakes. Hurtful, marriage-killing mistakes. But there was a time when he truly loved me."

She threw her hands in the air, propelling the remote control onto the floor. "Stop acting like he's such a hero. He knocked you up—with twins! Made you quit school and give up any hope of taking care of yourself."

My blood had already reached a slow simmer. Dear God, don't let her crank the burner too high. "He married me because he loved me."

"Don't kid yourself. He loved the idea of you. A pageant queen wife, perfect kids. For goodness' sake, you even have a Labrador retriever."

I clenched my teeth while I searched for words she wouldn't throw back in my face. "Mom, you don't know all the facts. If you did, you might have more respect for Michael."

"I doubt it. I've known men like him my entire life."

My skin itched with the need to set her straight and shut her mouth for once in my life. "Mom—"

"There's something in those Y chromosomes that tells them to take and take and take until they've bled us dry." She retrieved the remote from the floor and turned off the TV.

"Mom—"

"I thought I raised you to be strong and independent but apparently—"

I lurched forward in my seat. "The twins aren't his!"

In the resulting quiet, I fanned the blanket out, wishing it could soak up the blood I'd let boil over, but there was no way to put it back inside. It was out, and all I could do was contain the mess.

In my periphery, Mom glowered. I couldn't bear to meet

her eyes for this part. My throat felt thick as I attempted to cough up my next words. "Eighteen months into dating Michael, we discussed the future. He wanted to go on to get his MBA after college, then move to New York City. I knew I wanted to move to Southern California after graduation and begin my career in interior design. We loved each other too much to let the other person sacrifice their dream, so we decided to cut ties."

"You never told me this."

"Because I didn't want to see you celebrate when my heart was broken." I steeled myself for what was coming next. "My friend set me up with this guy. She said he would cheer me up. He took me out for dinner and dancing. I wasn't having fun though. I missed Michael, so I asked him to take me home. He didn't. He drove me out east of the city, onto a road I didn't recognize." I thumbed the blanket, afraid to close my eyes and relive the next part any more than I had to. Of all the memories I'd lost, why couldn't this be one of them? "He wouldn't bring me home until he got what he wanted. I fought him. I promise I did. But he was stronger than me."

Mom rose from her recliner and joined me on the couch. What I wouldn't give for her to pull me into her arms right then. I knew better than to expect it though. "What happened next?" she asked.

"He drove me home like nothing had happened. Like I wasn't sobbing in the passenger seat. He even had the nerve to walk me to my apartment and tell me he'd had a good time." A strangled noise left my throat—part laugh, part cry, part something else entirely that emanated from the core of me. I took a second to breathe in then out again before continuing. "Once I got home, I called Michael. He came over right away. I probably wouldn't have gone to the police if it weren't for him. He was there with me as they took samples and asked me all the questions."

My mom clasped her hands together in her lap so that the area around her knuckles mottled in red and purples blotches. "Why didn't you tell me?" The harsh tone of her voice awakened the shame that had lingered inside me for nineteen years.

I sniffled like a child. "I knew I'd failed you. I was supposed to be smart enough not to let this happen."

"Lori, you couldn't have known that man was a predator. And you shouldn't have to live in a world where stepping outside is a dangerous decision. What happened was not your fault."

I sucked my bottom lip between my teeth so it wouldn't quiver. Not your fault. I shouldn't have needed to hear that from her, yet I did. If I'd known she would have stood by me rather than shame me for being foolish, I may not have felt so helpless in the months that followed.

"I'm glad you weren't alone. And I'm sorry that happened to you, dear." She grabbed my hand and patted it firmly between hers before releasing it. "Did they catch the man?"

I heaved a deep breath in. "They did. I wasn't the only one he'd done this to though. When he got released on bail, the brother of another victim beat him to death." I spoke matter-of-factly, having never known how to feel about that part of my story. I was spared the trauma of a trial, of being publicly berated by the defense team as a girl "asking for it" simply because I'd agreed to a date. Yet, I never got to face him or show him that I made it through despite what he'd taken from me. "That was right around the time I discovered I was pregnant."

"And you know for sure that man is the father?"

I nodded. "Michael and I never slept together before we married. He'd made a commitment to wait. And once he sets his mind to something, he follows through. He must've decided he would be there for me from that point on because he went to every doctor's appointment. He held my hand when I decided to continue the pregnancy." A slow smile crept onto my lips. "He was there when I learned there were two babies instead of one."

I closed my eyes. I could still see their two profiles on the ultrasound, facing each other and forming a heart. A tear slid down my cheek and dripped off my jaw before I could catch it. Mom rose, retrieved a tissue box, and returned to my side.

"I knew right then that I didn't want to give them up for adoption, but I also knew I couldn't give those sweet babies the life they deserved without a job and a degree. Michael proposed to me that night. Yes, we loved each other, but more than that, we loved those babies. Michael wanted to be their father. So much so that he was willing to give up his New York City dream."

"What about your dream?"

I spread my hands wide in a half-hearted shrug. It was hard to be apologetic about this part. "God gave me a new one—to be the best mother possible for Avery and Austin."

"Did you ever tell them Michael isn't their father?"

"Their biological father," I said, hoping she got my point. "No. I didn't want them to know they were conceived in an act of violence, that their DNA was split between a rapist and his victim." I attempted to clear my throat. "Maybe that wasn't the best decision, but it's what we chose."

My mom nodded. Her lips pursed hard, causing wrinkled spokes to spread outward from them. I glanced around her family room. In between her nursing diplomas, her fishing tournament trophies, and her various knickknacks, framed photos of me and the kids graced the walls. Not a single picture of Michael.

"You know, Mom, Michael certainly hasn't been a perfect father, but he was there when I needed him all those years ago. So whatever happens from this point forward, he deserves more respect than what you've shown him."

# thirty-nine

"If it isn't my favorite patient." Dr. Klein welcomed me into his office. "I wasn't expecting to see you until June. Are you doing all right?"

"Uh, okay, I guess."

"That isn't exactly convincing. Take a seat." He nodded to the couch while he sat on a stool.

I settled into my usual spot.

"Any headaches?" he asked.

"Not really. But I hit my head against a door in the beginning of April, so nearly four weeks ago, I guess. It was right on my scar too."

Dr. Klein pitched forward in his seat. "Did you go to the hospital? Why didn't you come see me?"

"It wasn't bad enough for that."

"We still should schedule a scan just to make sure there isn't any swelling." He made a note on his tablet before returning his attention to me. "And how is your memory recovery going?"

"Fine. It's overwhelming, actually, the number of memories I'm recalling every day."

He beamed. "I'd say that's a good problem to have in your situation. What's your most recent pre-injury memory?"

I searched the timeline I'd sketched in my brain. "Avery designing her homecoming dress. Helping Austin pick out Sarah's corsage. It's not a continuous stream of memories, but I can recall the days before the accident."

"That's fantastic, Lori. Truly." His smile grew even wider. "How's your family doing now? Are they being supportive?"

"That's . . . complicated. I've been living with my mother for the last month."

He nodded, suspending judgment. Boy, did I appreciate that. "Tell me about that decision."

"The more memories that come back, the more I remember how my life and my marriage had been. It wasn't good," I said, my throat thick with gathering sobs. Dr. Klein had seen me cry more times than I could count, and it seemed I was about to add another one.

"I'm sorry to hear that. It isn't unusual for a person with a closed brain injury or amnesia to struggle. New roles, new circumstances, new sensitivities, new goals even. They can shake up the family system. Sometimes a family member may actually sabotage the patient's recovery."

I looked down at my hands, clasped in my lap. The solitary diamond on my left ring finger reflected the office's harsh light. That and the thin gold wedding band seemed to be all that remained unchanged through the years of my marriage. The Michael who gave these to me would never do anything to heed my progress. But this Michael? The one who was hesitant with every breakthrough in my memory recall? The one who knew I'd had enough neglect and adultery? He might.

My lungs fought to expand. Michael was the only person who had motive to keep my memories hidden. I had been finding my voice. He was about to lose me. Was that why he hid my Momentso account from me? To save our marriage?

Dr. Klein's question brought me back to the present. "Was there any memory in particular that bothered you?"

"That's why I scheduled this appointment." I struggled with how to word my thoughts. "Dr. Klein, do people with my condition ever remember things that didn't happen?"

"Yes. It's called confabulation, and it's fairly common. Some people refer to it as honest lying. They aren't trying to deceive anyone. It's their subconscious filling in memory gaps to help their world make sense."

I dug my fingernails into my palms. Was the memory of Jade and Michael confabulation? Maybe Michael was telling the truth after all. Relief and embarrassment added themselves to the swirl of emotions inside me. "Is it permanent?"

"Not normally. Since confabulation is a response to memory loss, patients can combat it by strengthening their memory skills. It's usually caused by trauma to both the basal forebrain and frontal lobes. Your swelling was extensive, so it is possible."

"Possible, but not probable?"

"Correct. Possible, but not probable."

❖

"Lori, thank you for coming to this final PTO meeting, even if it's simply to help pull off prom," Peter said as he took the seat across the lunch table from me. "How's your healing going?"

"Really well. Physically, I've gotten all my strength back. I've been working, goodness, fifty hours a week."

"At that store, um . . ." He snapped his fingers a couple of times.

"Lake & Hearth."

"That's right. You'd think I was the one with amnesia." He laughed at his insensitive joke. "By the way, my mother loves her front room. Thanks for hooking me up with Kendra."

"I was happy to help."

"Lori Mendenhall—happy to help. That's been your MO

as long as I've known you. Speaking of, how is your memory recovering?"

"Okay. There are still some gaps though."

He scratched his jaw. "That has to be enormously frustrating."

"You have no idea."

Again, he laughed, although there was a nervous edge to it this time.

I looped my purse strap over my shoulder and pushed myself up from the table.

"There's something else. I heard about you and your husband splitting up. Is Avery doing all right?"

A foul taste hit me. "We haven't split up. My mom wanted me to stay with her while she worked through some issues. She has a lot of issues." It wasn't a lie. "As for Avery, she's doing great. Michael has been calling around to college admissions offices to update them on her progress. We're hoping for good news soon."

"Excellent. Between that and prom court nominations, she must be on top of the world."

My next breath sputtered out. "I have to get to work. I'm sure I'll see you tomorrow at the dance."

"Yep. Make sure you prepare yourself for what you may see while chaperoning." He chuckled. "Their style of dancing, if you can call it that, is far different from ours. Michael is coming, correct?"

I pretended not to hear his question. Michael and I hadn't discussed chaperoning prom since I left. Most of our conversations consisted of accusations and deflections, not dance duties. And we certainly hadn't discussed Avery's nomination. My girl was up for prom queen, and she hadn't even told me. I had to find out on the school's Momentso page. "I've handled a lot. I can manage some kids dirty dancing."

"Gotcha. Let me walk you out. I'm heading to my office

anyway." He prattled on about his summer vacation plans—something about taking his kids to Mount Rushmore and a solo camping trip to the Grand Canyon. Funny, he didn't look like the camping type. More the "sport Patagonia clothes then book a room at the Holiday Inn Express" type.

The bell rang and students filled the hallway. One student in particular caught my eye. Bright as day, Avery pranced through the monotonous throng of kids shuffling to their next class until she got to Xander, who was standing at a locker shelving a binder. She tapped on his shoulder, and when he turned, she jumped into his embrace, locking her legs around his waist like she was on *The Bachelor* or something. I'd once felt that for Michael—that desperate need to be near him, kissing him. The feeling that time was endless and dreams were as close as a lover's lips. A teacher broke up their moment with a soft scolding, but Xander and Avery merely paused their kissing long enough for the teacher to turn away. Finally, we passed by, and Avery noticed me. I waved to her, but my girl grabbed her boyfriend's shirt and pulled him down the hall.

"Lori, one last thing," Peter said. "If helping with the dance is too much, please let me know. I'd hate for it to cause you any harm." Something in the way he looked at me set my skin crawling.

I forced a smile. "I know my limits. Gotta go," I said, cutting through the students and heading straight to the exit doors. Once I got to my car, I unlocked my phone and discovered a text from Michael.

> Would you still like me to chaperone prom with you tomorrow night? I'd like to, but I'll respect your wishes. Just let me know.

There was something about that man. Even though he'd broken my heart, part of me still yearned for his affection, his care.

There was nothing wrong with me. We were made to love others with the fullness of our hearts. To sacrifice, to forgive, to show compassion. The wrong lay with those who made others feel worthless and unlovable.

If only *that* could brand itself on my memory.

*forty*

"So your daughter is on her way to prom? How are you not a weepy mess right now?" Andrew stacked some books from local authors on a teak shelf. "Or is that a mom stereotype?"

I checked my watch. Xander should be coming over for pictures at 5:15, which meant I needed to duck out of there in the next ten minutes. "It's only a matter of time before the waterworks start, I assure you. I should get going."

"Excuse me, I have a rather odd question," a man to my right said. He was short, a good three inches shorter than me. His round glasses made such a statement that they'd be better labeled spectacles, and his mustache made him look like a nineteenth-century Russian czar. A combination of features that was unique to only one man that I knew of. And suddenly, I was remembering escargot.

"Are you . . . Herschel Irving?"

"The one and only." His grin forced the thick ends of his mustache to touch the bottom of his glasses. "I'm teaching a series of interior design courses at the University of Colorado. As a project for my students, I'm looking to furnish a home completely."

"That's wonderful. I was enrolled in that program a long time ago."

"It's a good testimony for the school that its alumni are doing so well. This shop is curated marvelously."

"Oh, well, I never graduated, so I'm not sure I count as an alum. And this isn't my store. I'm simply the acting manager."

"Don't be so modest," Andrew butted in. "Everything you see here is all Lori's work." When my face flooded with heat, he winked.

"You have a good eye for design, indeed," Herschel told me. "Maybe you should consider finishing your degree. You'd be an excellent asset in my classes." He pinched the corner of a pillow, then stroked the velvet fabric with his thumb. "Listen, Lori, I'd like to partner with local artisans and local shops to furnish and decorate the home. The work will be featured in my magazine. This shop came highly recommended by a friend of mine. Could you tell me a little about it?"

My heart sank. I didn't bother to check my watch. I knew it was time for me to leave. "Andrew has worked here longer than I have. He can tell you all you need to know."

Andrew's eyes widened, then he turned to Herschel. "There's a dinette right over there that would be a perfect spot to chat." He waited for Herschel to step away before he turned to me. "This is your chance to make yourself known to The Herschel Irving. He's already impressed by your work. You sit down with him."

"I can't. Avery."

"Look, I was a teenager six years ago, and I can tell you that she'll be mad for a day or two, but she'll get over it. And one day, when you're some hotshot interior designer, she'll be glad you didn't miss this opportunity."

I shook my head. "No. I promised."

"Lori, this is your time. Don't let it pass again."

———◆———

**AVERY**

"Ahem," I cleared my throat loudly upon entering the office. Dad kept his focus glued to his laptop screen for another ten seconds before raising his eyes to me. Even then he didn't smile as I'd expected.

I fidgeted with the ribbon at my waist. Perhaps he didn't like that I'd hacked up Mom's Miss Colorado Teen dress to make my prom design. Or maybe he'd eaten expired deli meat for lunch. I don't know.

Finally, he stood and came to me. He squeezed my upper arms. "I don't think I'm ready for you to stop being my little girl."

"Oh, Dad. What if I promise for the rest of my life to always act like an immature, self-absorbed teenager?"

"Avery, you're my daughter. I don't think you'll need to make a promise to remain self-absorbed," he teased, pulling me in for a hug. "You look beautiful. Just like your mother."

I dabbed my eyes with my fingertips, trying not to smear my eyeliner. "Why isn't she here, Dad? Isn't this why mothers want a daughter? For days like these?"

"She must have gotten delayed at work," he answered curtly.

"She wouldn't have missed Austin's prom."

"She'll be here. Now, before your date arrives, I have something for you. I don't know if you'll like them or not. I won't be offended if you don't." He reached into his laptop bag and pulled out a Tiffany-blue box.

Stifling a squeal, I accepted it and tore off the lid. I gasped at the sight of the earrings.

"They're Akoya pearls with 18K white gold. That's what the young lady said when I ordered them from New York. Like I said, you don't have to wear them. I don't want to mess up your style."

"Dad, I love them. Thank you."

He held the box while I took each earring out and placed it in my ear. When the doorbell rang moments later, I danced in excitement before lifting the hem of my emerald dress to leave the room.

"Sweetheart, that's not how this works. I answer the door, and then you make your grand entrance from the hallway."

"Yes, Dad." I remained in the office and listened as he answered the door.

"Alexander Dixon, you're looking sharp." Dad's voice carried across the house so I could hear his every word. "Who are you wearing, Armani?"

"Yeah, right. This is, however, the finest tux you can rent for ninety-nine dollars."

"It'll do fine. She's almost ready."

"Cool. She looks pretty, huh?" Xander's words came out quickly. Was he nervous for our big night? So cute.

"She does. I don't have to tell you my expectations, do I? What you can and more importantly cannot do with my daughter?"

"Oh, no, sir, Mr. Mendenhall. I won't even touch her."

I straightened. That was a bit extreme.

Dad laughed, and a noise that might have been him patting Xander on the shoulder—hard—sounded. "You can touch her to dance with her. But none of that grinding stuff. Keep this in mind. Dancing is good. Friction is bad."

I cringed. Poor Xander. I could just picture his face turning red.

"Absolutely, Mr. Mendenhall. I mean, absolutely not."

"Relax, kid. I trust you. Here's some money for dinner."

"Thanks, but I've been helping my stepdad at the restaurant to pay for this."

"That's too admirable for me to deny. Next date's on me though."

"Fair enough."

"I'll call her. Don't forget to breathe. And don't lock your knees or you'll pass out. Avery, Xander's here!"

My cue. I left the office and glided down the first-floor hall. When I rounded the stairs, Xander rocked back on his heels.

"Whoa," he said.

Dad playfully shoved him toward me, and I caught him by the waist.

"Hey, handsome," I said.

He leaned down until his forehead touched mine. "You are so, so pretty," he whispered.

The door burst open behind Xander. "Am I too late for pictures?" Grandma Anita's shrill voice set Wynton to barking. Not normal barking but, like, if-his-stuffed-lamb-took-a-shotgun-blast-to-the-head barking. While Dad worked to calm the dog, I worked to calm Grandma.

"You're good. Xander just got here."

She moved to hug me—scratch that. Not hug. She was simply trying to pull the waist of my skirt higher and the bottom hem of my halter down. "Goodness, girl. Cover your belly."

"Grandma, it's only an inch of skin, and you can't even see my belly button."

"And now it's only a half inch. You know, I have a cute cardigan at my house that would look darling with that dress, and it will keep you from getting cold too."

"I'll be all right. If I get cold, Xander will let me wear his jacket. Hey, have you heard from Mom?"

"I have. She got held up at work. Something about some fancy-pants big shot coming into the store. She said she'd miss the picture-taking, but she'll see you at the dance."

I fumbled for Xander's hand.

"Don't give me that look," Grandma said. "Your mother is finally doing what needs to be done. You're almost out of here, graduated. Let her work if that's what she wants to do."

"Come on, Ave," Xander said close to my ear. "Let's get our pictures so we can get on with the best night of our lives."

If it weren't for him, I probably would've looked like I just smelled something rotten in every picture we took. But he knew what to do to make me smile a genuine smile. A tickle to my ribs here, a few whispered compliments there, and soon we were finished with the backyard modeling shots.

After a not-so-quick, lipstick-ruining kiss, Xander held the Bronco's passenger door open for me to climb in.

"I forgot my bag for the after-prom party." I kicked off my heels and handed them to Xander. "I'll be right back." I jogged to the door that led into the mudroom, opening it quietly so Grandma couldn't put a bathrobe on me or anything.

"Will you listen to me, Michael?" Grandma asked. "I have something important I must say. It's about Austin and Avery."

I tiptoed closer but stayed hidden from view.

Grandma sighed. "Lori told me."

"Told you what?"

"About what you did years ago. For her and the twins."

I'd never heard Grandma sound so . . . kind? Especially when talking to Dad.

"I owe you an apology," she continued. "All this time, I thought you were the one who got her in trouble."

What on earth was she talking about? I breathed out so deeply, my lungs seemed to collapse in on themselves, and for some reason, I couldn't welcome any air until I knew what was going on.

"I thought you knocked her up and married her to keep her under your thumb," Grandma said. "I've treated you as such all these years. But I was wrong, and I'm sorry. It was noble of you, the way you stepped in to be the twins' father like you did."

I steadied myself against the wall physically, while internally, I crumbled. It had to be a lie. One more ludicrous so-called truth that Grandma claimed to be so sure of. She'd always hated Dad. Always tried to convince Mom to leave him. Now that she had, what sick game was she playing?

One thing was for sure: I was tired of people, death, God, and whoever and whatever was trying to rip my family apart.

"It's not true," I said, charging into the kitchen, nearly tripping on my dress in the process. "Dad. Daddy, tell her she's wrong. She doesn't know what she's talking about."

Color drained from Dad's face, and he stepped back, away from me. Why? I skewered Grandma with a glare.

"Avery, I thought you'd left, dear." Grandma moved quickly, as if to block me from Dad, but I skirted past her.

"Yeah, well, I didn't." I threw myself at Dad, tightening my arms around him. "Tell her she's wrong. Tell her you're my father. My real father."

His silence sank within me, grabbing hold of anything in its path and pulling it all down to the depths. He combed his fingers through the ends of my curled hair, but instead of bringing comfort or peace, it tore at my scalp, searing and seizing everything I thought I'd known about my family. I pushed away from him. "Tell her. Tell me."

He shook his head.

"I don't get it. We have the same personality, the same strengths and weaknesses. We roll our eyes the same way when something is dumb. We have the same chin—Mom said so." I touched my jaw, finding it wet. My fingertips glistened with tears and streaks of mascara.

"This doesn't change any of that," he said, his voice wavering a touch, before he cleared his throat loudly. "You're my daughter, and Austin, my son. Even before you took your first breaths. I love you more than any biological father could."

"Avery? Is everything okay?"

I spun to find Xander stepping lightly toward me, concern blazing in his stormy eyes. "No, it's not." I grabbed Xander by the lapel and pulled him to the door. "Take me out of here. Now."

# forty-one

Rather than meeting Matt and Sarah for dinner, Xander and I parked at the trailhead for Eldorado Canyon and sat in silence. Everything hurt. My heart, my head, my throat. When not-my-dad called me for the fifth time, I tried to throw my phone out the window, but Xander intervened by texting "This is Xander. Give her some time," then turned off my phone and stored it in his glove box.

Once the tears had dried up, we headed for the dance, opting for distraction over self-pity. Not gonna lie, I looked a mess. Puffy eyes washed free of makeup. Patchy skin where the foundation had smeared. Tendrils of hair frizzy and unkempt. Xander, however, still found me beautiful. He reminded me about every five minutes.

It was a little easier to forget that everything in my life was a fabrication once we arrived at the school. We hit the snack table first since dinner had been a bust. Then we were drawn to the gym floor by Harry Styles. Turns out Xander was an outstanding dancer. Those skills carried over to a slow swaying when Taylor Swift's "Wildest Dreams" played. It's funny how a few kisses can dismiss all your worries—at least for a few moments. My anxious thoughts were never far from reach. What would happen if I didn't get into any of the colleges I'd applied to? I still hadn't heard from any regarding my unique circumstances. Would Xander and I survive as a couple if he went to Belmont in Nashville and I stayed to attend Red Rocks Community College?

"You're pouting again," he said. "Even if he isn't your father by blood, he's still your father."

"That's not what I was thinking about. Not this second, anyway," I added when he raised his brow. "I was wondering if we'd make it in a long-distance relationship." My gaze lowered to my bodice.

Xander hooked a finger beneath my chin and gently raised my face so I could peer at him. "I waited years for you. I could do it again." He lowered his lips to mine and pressed the sweetest kiss to my mouth. It was a forever kind of kiss. One I could imagine receiving at the altar someday or in the kitchen, dancing like Mom and Dad used to while dishes soaked in soapy water.

After the kiss, I nuzzled his neck with my nose before settling my gaze over his shoulder. Near the doors of the gym, I caught sight of my parents, deep in conversation. I clutched tighter to Xander as the weight in my chest grew heavier and heavier. They both eyed the crowd, and I shrank behind my date.

"What's going on?" he asked.

"My parents. I don't want them to see me."

Xander looked over his shoulder. "Too late. They're coming this way."

"Avery, honey, can we talk?" Mom, who'd already made it clear where her priorities stood tonight, now had the nerve to act like she cared about my needs. Her sorrowful eyes and soft voice sent splinters into my heart. "Your dad told me—"

"My dad? Really? My dad?" I stomped my foot, nearly catching Xander's in the process. "I don't wanna talk now. Not at prom. Can't you take your lies over to the snack table for your chaperone duties?"

Around us, couples had slowed their steps to eavesdrop on our family drama.

"We never meant to hurt you." Dad spoke the same words I had said to Sarah in Moab, a realization that jabbed my core.

"Can't I be a normal teenager dealing with normal teenage drama for one night?" I tried to keep my voice down to avoid more stares, but it was getting more difficult by the moment. "Can't I pretend that not winning prom queen would be the biggest heartbreak I could ever face?"

Mom's chin quivered. It was a bad look considering how pretty the rest of her face was. In that little black dress, she was sure to make not-my-dad pine for her, whether that was her goal or not. Not that I cared at this point. My family had unraveled entirely, if it had ever been knit together at all.

"Come on, Lori. We'll discuss this later." Dad, er, Michael offered my mom his hand. She denied him, of course.

For the next half hour, I leaned into Xander and tried to pretend it was only him and me in this world. Reality came too soon as Principal Wright climbed onto the stage and announced it was time to crown prom king and queen. Two weeks ago, voting had been held. To be honest, I wasn't too surprised to be nominated. After all, I'd been on homecoming court every year except the past one. The real pleasant surprise was having Xander nominated for king.

I couldn't have been prouder standing on that stage holding his hand, even though he was utterly embarrassed to be in the spotlight, not for his music but for being well-liked. I hadn't felt his sweaty palm for a long time. It was kind of sweet.

On my left, Courtney stood motionless. The arm closest to me hung loose at her side while the other crossed her stomach, her hand clutching her elbow and her manicured nails pinching her skin. I stole a look at her face. Pale streaks stretched from her eyes down to her jawline.

Principal Wright stood behind the microphone with a crown

in hand. "And now, I present this year's Front Range High School prom king . . . Jake Powers." The crowd clapped unenthusiastically as Jake stepped forward to accept the crown. Courtney didn't react.

I felt myself leaning toward her as my mind rattled with possible things to say. *You look pretty. I like your dress. Are you okay?* I told my mind to shut up.

"Now for your queen," the principal said.

Xander squeezed my hand. I offered a half-hearted smile.

"And this year's prom queen is . . . Avery Mendenhall!"

The crowd cheered much louder this time. I stepped forward, hesitant to let go of Xander's hand, but I did. As Ms. Crandall placed the crown on my head, I stared at Courtney. Those lines on her cheeks now glistened, and her chin puckered, showing the dimple she'd always hated.

Next, Jake and I were forced to pose for pictures at the side of the stage. The whole affair took way too long as the photographer had to switch out batteries on her camera.

Jake, smelling faintly of cheap beer, kept close to me. "You look hot."

"You look drunk," I said, pointing to his red nose and flushed cheeks.

"Not yet. Give me an hour."

"No, thanks. Hey, what's Courtney's deal?"

"What do you mean?"

"She looked upset on the stage."

Jake uttered his best *idunno*. "Maybe because she lost to you."

"Before that."

Finally, the photographer was ready. She directed us where to stand and had us put our arms around each other. Despite that, I held my smile for the camera.

"Maybe she was upset because we broke up," Jake slurred.

Trying hard not to let my face fall into shock, I spoke through my smile. "When?"

"Right before we got here."

"Why?"

"Well, she saw me looking at an old picture of you and me. She said something about always having to compete with you. I don't know. I was two cans in by that point."

"Hold those smiles," the photographer said. A series of flashes blinded me, and Jake's breath blazed against my ear. "She's right," he whispered, as his hand slid from my waist downward.

I jerked out of his reach. "Let me tell you something I learned. You can be given everything in life—love, money, friends—but if you don't treat people well, you're just a—"

Jake unleashed a flood of vomit onto the floor between us. I had to hop backward to keep it from hitting my shoes. While my classmates cawed and cackled at the scene, Jake tumbled onto his backside.

"Have a good life, *Jock*." I cut through the onlookers, searching for my boyfriend. I found Sarah and Matt instead, chilling by the snack table. "Hey, have you guys seen Xander?"

Sarah peered through the side doors of the gym. "He's, uh, on the stage. He said he had a surprise for you."

A flutter in my heart forced me to take a quick breath. "Thank you." Hurrying, I returned to the dance floor. The music had stopped, and Xander's voice came through the speakers.

"I hope you all don't mind, but I've been asked to play a song up here. I wrote this one for my best friend, Avery. This is called 'Awaken.'"

I stepped toward the stage. Someone grabbed my hand though.

"Courtney." My mouth refused to say anything else. The girl was a wreck. Physically, emotionally—every *-ly* there was.

She wiped her nose with the back of her hand. "I'm sorry. Sorry for what happened."

My eyes flickered to the stage where Xander strummed the opening chords of his song.

I set my focus back on Courtney. "It's fine."

"No, it's not. I was a terrible friend to you. I wanted what you had. Your perfect relationship, your perfect life, your perfect family."

Oh, if she only knew.

"And that dumb bicycle post about you being easy. I meant it as a joke. I didn't think it would stick with you."

Fire rolled through my veins, singeing my ears, my cheeks, my hands. She'd been the one to comfort me after that "joke" spread through the school.

But then the first few lyrics poured off Xander's caramel voice.

> When I look at you, I'm breathless
> When I take it in, I lose myself
> All the little things that I never knew
> That you loved me before I knew you

My eyes locked with his, and my heart led my feet a step closer to him.

Behind me, Courtney heaved a sob. "Also, thanks for not telling everyone about the picture."

I spun around to face her. "What picture?"

The disco ball's colorful lights formed a kaleidoscope in Courtney's dark irises. "Trey's picture. Thanks for not telling everyone it was me."

Rocking back on my heels, I pictured the wretched image that had been burned into my brain after only a one-second view. Nothing I noticed could've given away her identity. "That was you?"

Courtney stammered. "I thought you knew. That you'd recognized my bedroom. That you were protecting me."

"I'm not that nice," I said, straining to hear Xander's lyrics over the loudspeakers.

"Jake and I had a fight, so Trey came over to watch a movie—"
"Look, Courtney." I grabbed her hands. "You want my forgiveness? You got it. I was an awful friend. You were an awful friend. All that is in the past. But right now, an amazing guy is singing me a love song, and he's my future." I squeezed her hands once before releasing them. "So I'm gonna go."

I nodded swift and hard, and then found my way to the stage, giving Xander all of me as his serenade continued into the chorus.

> Awaken love that finally overwhelms
> Awaken love to find its place in me, take me over
> Awaken love that finally paid the price
> In me, in me, in me . . . you finally answered.

My heart grew close to bursting when the crowd whooped and hollered with applause at the end of the song. When Xander hopped down from the stage, I thanked him with a sweet, tender kiss. Yes, this love had awakened right when I needed it, and it was one worth waiting for.

# *forty-two*

**LORI**

After watching Xander's performance, it was hard not to be moved, especially as Michael's arm grazed mine where we stood in the doorway of the gym.

"How about one dance?" he asked.

I took his hand and led him to the dance floor. Despite everything, it still felt good to be in this man's embrace again. His touch held so much history, most of which I now remembered. Then again, how would I ever know if I remembered it all?

Several measures went by before Michael spoke. "We should never have kept that secret from the kids. I know why we did. It was an impossible situation, and we did the best we could. Still . . ."

"I hate that we hurt her." I chewed my lip and willed the tears to retreat.

"I hate it too, Lor. She'll be okay. She's tough."

"A whole lot tougher than me."

"Nah. Look at what you've done. How you've recovered after an injury that could have killed or permanently disabled you. On top of that, you're doing amazing at your job. Kendra trusts you to handle all the operations at Lake & Hearth. Pretty soon, you'll have your own store. You're amazing."

"I didn't know you believed in me so much."

"I've always believed in you. The problem was I didn't believe in myself. Not in my ability to make it without having you there to lend support whenever I needed it. That makes me sound incredibly selfish. It was never my intent to hold you back from achieving your goals, but that's what I did."

My chest swelled at his confession. Finally, he was speaking honestly. "Michael, I was happy to support you. But I needed support back. To do all I wanted to do, I needed you to be there for me too."

"I know that now. I'm so incredibly sorry for neglecting you how I did. If I could go back, I would do many things differently." Such earnestness in his eyes. Was it enough though? To allow me to trust him again with my heart? Or would I forever question his faithfulness? Would I fret every time he worked late? Would I have to attend business dinners with Jade, smiling and pretending she hadn't tried to take my husband from me?

"Excuse me." Margot Lowry held out an empty plastic bag and a two-liter of Sprite. "There aren't any more cups at the drink table."

Michael tensed and huffed a breath. He and the Lowrys would never be good buddies.

I patted his arm. "We always kept extra plasticware and cups in the PTO storeroom. I'll check there and be right back."

I turned left out of the gym and headed down the poorly lit hall toward the designated PTO space between the band and art rooms. My steps slowed, however, when I picked up the first scent of fresh-cut wood. The woodshop classroom was fifteen yards ahead on the right. Only the band room stood between me and the full, choking smell of sawdust. I clasped my hands together, pressing them to my breastbone. No memories tonight, I pleaded. To God? To my mind? To whatever or whoever held my memory captive all this time?

I caught my reflection in the trophy case by the door to the band room. Austin's picture was displayed—a small memorial to the school's best ever trumpet player. Beneath his individual picture, a five-by-seven frame held a picture of my family. Austin in his uniform full dress, Avery in her cheer outfit and homecoming princess sash, Michael, and myself standing on the football field's fifty-yard line. I moved closer. A yellow sweaterdress. I was wearing a long-sleeve, yellow sweaterdress cinched by a brown belt. Images flickered through my mind, too fast to make out, fast enough to send panic through my veins. I walked a few feet more, to the PTO's unmarked door. The knob, ice-cold in my hand, turned easily.

The door gave way to a dark abyss. I ran my hand along the interior wall until my fingers found the light switch. I flicked it on. Shelves held office supplies. The kind teachers and PTO members would use, not financial planners. I stepped inside and worked my way around an old laminator, until I stood where Michael and Jade . . . had never stood.

"This sure does bring back memories."

I whirled around to see him closing the door. "Peter?"

The light seemed to grow brighter then. I squinted. I wanted to shield my eyes—my mind—from this memory I didn't want to get back.

He closed the distance between us. "You remember, don't you?"

I backed up until the shelves held me still. "I don't . . ."

"You don't remember how this"—he motioned between us—"had been building for months, begging us to do what we both wanted."

"No. I was married."

"To a man who didn't love you, didn't meet your needs, didn't notice how gorgeous you are. He had a diamond in his hand and couldn't care less. But I cared. I listened. I was the husband you deserved to have in all ways but one."

Bile rose in my throat, burning up any words I tried to speak. A carousel of moments sped through my mind. Peter smiling.

Peter tucking my hair behind my ear. Peter caressing my wrist. Peter whispering in my ear all the things he wanted to experience with me if I'd only give him a chance.

His eyes had lost their simpleminded gleam and instead shone a hunger. "The day of the homecoming football game— I'd been waiting for that day all summer and all fall. So when you asked me to unlock the school doors so you could get the crowning supplies, let's just say I've never been more excited to see the inside of this supply closet." His hands slid across the waistline of my dress, pinning me against him.

"I don't want this," I eked out. But I had back then. I'd wanted him to kiss me that day. I'd wanted to feel wanted. I'd wanted to feel seen, cherished, honored. He made me feel like that with every intimate conversation on the phone and each Momentso message—what had happened to those?

"Lori, please. I've been so patient."

Looking down, I saw Peter's fist clutch the fabric of my dress by my hip. Only my dress was no longer black. It was yellow. Front Range High School yellow. His lips had started on my neck. I had known what I should do: shove him off and return to my husband. But his attention had felt too good, so I not only welcomed it, I pursued it. The kisses had been sloppy, reckless, wanton. The groping had been clumsy and vile. Yet that day, it felt wildly romantic.

Until we were interrupted.

Austin stood in the doorway, heartbreak written all over his face. "Mom?"

My good sense returning, I pushed off Peter. "I shouldn't be here," I said. What had I done? In one uncontrolled moment, I'd splintered my family and tainted my sweet boy's innocent view of the world, of marriage, and of me. "I'm sorry, Austin," I cried. "I'm so sorry. Please don't tell."

Austin's chin trembled and heavy tears pulled at the brim of his eyes. "If you don't, I will."

I reached for Austin then. He backed away, then ran out of sight. "What have I done?" I had asked then.

I repeated the question now, soft as a whisper.

"What your heart told you to," Peter said while his hands greedily pawed me. "Nineteen months I've been replaying that kiss in my mind. Nineteen months I've spent waiting for you to remember what we had built, creating hoops for your daughter to jump through, all so I could see you grace my office."

I gasped. He'd done what to my little girl? My fight-or-flight instinct kicked in. Confused as I was about my marriage and myself, this I was sure of: Peter Wright was not welcome to touch my body or my heart. I slapped his hands repeatedly until he recoiled.

His eyes were wide with confusion. "I don't get it. You wanted me."

"I wanted to feel cherished. I wanted to feel honored. You did neither." I fought my way past him and bolted through the door but stopped on a dime when I saw Michael looking at our family picture in the display case. "Michael."

He turned to face me. I'd never seen him so broken as when Peter exited the closet after me, feigning dignity and retreating to the gym. Part of me expected Michael to go after the man, to shed his anger through his fists. Part of me wanted him to. And yet all of me knew that Peter Wright was simply a pawn.

"You knew, didn't you?" I asked Michael.

He nodded. "Austin told me after the game. Right before we got to the car."

Trembling, I wrapped my arms around myself. "It was my fault. And all this time, I've been blaming you for the accident, for breaking our family apart. It was me." I looked up to the dark ceiling. "God knows and I know it was my fault."

"I drove you to him." Michael quick-stepped to me, but I rejected his touch.

"If you knew, why didn't you tell me? All those times I went after you and Jade, you knew it had been him and me." I paced back and forth over the same few tiles. "The Momentso messages from Peter. What happened to them?"

Michael held his hands out in surrender. "When you were in the hospital, I logged into your account. I saw the history between you and him. I read how it went from questions about school functions to you confiding in him about us, about everything."

I struggled to breathe. I needed to get out of this tight dress soon or I'd end up back in the hospital.

"Once you came to and we learned the extent of your memory loss, I went back online. I deleted the messages and shut down your account. I thought this might be God's way of giving us another chance. I could make things right. I could make you love me again."

My gut twisted. What had I done? The full breadth of my betrayal slathered over me, making my body feel heavy. All the pain, insecurity, sorrow, and jealousy I'd felt when I thought Michael and Jade were having an affair, I heaped on Michael. He had to carry that every single day that he sat at my hospital bed, visited my rehab clinic, and slept beside me in our home.

Dark spots blotted my vision, and I began to sink beneath the surface of consciousness, but not before Michael was there to catch my fall. Again.

# *forty-three*

"You look like death warmed over." My mother shoved a mug of coffee across the kitchen table the next morning. "Late night?"

"No, just a bad one." I rubbed gentle circles on my temples. How had a day that started with a major career opportunity ended with my life crumbling in my hands?

"Serves you right for choosing to chaperone a high school dance." She tsked. "I believe Dante wrote about those in his *Divine Comedy*."

"It wasn't the dance. It was everything else that happened. For one, you told Avery that the man she's always thought was her father wasn't."

"Don't you for one second put this on me. No secret lasts forever. Give it another five years, and I bet we'll know where Jimmy Hoffa is buried."

I wouldn't put it past my mother to have Hoffa locked in her attic, alive and well. I never have and never would understand her. "I'm sorry. I'm not blaming you. It was my decision to keep the truth from the twins. I only wish it had come from Michael and I, at a time and place where we could have helped her through it."

She handed me the cream, sugar, and a spoon. An extra teaspoon of sweetness was definitely called for today. I mixed it in with my normal fixin's, hoping it would do its magic and keep me from hiding beneath my blankets all day.

"Yes, that would have been best. The good news is Avery annihilated the competition for prom queen. You should've put her in pageants, I'm telling you."

"Have you spoken to her?"

"No, but the school posted about it. She looked pretty, even after starring in her own Maury Povich episode."

I clanged the lid of the sugar bowl onto the base. "Is everything a joke to you?"

"Humor is a perfectly acceptable form of coping."

"For it to be considered humor, it should be funny to someone other than you."

My mother looked down her nose at me. "And you're such a comedian? You took after your father in that respect."

I laughed bitterly. "What father?"

"Don't scowl, Lori. You'll get frown lines. I wanted a child, and Gregory and I made a calculated decision so I could conceive. I've never kept that secret from you."

My sigh sent ripples across the surface of my coffee. I'd never convince her it was just as damaging to know my biological father lived a few states away, content to have zero relationship with me. "You win, Mom."

"Other than your paternity drama, what reason do you have to be so crabby? Let me guess. Michael did something last night at the dance?"

"Michael didn't do anything. I can mess up my life without any help, it seems."

She waved a dismissive hand in the air. "Whatever it is, it can't be as bad as anything he's done."

I couldn't believe I was about to tell her something else since she'd handled the last bit of sensitive information so well. But she was honest to a fault. Right now, I needed honesty. "I remembered something last night. That I'd been the one having an affair, Mom. An emotional one that was turning physical, but Austin caught us. He told Michael right before the accident."

Mom sipped her coffee like I'd merely told her the sky was blue.

"You're not surprised?" I asked.

"Not really. Not many women could have been so faithful for so long in a marriage like that. I've seen this happen over and over with my friends."

"I don't expect you to condone my actions."

"Oh, I don't, but Lori, relationships are hard. Why do you think I've avoided them my whole life? 'The happiest of all lives is a busy solitude.' Voltaire said that. I tried teaching you, but you had to go and learn the hard way."

Anita Stowe, always there to keep it real.

"However, before you make any decisions about your marriage, you need to talk to Avery. You tell her the truth about everything."

◆

"Every rose has its thorn," Avery sang in harmony with the song's title line. From the doorway, I could see her lying on Austin's bed with an arm and a leg hanging off the side.

"Knock, knock," I said a bit louder than the music. "Can I come in?"

She lifted her head off the pillow for a moment, then rolled to her side and hugged Wynton. "Didn't you move out?"

"Honey—"

"That's why you tried to get me to go to Grandma's with you. Because Dad's not my dad?"

"Avery, he *is* your dad. Will you give me a chance to explain?"

She buried her face in Wynton's fur and growled.

I sat on the foot of the bed and traced the lines on Austin's quilt. "I met your dad—Michael—at my first-year college orientation. He was a junior, helping out with Welcome Week. You know how you can lock eyes with someone, a stranger even, and there's an instant connection? That was our story. Then I talked to him, and *whoa*." My attempt at lightening the mood failed. Avery remained frozen, her face hidden by the extra skin Wynton had gained around his neck in his old age. "He was funny, sweet, flirty, smart—all things my mother told me a man couldn't honestly possess together. We were deliriously happy for a while. But reality set in two years later. He wanted to pursue a financial career on Wall Street. I wanted to finish school and become an interior designer in California."

I blinked hard and long. "As much as we cared about each other, we were stubbornly focused on our goals, neither willing to bend. So we took a break. What happened next is something I've only told Michael, Grandma, and the police."

Avery craned her neck until I could see her eyes.

"I went on a date with a friend of a friend. He wasn't a good guy." I went on, explaining how Brolin McIntyre sexually assaulted me.

As that information seemed to echo around Austin's room, Avery sat up, her focus deadlocked on me.

"That's how you and Austin were conceived."

She parted her lips, and I could see all the thoughts and emotions warring in her irises.

"Michael was the first person I called. He took me to the police. He cared for me. I don't know when we technically got back together. We just were. All the things that had seemed like deal breakers didn't matter anymore. When I discovered I was pregnant," I said on a sigh, "the doctor told me I had a choice to make. But truly, there was no choice. You were my children—innocent when the whole world seemed dark. I chose to carry you, still unsure what I would do when you arrived. Your father—Michael, I mean—offered to marry me, not only to provide financially so I could keep you but also to be your father."

A tear slipped down Avery's cheek, and she caught it with the back of her hand before it dripped off her jaw.

"I never knew my father, but I knew of him," I continued. "I knew he wanted nothing to do with me. That's a hard truth to live with when you're little. It's a hard truth even now. So when I had this amazing man who wanted to love you and your brother as his own, I didn't turn him down. And as far as telling you the truth about your paternity, there was never a right time to tell you and Austin that you were brought into this world through an act of violence."

I explained Brolin's fate next, and Avery was quiet for a long time. Finally, she pushed her way into my embrace, squeezing Wynton between us. "I'm sorry you went through that."

"I'm okay now, thanks to a lot of faith and counseling. Don't be angry with your dad. If you're going to be mad at anyone, let it be me."

"I'm not mad. I-I want to go find Dad." She backed off the bed.

"Wait. There will be time for that. First, there's something else I need to tell you." I patted her spot on the mattress and waited for her to reclaim it. "I'm sure you remember the memory I had about your dad kissing his colleague."

"Yeah," she said, dragging out the single syllable.

"Last night at the school, the truth behind that memory came back to me." I caressed Wynton's fur while I willed myself to continue. "The day of the accident, right before the game started, Austin didn't see your dad kissing someone. He saw . . . me kissing someone."

Avery's mouth fell open. "What? Wait . . . what?" Her shrill tone gave me shivers.

"I let a man kiss me."

"At the school? Who was it?"

"I don't think I should—"

"It was the principal, wasn't it? Ew. Ew, ew, ew. Why?"

I swept the hair off the back of my neck, but it didn't relieve the stifled feeling. "I lost myself. Simple as that."

"Do you still have feelings for him?"

This truth was easy. "Not one little bit."

Avery processed my words. "That's why Austin was upset after the game? It wasn't about me?"

"I don't think so."

Avery's eyes glazed over.

"I'm sorry, honey. You, Austin, and your father didn't deserve what I did."

"Mom, you didn't deserve to be treated like you were. I know I took you for granted. Dad certainly did. I think the only one innocent in all this was Austin."

It's funny how innocence is so easily confused with naivety. Austin saw the world as a beautiful symphony during which he got to play a single note. When an instrument went off-key, all it took to be righted was a good tuning or a skillful move by the conductor. The last day of his life, he saw inside the instruments and got tangled up in the strings.

My gaze landed on the picture of Austin and Avery in front of the school bus. "We were blessed to have him in our lives, even for a short time, weren't we?"

"Mom, Austin loved more than anyone I've ever known. And he didn't hold grudges. Heaven isn't a place for unforgiveness. Maybe we shouldn't hold on to our grudges either."

A light knock sounded. Michael stood in the doorway, still wearing pajama pants, a plain white T-shirt, and a day's worth of scruff. After a slight nod in my direction, he shifted his focus to Avery.

"Oh, Dad." She scrambled off the bed, straight into Michael's arms.

# forty-four

In all of my recovered memories, I'd never seen Avery so happy as she was wearing that cap and gown. Graduation, perseverance, and accomplishment looked good on her.

"Mom, you promised not to cry until my name was called," Avery said, placing her hand on my shoulder. "I hope you brought tissues, Dad."

"Are you kidding?" He pulled a travel pack of Kleenex out of his pocket. "I brought these for me. We're proud of you, goof."

"Thanks. And thanks for pushing me to go back to school."

"We knew you could do it," he replied.

"Is Xander nervous about his speech?" I asked.

"Xander lives for the stage. But his mom wants to get a picture of us, so I should find him." She cavorted between the various families fawning over their seniors, leaving only Michael and me. Since prom, I'd debated coming back home but each time, the seams I'd torn in our family felt too large to mend. Michael must have thought so too. He'd stopped pushing for me to come back. Now, his resigned stare fell heavily on me.

"I should see if my mom is here." I withdrew my phone from my purse. Three texts from my mother filled my home screen.

This parking lot is crazy. You'd think a school
this rich could afford some parking attendants
or police. I had to park by the tennis courts,

273

right next to some kids that I'm sure will ding
my car with their door.

Did you bring bug spray? We'll be eaten alive.
Why would they have a graduation outside so
late in the day? Makes no sense.

I went straight to the stadium and got great
seats. I don't know how long I can save them
though. People are giving me the ugly eye. I'm
giving it right back.

"She's saving us seats," I told Michael. "Could you head out there before she starts a feud with another family? I'd like to stick around in case Avery needs me for anything."

"You sure? I can wait with you."

"It's fine. I'll see you in the stadium."

As Michael exited the school, Enid attacked me with a hug. "Can you believe our babies are graduating? Lori, I'm not okay with this." Pulling back, she smiled. "How are you holding up?"

"I'm . . . okay."

"I've missed seeing you around the neighborhood. I haven't been able to share my news with you."

"What's that?"

"We're selling our house. With Margot heading to college, we're downsizing to a place over on 80th. Basically, we're tired of being house poor. After we move in, could you help me decorate?"

"Of course. I'd love to."

She hugged me again, then flitted away almost as fast as she'd appeared. The crowd began to thin. Graduates went one direction, families another. One group remained, the members sporting various shades of blond hair, save one. A single dark-haired beauty stood on the outskirts, her hand tucked in the grasp of a tall lawyer-type. When the woman turned her face toward me, her identity was undeniable. Jade Jessup. Her gaze zeroed in on me. She offered a dainty wave like she thought I might swallow her whole. I didn't blame her considering our last encounter.

Instead, I waved back. Oh goodness, that seemed to invite her over.

"Hi, Lori. Your hair looks amazing."

"Thank you." I touched the razored ends of my new shoulder-length bob. "What are you doing here?"

"My fiancé's niece is graduating." She pointed to a girl inside the group's circle, her blond curls protruding from beneath her cap. "Are you doing well?"

"Physically, yes. Life and all its circumstances are still a bit overwhelming."

"Trust me. I get it. Trauma is something I've had to get used to in my life."

My mind slipped back to the text I'd seen from her in January. Something about people finding out something and losing respect for her. At the time, I assumed it related to adultery. Now, I wasn't so sure. "I'm sorry to hear that. Is there anything I can do to help?"

"Oh, no, it's all in my past. And, as you once pointed out, nothing like losing a child, thank goodness." Jade itched her ear with her shoulder. "Basically, my father was recently released from prison. It was quite a shock to me and my family. I worried that if people discovered my connection to a felon, they'd not trust me to handle their finances. Michael assured me I'd be okay though."

I worked my jaw until some words found their way to my lips. "That sounds like quite a story."

"I guess it is. Hopefully it's one that never gets told." She smiled awkwardly. "Speaking of shock, Michael surprised us all with his decision. But he isn't the type to do things halfway."

"Sorry?" I angled my ear to hear her better.

"You know. Selling the business to my future father-in-law."

The news struck me right in the breadbasket. Michael's business? The one he'd sacrificed our family to build? He was selling it?

Her smile fell. "Oh, you *didn't* know. I didn't mean to be the one to break the news to you."

"Did he say why?"

"He was vague. You should ask him directly. But if I had to guess, the biggest reason is he misses you." She squeezed her eyes shut and scrunched her nose. When her thick lashes lifted, her green eyes carried sorrow. "There I go again. Somehow I keep barging in on your family. It's not intentional."

"Oh, uh, it's okay."

"No, it isn't. Look, Lori. I appreciate how Michael has taken me under his wing and showed me the ins and outs of the wealth management industry, but I'm afraid that might've taken time away from you and your children. I'm very sorry for that." Her cheeks, already dusted with blush, deepened in color. "This is awkward. I don't know if this was ever a question in your mind or not, but my fiancé thought there might be something more happening between Michael and me."

An uncomfortable laugh snuck out. "He did?"

"Yes. In case you were worried, let me put your mind at ease. Nothing ever happened or would ever happen. Michael is like the older brother I never had, so that would be disturbing. And he loves you too much to lose you. I can tell you're not the kind of woman who would put up with adultery."

My legs felt heavy, bogged down as if all the blood in my body had pooled there. When a woman declared that graduates should begin lining up and parents should exit to the stadium, I struggled to move. I seemed to be right back to the first days I'd returned home, needing a walker to do even the simplest things.

I'd been wrong about Jade. I'd been wrong about Michael. I'd been wrong about myself, or at least my former self. Had I gotten anything right? It didn't seem so. And at what cost? My marriage? My husband's beloved business? My peace of mind?

I needed to talk to Michael before he made an irreversible mistake.

But the horde of people climbing the bleachers didn't help. By the time I got to Michael and my mom, the graduation processional had begun. When the crowd stood to snap pictures and ooh and aah over their seniors, Michael cradled my cheek with his palm. Then, too soon, he moved his hand to feel my forehead. "What's wrong? You look like you just ran a marathon."

"You're selling your business and you didn't tell me?" I tried to whisper, but the sound didn't carry with all the applause around us. I repeated my question, louder.

"Who told you?"

"Jade. She's here with her fiancé's family."

"I didn't tell you because it's not finalized yet."

I tugged on his shirtsleeve. "So you can still stop it? You put in so much time and effort to build your business. Why on earth would you sell it?"

"Because it got in between us. And because, without selling it, I won't have the money to buy Lake & Hearth for you."

This was too much. I gripped his forearm with both hands to steady myself. "Buy it?"

"Yeah. I've been in touch with Kendra. Depending on what happens with her family, she may be interested in off-loading it." Michael placed his hands on my hips and stared deeply into my eyes for a full measure before he spoke next. "Lori, the only reason I was able to build my business was that you were home, raising our beautiful, smart, funny, and caring children. Cooking for them, doing their laundry, helping them with homework, driving them to and from practices, even praying for them. You've earned this opportunity way more than I did. It's time for your dream now."

—◆—

## AVERY

"Please welcome this year's valedictorian, Alexander Dixon," Gross Principal Wright announced. My jaw ached from how hard I'd been clenching my teeth every time the sleaze spoke. If I could figure out a way to show everyone the man's misdeeds without bringing more noise into my parents' marriage, I'd do it. The school board wouldn't appreciate their high school principal using the PTO as his dating pool.

Xander climbed the steps and took his place behind the podium. His presence loomed as large as a country music star. I wouldn't be surprised if he shed his cap and gown right then and there. I hardly recognized him as the boy I'd loved and sometimes hated over the last thirteen years.

He adjusted the microphone height and then let his gaze span the crowd before it landed on me. "It's an honor to look out over all these familiar faces today. But there's one missing. My best friend, Austin Mendenhall, was killed homecoming weekend of our junior year."

I inhaled sharply. No wonder Xander wouldn't let me read over his speech. I sucked my bottom lip between my teeth and fought to keep the tears away.

"Many of you knew him, and if you knew him, you liked him. He was the first person to ask how the game or recital went. He was always willing to help someone out, put someone else first, and encourage people during their challenges. Rather than giving the same old valedictorian speech being shared across the country right now, I thought I'd simply write a letter to my friend and tell him all he's missed around Front Range High School in the twenty months he's been gone."

Xander took his phone from his pocket and read off the screen. "Dear Austin, it seems like just yesterday we were daring each other to jump off playground swings, peeling dried glue off our palms, and forging our parents' signatures on our practice sheets in beginning band—wait, that was just me." Xander paused as the crowd chuckled. "As we got older, it was looking forward to Taco Tuesdays, counting down the days until summer break, blowing up your sister's Minecraft creations—oh wait. Again, that was only me."

I caught his eye and shook my head.

"If we'd known how quickly childhood would end, maybe we wouldn't have been in such a hurry to grow up. As it turns out, life without you is a lot harder than I ever could've imagined. But we've come a long way. We're doing all right now. That said, you've missed a lot of good times.

"Our cross-country girls won the state championship this year. The spring musical won Colorado's Bobby G Award. And one time, someone let a stray dog inside the school, and we all teamed up and helped him evade capture until sixth period."

"Front Range Fido!" one of the seniors yelled the honorary name we'd given the Jack Russell terrier.

Xander responded with a fist in the air and said, "Three cheers for Fido."

As a group, we pumped our fists in the air and yelled, "Rah, rah, rah!"

Xander waited for the laughter and chatter to quiet down before continuing. "Dear Austin, now it's time to move on to a new phase of life. Despite all we've been taught within these walls, it still feels a bit like walking into the fun house at the sixth-grade carnival. We don't know what's real or fake, and the path forward isn't always clear.

"To put it in words we band kids understand, the life ahead of us is like a song. Right now we stand on the first note without any clue how the song will sound—its tempo, its range, even its genre. It may be hard rock, classic country, or an '80s ballad. Will it remain soft and quiet or will it hit a new crescendo in each stanza? Will it resound over a sold-out arena or be sung to one sweet soul in a serenade? Finally, will we sing solo or will we join in with others for a fun K-pop vibe? Personally, I'm hoping for a duet." He winked at me, and if I weren't already sitting, I'm sure I would have swooned.

"As we forge ahead with our life songs, we know that if we ever get lost in the lyrics and melody, we can trust in the experience we've gained here in these halls and classrooms, on the athletic fields, and in the art room, gymnasium, and theater. And we can trust those we've experienced it with. You taught me that, Austin. I promise to spend my life looking out for those you left behind. Rest in peace, brother. And one last time, three cheers for Front Range."

Again, we cheered, "Rah, rah, rah!" No one, of course, cheered louder than me.

After the crowd gave Xander a standing ovation, Principal Wright returned to the podium. The first group of my classmates rose and proceeded across the stage to receive their diplomas. Halfway through the procession, the M row headed to the stage. In a few moments, the assistant principal would announce my name while Wright presented my diploma to me and then offered me a handshake.

A million insults clambered over each other in my mind for the chance to tell off the man who tried to break up my family. Some funny, some mean, some funny *and* mean. No matter which one I decided to go with, he'd be put in his place. After all, Austin was the sweet one, right?

"Avery Wheeler Mendenhall."

Applause erupted the moment I set my foot on the stage, reaching down deep in my soul. The scene whirled around me, and the stadium lights streaked comets of radiance across the cheering crowd. I took a few more steps toward the principal, fumbling over my barbs. I reached for my diploma, but Principal Wright held two paper rolls, each wrapped in yellow and green ribbon.

"An honorary degree," the assistant principal said, "goes to Austin Alan Mendenhall."

The applause thundered louder. Rising from their seats, every person in the stands and on the field honored my brother for his place in this school and this community. A breath trickled out of my lungs as tears spilled down my cheeks. I spied my parents halfway up the stands, in the center. My father stood behind my mother and put his arms around her the way he used to in our family pictures. Mom blew me a kiss, and I smiled before turning back to the principal. I accepted both diplomas. Then he extended his palm to me for a handshake.

I locked my stare on him. Every ugly word had retreated off my tongue, hurrying back to find all the dark places within me. Good luck to them. "I know everything, Principal Wright," I said. "And I forgive you, because that's what my brother would want me to do."

I walked past him and proudly moved my tassel from one side of my cap to the other.

# *forty-five*

## LORI

Eighteen years had flown by. What I wouldn't give to grab hold of time's wings and keep things still a little while longer. It felt like just yesterday that Avery, with her hair pulled into two pigtails and a dress that matched Austin's jumper, had headed to kindergarten, holding her brother's hand.

Now she'd conquered high school. Next up, the world of fashion.

We all reunited in the school's parking lot after graduation ended. Michael clapped Xander on the back. "So, Mr. Valedictorian, Belmont's School of Music?"

"Yes, sir," Xander said. But rather than excitement, a certain soberness washed over the boy's face. He tugged Avery to his side. "I'll call every day from Nashville."

Avery's brow pinched, and she pouted. "That won't work for me."

The entire group of us—Michael, my mother, Xander, and myself—pressed closer, figuring we hadn't heard correctly.

She reached into her handbag, withdrew an envelope, and waved it in the air. "I think I'd rather see you in person."

Xander's eyes grew large. "Vanderbilt?"

She beamed as she nodded. "I've been accepted for spring semester. But there's a company in Tennessee that repurposes textiles for new clothing. They like what they've seen in my videos and want to partner with me to bring back some '80s styles. It looks like I'll be eastward bound in August after all."

Xander lifted her off the ground and spun her in a circle.

Even as joy filled my heart, tears pricked my eyes. My sweet girl, across the country. A hand warmed the small of my back. Michael watched me with a knowing glint in his eyes, then he offered a reassuring smile.

"Promise me one thing?" Xander asked Avery.

She hugged his waist. "What's that?"

"When you move to Nashville, don't pack the clarinet." That earned him a playful shove.

After giving Avery our approval to stay out all night as long as she promised to make good decisions, Michael and I walked my mom to her car. Once Michael had inspected it for door dings—none were found—he offered to drive me to my mom's house. We'd arrived at the ceremony together, it only made sense we leave together as well.

Silence reigned until we got in the car.

"I don't want you to buy Lake & Hearth," I said in a shaky voice.

"You'd rather start up your own shop instead? We can do that."

"No. I don't want you to sell your business. Call it off." My voice sounded meek. That wouldn't do. Not if he'd already set his mind to it. I took a big breath, straightened my spine, and summoned my mother's voice. "Call it *off*." Much better.

Michael thought a moment, then started the engine and backed out of the parking spot. "I won't."

"I'm asking you to."

He shifted into Drive and drove the Lexus toward the lot's exit. "Please, Lori. Give me one more chance to help you build the life you deserve. Maybe Avery's graduation has got me sentimental, but it doesn't feel like long ago that I promised to do that. To provide and protect you and the kids. I know I've failed on both of those promises more times than I can count. Give me one more chance."

My hands clasped the seat belt across my chest. "Aren't you afraid too much has happened? What if we try and try and we're still broken at the end of this?"

Ahead of us, the traffic light turned green. Instead of turning right toward my mom's, Michael switched his blinker and turned left out of the school's lot.

Dread flashed through me. "Why are we going this way?" The question shrilled, ripe with pure panic. Ever since I'd regained my ability to drive, I'd detoured around it, adding ten minutes to every drive. All to avoid what surged through my body right now. "Turn around. Michael. If you want to do something for me, turn around."

The road curved. What used to be a clear view of the Flatirons was now blocked by a bridge—the town's recently completed construction project to prevent any future car-train collisions.

"We have to face it, Lori. This may not be where our troubles started, but this is where our family's song hit its crescendo." He steered the car to the shoulder before the road dipped into a tunnel. The car came to a rest next to a white cross that reflected the moonlight. Yellow and green ribbons, some tattered and faded, some fresh and lovely, formed bows around the vertical beam. Horizontally, shadows spelled out Austin's first and last name where the letters had been etched into the wood. How many years before high school kids would turn his memory into an urban legend? Turn this bridge into a haunted site to visit in the middle of the night? Would this cross be enough to remind the world what a beautiful soul Austin was?

I struggled to find air to breathe. After manually unlocking the door, I opened it and then tumbled out onto the gravel, welcoming the sting of it on my knees and hands. Michael was there to help me to my feet.

In the shadow of the bridge, he held tight to my hands. "I'm not giving up on our family. I refuse, so stop asking me to."

I couldn't speak a single word.

"Lori, I fell for you the first time I saw you. I fell for your laugh, your smile, your ability to walk into the ugliest room and see its potential. The stupidest thing I ever did was think I could live without you."

"Michael, stop. You're only making this harder."

"What happened to you in college wasn't fair, but even then, you had hope for what could be. You let me be a part of it. What happened here that night wasn't fair. But look at you. You've somehow come out stronger. Even in the worst scenario, you had hope."

"I don't want to do this. Not here."

"Then where?"

Faint in the dark, graffiti spelled out "RIP" on the bridge wall. Below that, a bird with wings outstretched soared in dove-white paint.

"You know I can still hear him calling out to me," Michael said. "All this time you've been trying to remember, I've been trying to forget. I've tried to push away the thoughts of him, but I keep seeing him run across the church lawn with Avery in their Easter clothes. I see you wearing that sundress, smiling at me. Our house was falling apart. The car had broken down. The bills were piling up. I wanted to give you more. You deserved more."

I felt my heartbeat everywhere—even in my fingertips. My blood rushed past my ears, roaring like a building wave looking for a place to crash.

"If I'd known what that job change would lead to, I wouldn't have done it."

Headlights approached. A pickup truck sped past with a triple honk, its bed full of teenagers, their graduation gowns flowing in the wind as they disappeared into the tunnel below the tracks. Another noise remained though, growing louder every second. Oh, Jesus, I prayed. Not another train.

Michael was yelling now. "I drove you to bitterness, to resentment, to the arms of another man. I made you hate me."

"I didn't hate you," I yelled back, but my voice couldn't compete with the thundering sound.

"I realized my mistake when Austin told me about that kiss. And when you asked for a divorce."

The memory was clear now. Michael had just reached the car after finishing his conversation with Austin outside the stadium. I hadn't needed to ask what Austin told him. I could see it rising into the air like smoke from a burning house. I could smell the way it had charred Michael's body down to the bone. I could taste the ash on my tongue as I'd looked across the hood of our car and told Michael I wanted a divorce.

"Driving away from the school that night, all I could think about was how I'd caused you pain. I went blind with it. I couldn't see or hear anything until the train was upon us and I heard the screams."

The past and the present collided. The wind picked up, whipping my skirt around my knees painfully, and it seemed all of the angels above shrieked and wailed in their grief. I palmed my ears to shut out the blaring noise. The earth shook and the bridge walls trembled. Dirt rained down as a train overtook us. Michael grabbed me by my waist and although I couldn't hear him, I read his words as they spilled off his lips: *I killed Austin.*

I begged my body, weak as it felt, to do this one last thing. I circled my arms around Michael's neck and pressed myself against him. My lips found his ear. "You didn't. If you believe that, then I killed him too."

He shook his head.

"We may never know why he had to go except that it was just his time. But it wasn't your fault, Michael."

His chest heaved in brutal harmony with my racing pulse. We held each other like our lives, our futures depended on it. We held each other until the wind settled and the clamor faded. I felt his sobs before I heard them. "Will you forgive me for not seeing you and not hearing you?"

I nodded. "Will you forgive me for forgetting how much I love you and you love me?"

His lips cracked into a tired, solemn smile. I kissed his wet cheeks. Or maybe he kissed mine. We were a beautiful, broken mess, but we'd made it to the hope that lies on the other side of the tracks. Once our ragged breaths eased to soft wisps, twining together with the hope of new memories, I swept my lips over his. "Bring me home."

# *epilogue*

## AVERY

The sweetest little girl in the whole world ran down the church hallway as fast as her Mary Jane–clad feet could carry her. She had my blue-green eyes—the same ones as Austin and Mom—but her hair was dark and cascaded past her shoulders in ringlets. My wedding dress, with its billowing folds of satin repurposed from secondhand gowns, caught her like a net. In her hand, she held a note.

"Is this for me?" I accepted it, unfolding it with the steady hands of an expert seamstress. The note was simple. White paper, black ink—two doves sitting on a line. I kissed it before handing it to Sarah. "If it isn't too much trouble, will you put that in my purse?"

"Of course it isn't any trouble. Isn't that what a maid of honor is for?"

I kneeled and spread my arms open for my little sister, who happily accepted the hug. "Ainsley, you are the prettiest flower girl ever."

She kissed me on the cheek. "Xander told me to give you that."

"Well, thank you! Does he look handsome?"

She smiled and bounced her chin excitedly.

Mom, about to steal the show in her knock-'em-dead mother of the bride dress, put her hands on her hips. "My girls." Somehow, between graduating with an interior design degree and having another baby, Mom had managed to start her own business, curating homes for the rich and famous. "What did I do to be so blessed?"

"You were raised by me," Grandma Anita said. She'd visited me multiple times in the four years I spent in Nashville attending school. And every time she'd remind me that I didn't need a man to have a happy life. Most of the time she didn't even wait for Xander to leave the room to say it. It didn't help that he always agreed with her. "Lori, we should take our seats. I really hope my sisters didn't take my spot. It was supposed to be saved right there on the front row."

Mom rolled her eyes so only I could see. "I'm sure it will all work out fine, just like it always has."

Twenty minutes later, I peeked through the window in the sanctuary's side entrance. My cheeks ached from smiling. Now, seeing Xander in front of our families and friends? A smile was worth the pain. I turned to Dad. "I never thought I could be this happy."

He grinned as he lowered the veil and placed it over my face. He glanced at Ainsley Jane waiting in front of us. "I know what you mean."

Sarah, holding Ainsley's hand and Wynton's leash, led them into the sanctuary. It took some convincing for our pastor to allow a dog in the church. But at thirteen, Wynton wasn't about to tear the place to pieces. And it helped that our pastor was still a bit starstruck by my future husband.

Xander's band began playing an instrumental version of "Awaken," making sure to tone down the folksy-rock style he was starting to be known by outside of Nashville. When it was my turn to walk down the aisle, the storm in Xander's eyes cleared, leaving only calm seas for our voyage together. Who would have thought that the boy who put gum in my hair would be the man I'd wake up next to for the rest of my life?

As the music faded, Xander whispered in my ear, "You look heavenly."

The pastor welcomed the guests and then asked Dad who was presenting the bride.

Dad worked his jaw, then blew out a breath. "Her mother and I do." He raised my veil and kissed my cheek before taking his seat next to Mom. Ainsley bounced onto his lap, and Mom kissed him for longer than should be allowed in church.

Xander took my hand, and we climbed the steps to a white chair that marked the place where the best man might have stood. Xander's stepbrother handed him Austin's bomber jacket—the one I'd sewn long ago—and trumpet. He placed the jacket on the back of the chair and laid the trumpet on the seat. From my bouquet, I withdrew a single rose boutonniere and pinned it on the lapel, touching the trumpet delicately before withdrawing my hand. I moved to take center stage, but Xander stopped me. He reached into the jacket pocket and then held out a bracelet. Emerald green gems on an elastic string— the gift from Austin thanks to a middle school summer of ticket-winning. I inhaled slowly, knowing I'd mess up my makeup if I let tears fall. "Thank you," I mouthed to Xander.

He slipped the bracelet on my hand and wiped my tears away with his handkerchief. Sweet Swayze, he was handsome. It was all I could do to nod and match his smirk with one of my own.

"What do you say, Ave? Ready to make some more memories?"

# acknowledgments

It's always difficult to write about issues that real people experience on a daily basis. So many wonderful friends have shared their hardest moments with me, as well as their most joyful ones, so that I may write these characters' experiences as authentically as possible. Despite learning what true brokenness is, you've done all you could, you've loved deeply, and you've lived every moment believing what love was truly meant to be. Thank you to each friend who shared the pain of fighting for their marriage and either the heartbreak when their efforts weren't enough or the gladness when the relationship was restored.

Thank you, Michelle, for being so transparent about the challenges that come with a traumatic brain injury. You've inspired me since the first day we met, and I'm blessed to know you!

I'm so appreciative of my supportive publishing team. Tamela, thanks for your vision of where my stories belong. Kelsey, I've admired you from afar for years, so getting to work with you has been a dream. Your gifts and the hard work of the entire Revell group have lifted this story to new heights.

PW Gopal, I'm so in awe over your songwriting ability.

Thank you for sharing that with my readers through the song "Awaken."

Janyre and Rachel, I'll never be able to put into words what your friendship means to me. Maybe you can help me brainstorm that. :) My QTs continue to encourage me in my hard times and make me laugh in all the times.

To my Insiders and Outriders group—none of this would be possible without you all! Thank you for accepting me and spurring me on!

Mom, your help, especially through my deadlines and cross-state moves, has been invaluable to us! I hope you know how much we love you!

To William, Braden, Jonathan, and Corynn—you're the best kids ever. Thanks for the Sour Patch Kid gifts, encouraging notes, *Hamilton* and *Newsies* singalongs, hair brushing, laughs, and help with modern kid language. Not gonna lie, your help was dope. One hundred percent. Did I do it right?

Finally, George, your loyalty surpasses any other I've known. I love you.

*Keep reading
for a sneak peek at
Janine Rosche's next
engrossing novel...*

With moving themes and engaging characters,
Rosche pens a tale you won't be able to put down.

# prologue

Miles from any high-rise, the generations-old asphalt crumbles beneath the soles of my borrowed boots, and I wish my story would fall through the hot cracks of Route 66 as well.

Ahead of me, a sports car ignores the twenty-five-miles-an-hour speed limit through town. Before he's able to get a one-of-a-kind Jade Jessup hood ornament, I step off the road into the brush. The sound of the engine rumbles up my spine as it passes. This trip was supposed to help, not compound, my troubles. Only now do I hear "Take It Easy" by the Eagles blaring from the speakers. The tires squeal just beyond the neon sign for Tecoma Springs Motel, and the car whips into the same spot where I parked yesterday, only yards from my room. Will the Newtons let me stay gratis until everything gets sorted out? Even the kindest people have their limits.

The town of Tecoma is merely a rest stop on Route 66, otherwise undiscernible and undesirable for lingering, not like the tourist traps we've grown used to seeing. Perhaps that's why Dad chose it decades ago. One could hide here.

I pass the sole lamppost, which sits in the geographical center of town. Considering the amount of aged adhesive crisscrossing its pole, it likely still serves as Tecoma's news central.

It was at that post that I learned I was a missing child. Where the seams in my world ripped apart for the first time.

Another vehicle approaches from behind me. A glance over my shoulder reveals an older model Chevy 1500 creeping at my walking pace. A man—check that, a boy—wearing an ASU ball cap practically hangs out his driver window. His left hand slaps the door panel, and he rolls his bottom lip between his teeth. "Hey, baby, where are you going?"

Swatting my hand in his direction like he is a pesky mosquito, I focus on the roadside bar up ahead, the scene of last night's crime, or at least one of last night's crimes. What Tecoma lacks in entertainment, it makes up for in criminal activity.

"Aw, don't be like that," he went on. "It's too hot for a girl like you to be out here. You'll melt the asphalt."

I take a deep pull of Arizona air and shift my focus away from the road. The side entrance of the bar is propped open. Or should I say side exit? After all, that's the door the short man with the big attitude barreled out from last night with a bloody nose and, likely, a solid case of regret. I rub the tender place on my arm where he grabbed me so violently. Glynda, the bar owner, steps through the door now, carrying a large black floor mat. She promptly smacks it against the place's brick wall, releasing a cloud of Arizona dirt into the air.

The truck's engine revs to my right. "This AC feels real nice in here. I have some other ideas of what else might feel real nice if you're up for it."

Glynda looks up from her task and, upon seeing me, glares in a way that would intimidate Medusa.

My thirty-one-year-old self pulls my shoulders back, lifts my chin high, and latches my sights on the western horizon, where the famous road vanishes behind hills and buttes. Yet my eight-year-old self, with whom I've only just begun to reconcile, yearns to stick out my tongue at Glynda. The worst part is, it feels like her attitude is justified. I am my father's daughter. It's in my blood to bring harm to others, even lonely bar owners like her. That fact is inescapable, no matter how many miles I've driven—from Chicago to Santa Monica and beyond.

"Come on, baby," College Boy drones on. "You're not a tease, are you?"

I pause, my gaze shifting between the livid bar owner and this bum. I saunter—at least I think I'm sauntering, never done it before—to the front bumper.

"Well, all right," the guy says, shifting the truck into Park.

"Is this a '92?" Carefully, I reach between the grill and the hood, searching for the latch.

"Uh, yeah. Why? What are you doing?"

I lift the hood with one hand and disconnect the coil wire from the distributor cap. The engine stutters and dies, and I let the hood slam closed.

"What'd you do to my truck?" he yells while scrambling from the driver's seat.

With my best softball pitch, I send the wire into the desert flora. Ignoring the litany of sexist slurs he lets loose, I resume my trek to the last building in sight. With each step, my nausea increases, but I have no choice in this matter.

I tuck my fists under my chin and blow out a heavy breath before turning the toes of Sandy's boots toward the small jail that looks to be more tourist attraction than serious confinement. But I have no doubt those bars and locks are as real as the small cactus rising through the crack in the road. To think, I was a split second away from landing there myself. But Bridger.

Always Bridger.

Before I can take hold of the knob, the old door lurches open with a groan, revealing an older man with as jolly a face as Santa Claus and a beard just as long.

"Well, well, well. Mighty Miss Jade. I heard you'd come back to visit us. Been a long time." The light from the singular bulbs reflects off the too shiny, blushed skin on his round cheeks and even rounder nose.

I peek at the name tag on his uniform, and the vaguest of memories trickles back. "Sheriff Samson, hello."

"How're you doing? Folks 'round here wonder about you all the time."

"I'm . . . okay." There's no sense in sugarcoating it. "I'm here to see—"

"Me. She's here to see me." Bridger's voice holds more gravel than normal, and it scrapes over me like sandpaper.

My eyes move from Sheriff Samson to the direction of Bridger's voice. I push the door farther open until a cell comes into view. No. Two cells, sharing a wall of bars. In the nearest one, Bridger's lengthy form stretches across the concrete from one end to the other. He's in one of his yoga poses. A shiver courses over my skin when I see his nose brushing the floor that probably hasn't seen a mop in some time. "How is she?" he asks me.

"Good. The hospital's going to keep her for one more night, but that's simply for observation."

The sound of his exhale carries over to me.

"Bridge? Are you okay?" A foolish question if I've ever asked one.

"Peachy," he says, straightening his arms and lifting his hips upward until he achieves a downward dog position, although he looks less like a dog and more like a grizzly.

"Gotta say, this is the first time I seen someone do *that* in *there*." Sheriff Samson laughs heartily. "Been doing it all afternoon though."

"He's a unique one, all right. I'm here to post bail."

Bridger's attention cuts to me. Beneath a heavier than usual brow, his dark eyes are rimmed by red. Even if he was able to fit on the narrow, thinly cushioned cot, he couldn't have gotten much sleep. At once, he looks away and drops his knees to the concrete. "How'd you get money for that?"

"It's not important. All you need to know is I'm getting you out of here." I slide the bank envelope out of the back pocket of the Daisy Dukes I would never be caught wearing if I had any other real choice—which I do not—and hand it to the sheriff. As the man takes to opening the money that would likely cover this jail's entire operating cost for the month, I approach the cell with the enthusiasm of an accused witch to a pyre. I grip the bars, waiting for Bridger to regard me as anything other than what I actually am. Waiting for him to look at me the way he did not so long ago.

He stands but never quite reaches his full six-foot-five height before sitting on the edge of the cot. As he scrubs his hands over his face and then back through his wavy shoulder-length locks, the dull ache that has plagued me since Chicago stretches across my chest and sinks into my bones. Finally, his gaze meets mine.

I lean my forehead against the clammy steel and mouth, "I'm sorry."

"Me too," he says in the gentlest voice a man of his stature can find. And in his eyes, I see that somewhere, some part of him still cares about me.

"Twelve hundred," Sheriff Samson says. "It's all there. Pardon, Miss Jade." After I step aside, the sheriff fits the key into the door lock and turns it until the click releases my long-held breath. "Mr. Rosenblum, I'll grab your belongings and then you're free to go. And take that yogi stuff with you, will ya, big fella? If I tried any of them poses, I'd never get back up."

Bridger pulls a blanket off the cot as he stands. He folds it with care and hands it to Sheriff Samson. "Thank you for the extra blanket, Gill."

"It's not every day we have a celebrity in here."

"You'd have done it for anyone." Bridger claps his hand on the elderly sheriff's shoulder, and before I can think too long on any of it, I make my exit.

When I walk outside, the Arizona sun sinks deep into my skin like it somehow missed the flipping of the calendar page to September. College Boy's truck remains trapped in Route 66's westbound lane with its owner out in the dirt, kicking the brush and cacti in search of the coil. He doesn't see me. Probably good, lest Bridger decide to defend my honor again. I don't have another twelve hundred dollars to spare.

"I guess I should thank you," Bridger says, sidling up to me as I stare down the highway—close but not as close as he would've been even yesterday.

"You know it's the least I could do." I take a deep breath, then exhale slowly. "Bridger, I'm so sorry—"

"Jade, you don't have to do this."

"But I do. Now we're stuck in the middle of nowhere without a car, without clothes, without—"

Bridger steps in front of me. "There will be time to figure things out. For now, only one thing matters."

I nod and force myself to swallow the tumbleweed that seems to have wedged in my throat. "Benny."

**Janine Rosche** is the ECPA bestselling author of heartfelt stories that travel the peaks and valleys of life with the promise of hopeful ever afters.

Her longing to chase adventure, behold splendor, and experience redemption is woven into her novels as well as *The Love Wander Read Journal*, a digital quarterly magazine that provides inspiration for a life well-loved. When she isn't writing or traveling, Janine teaches family life education courses, takes too many pictures of her sleeping dogs, and embarrasses her four children and husband with boy band serenades.

# Connect with
# Janine

Find Janine online at **janinerosche.com** and sign up for her newsletter to get the latest news and special events delivered directly to your inbox.

**Follow Janine on social media!**

janineroscheauthor    janinerosche    janinerosche

# UNDEA

## BY
## BOREDMAN

 *Rocketship* ™ Rocketship Entertainment, LLC
rocketshipent.com

**Tom Akel,** CEO & Publisher • **Rob Feldman,** CTO • **Jeanmarie McNeely,** CFO
**Brandon Freeberg,** Dir. of Campaign Mgmt. • **Phil Smith,** Art Director • **Aram Alekyan,** Designer
**Jimmy Deoquino,** Designer • **Jed Keith,** Social Media • **Jerrod Clark,** Publicity

Created in December 2014 as an entry
for the Webtoon Challenge League Contest,
UndeadEd is the story of a dead man
trying to go on with his life.

Which, in addition to being paradoxical,
certainly isn't easy.

The series was later picked up
by Webtoon and became available
as a Slidetoon, updating three times
a week from the 8th of May 2015
to the 7th of February 2016

Special thanks to my friend Damien
for letting me know about the contest,
to my editor David for giving me a chance,
and to Elie, Anna and Vane for feeding me
ideas and support throughout the way.

UndeadEd is dedicated to my grandfather,
who passed away during its early beginnings.

# TABLE OF CONTENTS

# Chapter I
## -Denial-

As if
life wasn't
hard enough
without being
dead.

# Chapter II
## -Anger-

They say
life is pain.

But death
is no picnic
either.

# Chapter III
## -Bargaining-

The nice
thing with
being dead:

you can
relate to a lot
of people.

# Chapter IV
## -Depression-

So
what if i'm
dead ?


Life goes
on.

# Chapter V
## -Acceptance-

I'm already
dead.

What's the worst
that could
happen?

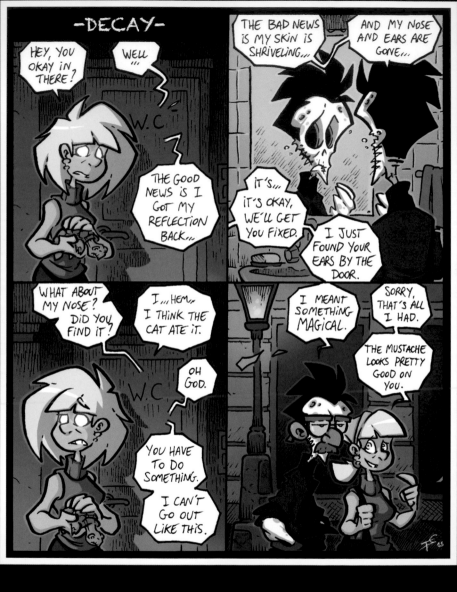

-THE TALE-

THE TALE OF STINGY JACK?

I THINK THAT'S WHAT IT WAS, YES... HE SAID IT MIGHT INTEREST YOU.

WHAT'S IT ABOUT?

THERE ARE DIFFERENT VERSIONS ...

BUT BASICALLY IT'S ABOUT SOME WICKED GUY WHO PLAYS TRICKS ON THE DEVIL TO ESCAPE DAMNATION.

WEEKEPEDIO

WHAT'S THAT GOT TO DO WITH ME?

AFTER HE DIES, HIS SOUL IS REJECTED FROM BOTH HEAVEN AND HELL, CURSING HIM TO ROAM THE EARTH FOR ALL TIMES.

REMIND YOU OF ANYONE?

ED? WHAT IS IT?

I THINK IT'S TIME FOR PLAN B.

111

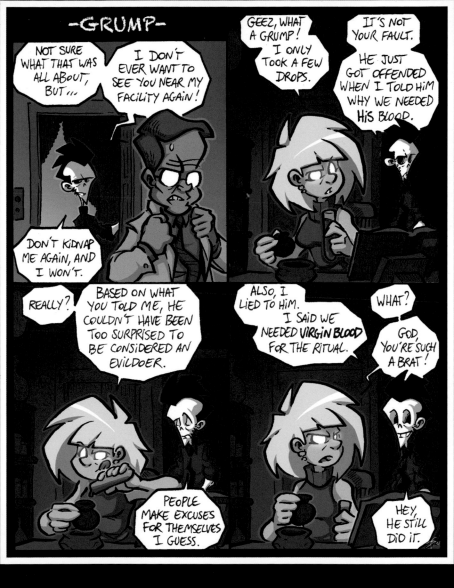

Searching yourself
can lead to
Heaven or Hell

But it still beats
not knowing

...

and roaming
the Earth

TO APOLOGIZE FOR THIS SAD ENDING,
I LEAVE YOU WITH A GAME:

IN EPISODE 55, THE INVISIBLE MAN
ALSO STOLE ED'S WATCH, AND HID IT
SOMEWHERE IN THE FOLLOWING EPISODES.

DID YOU SEE WHERE IT WENT ?

VON BELLSING,
PRIEST MATTHEW
AND LUCY
WILL RETURN IN

APOCALYPTIC
HORSEPLAY

# Concept Art
# & Illustrations

THE NAME OF THE STORY WAS ORIGINALLY GOING TO BE DEAD ED, BUT I SOON FOUND OUT THAT NAME WAS ALREADY TAKEN AND CHANGED IT TO UNDEAD ED... WHICH LATER TURNED OUT TO BE TAKEN AS WELL.

IT'S HARD BEING ORIGINAL NOWADAYS.

# DEAD ED

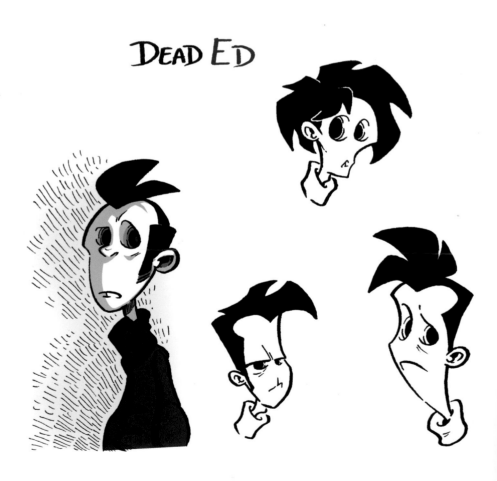

GHOUL

SHELLEY MONSTER

VAMPIRE

GHOST

Y THE TIME WEBTOON DECIDED TO TAKE UNDEADED OUT OF THE CHALLENGE LEAGUE AND INTO THEIR SELECTION, THE COMIC WAS ALSO AVAILABLE ON BOTH DEVIANTART AND TAPASTIC. SINCE IT HAD TO REMAIN A WEBTOON EXCLUSIVE, ALL EPISODES WERE THEN TAKEN DOWN AND REPLACED BY THIS ANNOUNCEMENT.

PIRATE SHARING LATER MADE IT AVAILABLE ON SITES LIKE MANGAFOX.ME, MYMANGAONLINE.NET, READMANGA.ME AND ON IMGUR AND REDDIT WHERE IT GOT HALF A MILLION VIEWS IN TWO DAYS.

UNFORTUNATELY IT WAS A WEEK BEFORE ITS CONCLUSION...

THANK YOU FOR READING! —E.

MY NAME'S ELIOTT, I'M A BONEY FRENCH CARTOONIST LIVING IN BELGIUM WITH MY WIFE AND OUR THREE HUNGRY BABIES, ONLY ONE OF WHICH IS HUMAN.

ARTISTICALLY BROUGHT INTO EXISTENCE BY BOREDOM, MY WORK IS NOW THE ONLY THING THAT KEEPS IT AT BAY, BUT THANKS TO THE WONDERS OF DIGITAL MEDIA AND MY COMPLETE DISINTEREST IN VITAMIN D, I'VE BEEN MAKING CARTOONS AND WEBCOMICS FOR OVER FIFTEEN YEARS.

SINCE UNDEADED'S OFFICIAL RELEASE IN 2015, I'VE BEEN PUBLISHING MY WORK ALMOST EXCLUSIVELY ON WEBTOON, BUT YOU CAN STILL FIND OTHER COMICS OF MINE ON DEVIANTART, PATREON, BLOGGER AND ON THE WALLS OF MY MOTHER'S KITCHEN.

22